DOES MY BUMP LOOK BIG IN THIS?

Amy Lynch

For mum.

What would I do without you?

Without my literary agent **Frank Fahy,** and the artistic talent of my good friend **Stephen Shortt,** this book would still be in a desk drawer… and it's far too pretty to be hidden away.

2003

'Listen, Becky, it's the easiest job ever, OK?'

Emma's been pleading with me all day to fill in for her babysitting job. She says I owe her one for doing my Biology homework last week.

'I don't know, Ems. I've never babysat before, I wouldn't have a clue.'

We've got to rush through the corridor and up the back stairs to get to double maths. I've already got a black mark in my diary for forging a sick note, and Smelly Kelly has it in for me.

'Becks, you'll be grand. Seriously, I've babysat for them for two years. It's a doddle.'

'But you said that there's three of them. And one's a baby!'

'Yeah, but they're grand! Very cute. Sure, all you've got to do is read them a bedtime story and then sit on the couch for four hours.'

Emma is doing the hard sell. You see, she promised the lady last week that she'd babysit this Friday night, but then an emergency came up. It turns out that Emma's ex boyfriend James (the one with the lush eyes) dumped her for Rachel (the one with the big boobs) and had been doing the dirt on her for ages now. It was so harsh, because they had been sneaking around behind her back for a whole two weeks. So now Rachel's ex Mark (the one with the Volkswagen Golf) has no-one to take to the debs' ball. Anyway, Emma's stepping in, because she's fancied Mark for ages now.

The plan is that they'll snog like crazy and make James and Rachel dead jealous.

'You'll make loads of dosh,' Emma continues.

'Yeah?'

'Yeah, like a tenner an hour. You'll be loaded.'

Emma has done so much babysitting this year that she's got loads of spending money for our end of school holiday to Ibiza. It's going to be insane, and Jack from Biology will be there.

'Hmm,' I waver. Dad's promised me proper driving lessons for my eighteenth, and if I show him I can save a bit of money, he might even get me a car. Besides, learning in mum's car is so embarrassing. It's so old and has a pathetic stereo. Also, it's quite dinged up on the side from when I reversed it into the neighbours Mini.

Anyway, a bit of easy cash might be handy. I mean, how hard can a little babysitting be? It has to be better than standing around a clothes store all day and pretending to help people devoid of fashion sense. Between minimum wages, tax and bus fares, I've flip all money left over. Oh, and also because the rest of my wages goes on the outfits. I get a staff discount, and I'm surrounded by sequin encrusted temptation all day. It's all very bitter sweet.

'You must have babysat before,' Emma narrows her eyes and sits next to me. Her mascara is clumped at the sides.

Smelly Kelly has terrible hearing, so we can keep chatting while he waffles on about some quadratic equation or other that we'll never need in the real world when we're rich and famous.

'Yeah, I mean... sure,' my cheeks flush, and I pick at my chipped purple nail polish.

'Good. Oh, and I forgot the best bit. They have a satellite dish. There are about one hundred channels!'

Mum's been banging on about me getting a babysitting job for ages now, so she's in a good mood when I tell her. She says I can catch up on a bit of study for the Leaving Cert when the kids are asleep, so I had to pretend to pack a French textbook. Dad's dropping me off at the house on their way to Killiney Castle for a bite to eat. He whistles as he pulls up to the black iron gates.

Mum's strains her neck out of the passenger window. 'Would you look at that, Gerry? They have a buzzer. Isn't that posh?'

'Right, go on then,' I shoo them away as the gates separate, revealing a sprawling red-bricked home. I don't want the family to see dad's beaten up 1995 Opel Astra.

Emma was right, Louise and Dermot are definitely minted. There's a silver Mercedes in the driveway, a giant TV in the corner of the sitting room, and a humungous chandelier hanging from the ceiling.

'Right. Thanks. Barbara, is it?' Louise has bright pink lipstick on her teeth, but I'm not sure I should say anything.

'Eh, Becky.'

'Right. Becky. Ok. Right then. The children are asleep, so…'

It's hard to keep the smirk off my face. I've just hit the jackpot.

'Oh, and baby Jamie had one of his vaccinations this morning, so I gave him some Calpol before he went down. I've a bottle made up in the fridge if he wakes. Martha and Ruth are fast asleep. Help yourself to anything.'

Dermot simply raises his eyebrows, smiles, and guides his flustered wife by the elbow to the car.

First thing's first. Emma told me where the goodies cupboard is, and I'm ravenous. The kitchen is massive, and I've snooped in every drawer and cupboard. I've got a Pepsi Max poured and the remote control at the ready. Watching MTV cribs on a massive screen just makes it even more amazing. It makes our crappy twenty-eight-inch TV at home look so sad in comparison. There's a new episode of 'Friends' on at nine, and then Big Brother at ten. Oh, and 'Ghost' is on channel four, it's such a delicious dilemma! Obviously Patrick Swayze out trumps Davina McCall!

At eleven, I'm just popping a bag of microwave popcorn when I hear crying coming from upstairs, so I creep up the stairs, my heart hammering in my chest. In the girls' bedroom, I can hear light snoring. One of them has kicked off their pink 'Little Mermaid' duvet, and I replace it. In the master bedroom, I can see a crying baby standing up in a wooden cot. Jamie's face is red and wet from tears, and his eyes are scrunched together in a howl. The sudden realization hits me: I have absolutely no clue what to do. I reach under his arms and lift him out of the cot. I'm holding him awkwardly like a football, now. In the movies, they put a crying baby on one shoulder and rock about a bit, but no joy. In fact, the baby is screeching even louder now, probably realizing that he has absolutely no idea who I am, or where his mummy is.

Panic claws at my stomach. I spot a telephone on one of the bedside lockers and dial Emma's mobile. She's probably slow dancing with Mark right now to Robbie Williams 'Angels' and snogging the head off him. No answer.

Then a light bulb goes on. No, not a metaphorical one, I mean an actual light bulb literally has come on. Two small girls in matching pink nightdresses are standing in the door frame squinting at me. One is a fraction taller than the other, with a gap in her front teeth.

'Who are you?' the slightly taller one asks.

'I'm Becky,' I try to smile, but the relentless baby shrieks in my ear.

The two little girls continue to stare at me, blinking.

'I'm Emma's friend.'

'Where's Emma?' the slightly shorter one wants to know. 'And where's my mummy?'

Her teeny chin wobbles and bit, and when I look to her sister's face, there are tears welling up in her eyes, threatening to spill if she blinks again. It's too late, the tears are rolling down to her cheeks now.

'I want mummy,' she whimpers.

'What's that burny smell?' the eldest sniffs the air.

When the smoke detector goes off, I connect the dots. The bloody popcorn is cremated. I'll just sort the baby out and then go downstairs to open a window.

Oh dear god. Please, please don't let them all start crying at once, because I swear, I will join in too.

'Right. Ok, then. Right,' I say aloud, starting to sound a little like their real mummy.

'OK, so Emma told me you like stories, is that right?'

The girls exchange a brief look, and nod their heads.

'Ok. Well, I promise I'll tell you any story you like, but first I've got to get Jamie back to sleep, OK? How does mummy get him quiet?'

The girls raise and then drop their shoulder in unison. No help there, then.

Think, Becky! What do babies need? I ask myself.

I haven't got a Scooby Doo, I reply.

Right. Well then call mum, I debate.

No, she'd panic. Then she'd insist on coming over here, and take over. Then the parents would return and see that I'm a completely useless almost-eighteen-year-old who calls her mammy at the first whiff of trouble.

Speaking of whiffs, there's a definite pong in this room. There's something damp on my left hand, and when I remove it from the baby's back to examine it closer, it's covered in a brown stain. I look down at the crying baby on my hip, and see that we are both covered in a kind of a toxic brown sludge. Louise's words circle around. 'He had a vaccination this morning.'

Oh, no. Don't babies get icky tummies after vaccinations sometimes? I demand my frazzled brain.

How should I know? Apart from various cousins, this is the first baby I've even held!

'We want a story,' the girls chirp in unison. It's hard to hear them over the noise from the smoke detector, so I put Jamie back in his cot, tell the girls to wait there and rush downstairs to wave a tea towel at the smoke detector until it stops.

'Right, I'm back. Just a sec, girls,' I look around for somewhere to lie the baby down so that I can figure out what to so.

'Martha and Ruth,' I say to both of them, as I have absolutely no clue which one is which. 'Will you be very good girls and fetch me a towel from the bathroom?'

Ten seconds later, they're back with what looks like a very expensive Brown Thomas white cotton towel – the kind you'd pinch from a five star hotel. In the hot press, I dig up an older one, and lay Jamie on top of it on the bed. Honestly, it smells like the stink bombs my brother Ian gets at the joke shop. I've peeled off the damp sleep suit, revealing the mud coloured vest. Getting the garment over his head means that his hair becomes covered, too. The nappy is bulging, way past saturation point. The brown gloop is all the way up his back and down to his chubby thighs.

'Right. Stay there,' I tell Jamie as I look around to try and find some baby wipes and a clean nappy. Thankfully, he has stopped crying, and is now kicking about on the bed. For someone who has never changed a nappy in their whole life (even on a baby doll), this is a baptism of fire. I've gathered up a few supplies, and turn to walk back to the bed.

'Jamie?' A chill runs through me. I can't see the baby anywhere.

There's a gurgling sound, and I see that he has managed to roll himself right off the king-sized bed and onto the carpet below, where he is crawling at a remarkable speed towards the top of the stairs.

'Jamie!' my hand shoots to my mouth.

Not only has he rolled all over the bedspread, but there is now a brown trail from the bedroom all the way to the landing. I grab him before he reaches the top step and put him back in the cot. Scrubbing the thick shag pile carpet with a damp towel is making the stain worse, and it feels like I'm shovelling snow in a blizzard. Perspiration runs down my face.

The baby wipes have removed most of the mess from Jamie's back, but the bit that's matted to his soft blonde hair is going no-where. I'm debating between opening a second pack of baby wipes and running a bath. The silk sheets are definitely going to need a boil wash, and his cot looks like a brown crime scene. The girls have gone awfully quiet in all of the chaos, I'd better keep them occupied while I'm tackling this mess.

'Good girls for waiting for me. Now, let's get you –.'

My speech is cut short mid-sentence. One of the girls has her whole fist in a family sized tub of Sudocrem, while the other is painting a handful of the white substance on the floral Laura Ashley wallpaper. The bedside locker, the lamp, their mother's purple silk nightgown, and the two girls themselves are also coated.

'Oh my God.'

I'm swearing to myself that I will never, ever take a babysitting job again. A clothes store might be boring, but at least I'm not on my hands and knees scrubbing.

The sound of the key in the door makes the blood drain from my face.

****

This morning's geography class is a total nightmare. And no, I don't just mean that it's the usual boring ramblings about oxbow lakes and volcanic dust or whatever Sweat Patch Patterson usually bangs on about. You see, my younger brother, Ian, had heard me crying to mum all weekend, and has now told the entire flipping world about Friday night.

'A tsunami,' Sweat Patch Patterson drones on, 'is a tidal wave causing massive destruction.'

The giggling at the back gets louder as he turns his back on the class to draw a diagram on the blackboard.

'Sir?' Rachel raises her hand, and looks over at me, smirking. 'What about a POOnami?'

The entire back row collapse in hysterics, and my cheeks flame. Sweat Patch Patterson is threatening detention if they don't all pipe down.

A scrunched-up note has been fired from a ruler, and hits me on the back of the head. When I pick up the note and open it at my desk, it reads:

Poonami.

I turn around and see Rachel laughing. All of her posse join in. Even Jack, who I was hoping would ask me to the debs, is laughing. I take a black biro, and scribble over the dozens of 'Becky Hearts Jack' designs on my school diary. I'm definitely not snogging him in Ibiza now.

One

'Honestly, Barry. Will you just go up there and tell them we're newly-weds. We shouldn't have to queue up like everyone else.'

'No, Becks, just leave it.'

The Cancun departure area is hotter than a sizzling burrito with extra jalapeños, and the check-in queue is taking forever. There's no air conditioning, and it's forty degrees.

Barry must be feeling like a baked bean right now, you should see the jeans he has on. We fan ourselves with the boarding cards. My blonde hair is starting to stick to my temples, and a bead of perspiration rolls down my tanned, freckled face.

'You'd think they'd have a separate line for honeymooners.'

Barry doesn't answer. He's too busy debating the cost of the additional suitcases at the check-in desk. Yes, that's additional suitcases, plural. Oops. My bad. Hopefully he's not implying to the check-in staff that I'm to blame for all of the extra luggage we have. It's with thanks to me that Mexico is currently enjoying an upswing in its economy. Eh, you're welcome, Mexico! Anyway, it's probably best if I swan off to the duty free while he sorts it all out.

At the security check point, the contents of my hand luggage are confiscated. A very scary looking member of the Policía Federal Preventiva has plucked two bottles of tequila from my Louis Vuitton deluxe brown leather travel bag with matching purse. How rude of him! The duty free is acceptable to bring through,

Señior Party Pooper explains, but the other liquids in my handbag are over the one hundred millilitre limit. Nightmare.

'That's ridiculous,' I declare, pulling myself up to my full five feet five inches. People are starting to stare. Well, let them, this is important. 'I mean, what kind of buzz would you get with one hundred millilitres or less?'

The female security guard then discovers two teeny vodkas from the hotel mini bar crammed into my jeans pockets. They're like little adorable alcoholic stowaways. She then throws them into a plastic basket, marked 'prohibido'. The staff here probably have a great Christmas party with all of the contraband booze.

'Let's take a seat at the boarding gate,' Barry leads me away from the security staff. The hangover from the last night of our honeymoon has reached throbbing point, and I'm not really in the mood for a Mexican stand-off, so I don't put up a fight.

We've finally boarded, and my head is banging. I swear on Patrick Swayze's grave, I'm never drinking again. Apart from in the next five minutes, of course, but that's literally for medicinal purposes.

'Airhostess! Airhostess!'

'Becks, she won't serve you 'til we're in the air. We're still on the runway…'

'Don't be daft. The service is great on these Trans-Atlantic flights. Sure, they love to keep the passengers happy. We've paid top dollar, and I'm going to get my money's worth between here and Dublin. Airhostess!'

The polyester-clad airhostess is definitely ignoring me. She's at the top of the plane doing some silly safety message or other, and pretending to toot-toot on a red plastic whistle.

'Eh, we all know how to buckle a belt,' I snort as Barry attempts to shush me.

Once we have reached the desired altitude, the trolley appears. About time, too. Dehydration can be a dangerous thing, you know. During the last few minutes, I've had to ask Barry to hold the sick bag out for me, just in case. Now, don't you go feeling sorry for him, right? He swore before God, not to mention our family and friends, that he would love me for better or for worse, in sickness and in health. Now might be his chance to prove it. Besides, maybe it's not my fault that I'm so ill. Maybe I was drugged by the bar staff last night. I saw that on a Channel Four documentary once, it was awful. Or maybe the food was off. Tequila couldn't possibly make someone feel this close to death.

'Gin and tonic,' I instruct the air hostess in between deep breaths into the paper sick bag. She pretends that she can't hear me as she rummages for change for the passenger two seats ahead of me.

'Next time, Barry, book seats closer to the top. They've all been served before us.'

'Uh huh.'

'And another thing. They should have upgraded us. I told them we were on honeymoon, but here we are slumming it in cattle class. We should be drinking free champagne.'

'Yes, Becks. You told them three times.'

'Exactly. It's a joke. I'm going to write a snotty letter. I'm good at snotty letters, Barry. I could type it up on your solicitor headed paper. It'll be the first thing I do when we get back. Well, the second thing. I want to squeeze my little fluffy Jessekins first, I miss him so much.'

I think of my hairy cat-baby at home. He's probably distraught, pacing back and forth on the lounge rug in that obese way of his, counting down the listless days until I return. Three weeks away from his mummy would have been like an eternity in cat years, he's probably traumatized. I just hope that mum remembered the little drops for his eyes, because he has cataracts. Oh, and if she didn't mash up his food, he'd choke. The poor thing doesn't have many teeth left.

'God, finally! Gin and tonic, please. Oh, and a packet of nuts.'

'Just relax and enjoy the flight, will you?' Barry shakes his head.

'Love you, baby,' I laugh. 'Isn't this fun?'

I don't want the other passengers behind us to think we're arguing. Newlyweds are not supposed to fight. They're meant to feed each other peanuts and clink champagne glasses as they smile into each other's smug faces in first class.

The complimentary pretzels are great for soakage, and I've also pinched Barry's packet. The heartbeat in my head has dulled, and I'm starting to feel a little better as the gin and tonic hits my fragile stomach. I plug in the earphones, drape the blanket around my knees, and close my heavy eyes.

Wiping the drool from my chin, I scan the plane to see what awful racket has woken me. There's a screaming baby at the back.

'Why would someone bring an infant on a long haul flight, Barry?'

'Poor pet probably has sore ears,' Barry is on his feet to admire the baby. 'Want to come and see?'

'Eh no, you go. I'll close my eyes for a bit.'

Barry is back half an hour later, gushing about the baby and a heart-breaking adoption story.

'Ah. She's beautiful, Becks. Stunning dark eyes, and long eyelashes. You should go and have a peep at her.'

'Yeah, sounds lovely. Maybe later.'

My hangover has gone down from a grade five to a grade four – it only hurts if I move.

'And just think, baby,' Barry smiles and his eyelids crease at the sides in that handsome way of his.

'Now that we're married...' he squeezes my knee. 'That'll be us with a little baby one day. I can't wait.'

There's a swirl in my stomach, and it's not the gin. I knew this day would come. Broody Barry has been talking about a baby since we moved in together. I kind-of-sort-of maybe said that we'd talk about starting a family when we were married. Then I distracted him with wedding bands and which variety of cake to choose for the reception. I've officially run out of time.

'Air hostess! Hello? Air hostess? Yes, you in the turquoise polyester! Another gin and tonic, please. Oh, and make it a double.'

Two

'Ah, welcome home, darling. Great tan!'

Mum is thrilled to see me and has the kettle on pronto. We have spoken every day on Barry's mobile since the wedding. His phone bill will be quite a stinker this month.

'I've some scones just made, darling. Grab some plates, will you?'

'Oh, I shouldn't. Piled on the weight on honeymoon.'

'Not at all, darling. Sure, you look great. Here,' Mum passes me the butter and jam for the table as she adds the scalding water and teabags to the teapot.

'No, thanks. Honestly, mum, I've got to cut back.'

I get the heavenly whiff of the scones as mum opens the oven door. It's intoxicating and I'm drawn to it, like a squiffy student to a kebab shop at three in the morning.

'Well. Just half of one. That can't hurt.'

I slice the plump scone in two and thickly smear the butter, followed by a generous slathering of jam.

'So....' Mum narrows her eyes. 'Something on your mind, darling?'

'What? No, nothing. Just thinking about having to face work tomorrow.'

'Sure, you'll be back into the routine by the end of the week. How's Barry?'

'Fine.'

There's no lying to mum, she can see right through me. I might as well spit it out.

'Look, it's nothing really, it's just that... Well, Barry really wants a baby...'

'Well, yes, that would be absolutely lovely, darling. Wouldn't it?'

'I suppose so.'

'A little grandchild,' mum smiles. 'A boy. Or a girl. Or one of each. You know Leslie in Bridge Club? The one who had her hip replacement done last year? Well, she has ten grandkids already. Ten! She keeps asking me when I'll be a granny. I mean, I don't know what to say to her.'

'Well, we mustn't disappoint *Leslie,* mum.'

I decide to push the other half of the scone away so that I'm not tempted, but, like an illusion, it has already disappeared.

'Look. All I'm saying...,' my mother soothes as she pours me another cup of tea, '...is that maybe you and Barry should talk about it. You know, now that you're married and all, darling. Barry's keen, isn't he?'

Keen doesn't even begin to describe Barry. He has always been like a mother hen, cluck-clucking every time we visit friends who have kids, talking about how great they are all the way home in the car. He's the type of guy who asks to hold the baby at a christening.

Mum's no better. She has been harping on about ticking biological clocks since before the engagement ring was even on my finger. Now that we're married, there's no stopping her.

'Tick tock,' she sing songs. 'Once you're in your thirties, darling, it's harder to fall pregnant. Something to do with the quality of the eggs. Saw it on The Discovery Channel.'

'Yes, mum. I know.' She has reminded me weekly of this fact since I turned thirty last November.

'I mean, I'm not getting any younger myself, darling.'

Here we go. I roll my eyes and she bends down to give Boy George a piece of scone, and coughs a wheezy splutter into her fist. Don't be alarmed, Boy George is her black toy poodle, she doesn't have the real Boy George under her kitchen table begging for scraps. That'd just be weird. Fun, but weird.

'Who knows how many years I have left, darling.'

'Mum! You're only sixty!'

'Perhaps I'll hold a little grandbaby in my arms one day, before I die...' She gives me a weak smile and coughs again. Barry says I have the 'drama gene' and I think I know where I got it from.

'Maybe next year, mum. We'll see...,' I throw her a bone. Perhaps it will keep her happy for a while.

Honestly, this whole *baby* thing is getting way out of hand. I have only just said 'I do' and already the pressure to reproduce is palpable. The tan from my tropical paradise honeymoon has yet to fade, and I haven't even unpacked. I haven't had Emer, my chief bridesmaid, dry clean my wedding dress yet! Can I not digest the flipping wedding cake before I have to consider babies? Can I not revel in my post-honeymoon bliss before talking about the pitter-pattering of feet? Everyone is ruining my wedded buzz!

'Lots of your friends have babies now, don't they?' Mum refuses to drop the subject.

'Yes,' I smile. 'Kids aren't a fashion accessory, mum. Just because my friends have one doesn't mean I should too!'

'Of course not, darling. That pal of yours…Karen, is it? She has three now, doesn't she?'

This is code for 'get your skates on'. Perhaps mum and Karen are in cahoots. My friends are even more pushy than mum. Just because they have been popping out sprogs left right and centre since they said 'I do,' they assume that I'll follow suit. Every time I log onto Facebook, I see them droning on and on about their brood. From new teeth, nappy rash and potty performances – they update their status with every gurgle, giggle and drool. Every Irish dancing medal is posted, even though I bet the teachers hand them out to everyone. Every vomiting bug is discussed in minute, stomach wrenching detail. It's never ending.

'But what if…,' I confide, '…I'm not cut out to be a mum?' my chin wobbles a bit when I say this, so it must be true.

'Don't be silly!' mum laughs. 'You'd be a great mum!'

'Yeah, but…I mean… some people always *knew* that they would become a mum. Remember Donna from primary school? Ever since she was four and pushing a doll's pram, she *knew* that she wanted to be a mummy.'

Mum nods. No doubt she remembers how Donna brushed the doll's hair lovingly, dressed her in an assortment of outfits, rocked her to sleep and kissed her angelic face.

'She has five little ones now. I saw her mum in Tesco.'

'Well, I was never like that, mum. Those baby dolls just did pees in a potty and said "mama". Creepy. What's the point?'

'Yes,' laughs mum. 'You and Anna had more of an interest in Barbies, I remember.'

Anna, my BFF when I was ten, would spend the afternoons with me, pooling together our impressive collection of Barbies, Cindis and Ken dolls. We had also collected Barbie horses, sports cars and Malibu beach houses.

I loved going to Anna's after school. Most houses use the space underneath the stairs for a clever shelving and storage area – perhaps a downstairs loo, or somewhere to store the Hoover. Not in Anna's house. In Anna's house, her dad had lovingly converted the under-stair area into a Barbie apartment. You heard me right. An entire flipping apartment block for Barbie, and her cool city-dwelling, couture-wearing friends. There was even a working lift and tiny furniture. There was somewhere for Barbie to park her Ferrari and keep her horses. Anna's dad was a lot cooler than mine.

'You'd spend hours at Anna's,' remembers mum.

Mum doesn't know this, but the games our Barbie dolls played were a tad grown up. No wonder we didn't have time for baby dolls and prams. The Barbie dolls wore sequined ball gowns and matching shoes. There was luxuriant blonde hair to style, and decadent jewellery to select. There were critical decisions to be made regarding various diamante tiaras and fur coats. My favourite was limited edition Manhattan Madame Barbie. She was quite the diva, making a scene at her friend's wedding and throwing wild parties in the penthouse. She would marry sensible brunette Ken in the serious beige corduroy trousers and plastic briefcase, and then have outrageous affairs with blond Ken with the six pack and Hawaiian shorts. Sometimes I would pinch my brother Ian's Action Man if Barbie was bored and needed someone macho to tell her that she was pretty. You know, because often Ken was consumed with fixing the Barbie deluxe holiday caravan, and didn't pay enough attention to her. Besides, he didn't understand her like Action Man did.

Anna and I would prepare Barbie for her vacation in the Malibu beach home (complete with deluxe kitchen and swimming pool) and then Barbie would boss the 'made in Taiwan' plastic imitation Barbie, and slag off her home haircut. There was no baby Barbie in our game. Barbie was having too good a time to worry about nappies and bottles. Now that I think about it, we might have been exposed at a young age to an excessive amount of Dallas and other TV unsuitable for our innocent minds. It would explain a lot.

'Yeah. Happy days.'

Last I heard, Anna was married and living in a three-bed semi in Wexford town, with two little boys. Boys! Imagine! There's probably not even a Barbie doll in sight. She's probably swimming in a sea of testosterone, Lego and Bob the Builder.

'Well, darling, I kept those Barbies in the attic. All of them, even the ones you got the scissors to. And the ones you stuck pins in. And the ones that were always naked apart from stilettos. Ah, bless your little imagination! You never know,' Mum sing-songs. 'Maybe a little granddaughter will play with them again one day.'

'Hmm. Maybe. But I've never really been overly excited by babies, you know?'

She knows. When I was younger, mum would stop strangers on the road to coo over their babies, admiring the drooling dotes in their prams. She would make gaga sounds and smile into their podgy faces. As a teenager, it was all very embarrassing and inconvenient. I would feign interest, just to be polite. I was usually distracted by the adorable little dog with rhinestone collar that trotted alongside the buggy. These days, it's Barry who stops people on the street to peep inside the buggy. I just smile and agree with him when he says how cute the kids are.

'Ah no. You'd be great, Rebecca. A wonderful mother. And sure, I'd babysit.'

The babysitting bit appeals, I must admit. Barry and I could jet off to Rome or Paris or some romantic European city, and enjoy a candle lit Table D'hote dinner while mum burps the baby back in Dublin, or whatever it is that grannies do with babies. Barry could buy me some staggeringly impressive diamonds in Amsterdam just to thank me for selflessly sub-letting my body out to the kid for a whole nine months. Oh, and a pair of those silky French knickers to reignite our passion. He could say 'there, there' and hand feed me croissants as I recover from stretch marks and stitches and other such horrors. I could call home and check on things from the Jacuzzi. It would be important that Barry and I invest in our relationship and not let a baby ruin everything.

'Hmm,' I consider.

Important questions run through my mind. Would I be patient? Would I be kind? Would I make papier-mâché creations on a wet Wednesday at the kitchen table?

'But babies are ...' I search for the right adjective. '...really hard work.'

I've never been one for hard work. Just ask my boss, I'm lucky to still have a job. I don't mind getting stuck in at the animal shelter every Sunday, but that doesn't ever feel like work, it feels like fun. Nothing's too much trouble for my fur-babies, whether it's mucking out pongy kennels or dragging sacks of dog food from the storage shed. If only I could be as enthusiastic about human babies!

'What do you mean, darling?'

It's hard to explain. You see, I like my civilized life and my designer clothes. I like my cream carpet and cream couch. I don't feel like losing either to sticky fingers and chocolate smudges. I like independence. I like parties. Having a dependent might mean rising at dawn. Hangovers and babies do not mix. So far in this life, I have chosen disposable income over disposable nappies. I've chosen bottles of wine over bottles of formula.

'A baby would be lovely, of course it would. And Barry would be a great dad, obviously. It's just that...' I try to explain my mixed emotions to mum, but the words are stuck, swollen in my throat.

A little image pops into my head. Barry and I have a baby, and the sweet little darling has colic, keeping Barry awake all night. Thankfully, I continue to snore like a fog horn, but Barry has black rings and puffy eye bags. It's not a good look on him. I'm stuck at home all day long while Barry swans off to work for twelve hours. I haven't lost the baby weight, and start talking like Peppa Pig.

My friend Sorca has a two-year-old who still doesn't sleep through the night. Can you imagine? She didn't come to the wedding because she and her long suffering husband Matt are so sleep deprived and run down, and couldn't get a babysitter. I mean, what if that happens to us?

You see, I've barely seen Sorca since baby Matthew was born. She hired a night nurse, but the woman quit. Nothing worked, the bedraggled nurse announced one morning last month, suitcase in hand. Sorca tearfully filled me in on the whole thing over the phone. The nurse was some kind of sleep specialist. Cost a bomb, apparently. Anyway, I think the child kind of... broke her. She hadn't seen a case like it, and is now considering stepping away from baby sleep coaching and moving to geriatric nursing, where the patients sleep loads more. I may have invented that last bit for my own amusement, so don't quote me on it.

If you ask me, Sorca should receive some kind of endurance medal. Or at least a Blue Peter Badge, if they still make them. Matthew wakes three times a night for a bottle and then starts the day at five in the morning. It's like a form of Chinese torture.

Mum takes my hand. 'It's just that …what, Rebecca?'

My mind flits back to that awful night so long ago, and the look on Louise and Dermot's face when they entered the master bedroom.

'It's just that..,' I attempt. 'I don't think that I'm cut out for it.'

Three

'Have you got that photocopying yet, Rebecca?'

It's the first day back to the dreaded office since the wedding, and already Harry the Horrible is being a pest. He seems to have failed to recognize that I, a golden bronzed newlywed, am in absolutely no mood to be in the slightest bit productive. For starters, I need to re-acclimatize back to the monotonous life I had before wedding fever took over. Secondly, I couldn't be bothered. After arriving late this morning, I reluctantly switched my computer on, opened the mini mountain of post, and made myself a strong coffee. Surely this is enough. Surely I should pace myself. I'm not a machine!

'In a minute, Harry! For goodness sake!' I can't hide my annoyance. Why should I? Radiant brides shouldn't have to enthuse over mundane tasks. Truth be told, if I could present my perfect-office-day in pie chart format (just, you know to impress the pants off you), it would be 95% web surfing and 5% work.

Dozens of emails spill into my inbox. They have built up from my four-week absence, and are of no importance. Some of them are marked as urgent. Well, tough! I absentmindedly hold my finger on the delete button. The emails disappear in a blur, as if by magic. Ah, that's better.

'Here.' I slop the papers across Harry's mahogany desk and he reaches to catch them. One slides off the side of the desk and flutters on to the carpet. Harry has to bend over to get it. Serves him right! Since my return, Harry hasn't even asked about the honeymoon. In fact, no-one has.

'Eh, you're welcome,' I make a clicking noise with my tongue as I exit his office before he can demand more soul-crushing menial tasks.

In the kitchenette, I add a heavy layer of butter to my bagel. I'm starving since getting back from the honeymoon. I think my metabolism adjusted to the 'full-board /all-you-can-eat /twenty-four-hour-buffet /must-get-my-money's-worth / yes-I'd-like-fries-with-that / make-mine-a-large-one' holiday.

'Ah, you're back, Rebecca.'

It's Brendan from Human Resources, stirring his tea. I'm eyeing up his packet of Jaffa Cakes.

'Hi, yes I'm back! Ah, it was great. Five star all the way. Real luxury. Opulent is the word I'd use. Very exclusive. No riff raff. Of course, Pearse Brosnan went there on his honeymoon, too. Here, I've a few snaps in my purse. I'll just get them...'

I turn around, but he's gone. Luckily, he has forgotten his biscuits in his haste, so I rescue them. I'd hate for them to feel lonely and abandoned.

Judy, my office BFF, sits in the cubicle opposite. I've guilt-tripped her into listening to tales of the honeymoon, and it would be rude of her to say no. She flicks through the snaps and yawns. Now, when I say flicks, I mean she literally flicks like a child showing you his home made cartoon.

'Hmm. Looks lovely.'

She glazes over as I describe the golf club. She looks positively bored as I tell her how the award winning spa made my toe nails look like little elegant shells. She barely raises an eyebrow as I recount tales to her of Roberto the hunky Latino lifeguard who lounged by the Olympic-sized swimming pool in teeny speedos. She reaches for her mobile to answer a call, raising her finger to indicate that this will only be a minute.

'Fine,' I take the photos back from her desk.

It's probably painful for her to hear about dips in the warm turquoise sea when her love life is dead in the water. It's possibly agony to learn how loved up Barry and I are, and how much honeymoon nookie we enjoyed in our deluxe suite four poster bed when she is going through relationship problems herself. Still, it's no excuse. She could at least pretend.

I go in search of a replacement ear.

'Amanda!' I wave my arms frantically at the accounts manager.

'Come and see the snaps. It was so great! So hard to be back to work. The cocktails were to die for. Such a luxurious hotel. Very exclusive. No riff raff. Of course, Pearse Brosnan went there on his honeymoon, too.'

'Welcome back, Rebecca. Sounds great. I'm late for a meeting. Better dash. Catch you later, yeah?'

Later, indeed! She wasn't in such a rush to leave when she was shoving cocktail sausages in her mouth at the wedding after party. She wasn't in such a hurry when she wanted to talk about the time that her and 'her Graham' got engaged. I had yawned politely through that!

Judy is off the phone and tapping away at her keyboard. Brendan is drinking his tea and searching through desk drawers for the Jaffa Cakes with a baffled look on his face. Harry is still trying to put the photocopying pages back in the right order.

Forget the lot of them! It was only four weeks ago that they were quaffing *my* Châteaux de Vin and chowing down on *my* succulent beef medallions followed by gateaux Diane. They drank *my* champagne and danced like drunken buffoons to *my* wedding band. They 'ooh-ed' and 'ahh-ed' at *my* fireworks. Now, it's all over and they don't want to know.

I call mum for a whine.

'Well, the honeymoon is officially over, mum. Life is so hard!'

'Never mind, darling. There's always an anti-climax after these things. Call around later for a chat.'

Even mum can't talk for long. She's on her way to a game of bridge with her retirement buddies and doesn't have time for her newly married only daughter.

Suzie from reception is at the water cooler, so I pounce on her like a lion on a gazelle at an African watering hole. She splutters on her Ballygowan.

'Hi! Oh, Suzie, you should have seen our waiter at the hotel! Fernando. Every morning he would lay out a selection of pastries and watermelon at the poolside. Oh, and the maid? Juanita. She made these little heart shaped towel things and sprinkled rose petals on our four poster bed. It was so classy. Quite exclusive. Absolutely no riff …'

'And so, will we hear the pitter patter of tiny feet any time soon?' she cuts me off.

'Pardon?'

It's my turn to splutter.

'Yes, any news?' Amanda appears behind my shoulder, startling me.

'What?'

The two gazelles have ganged up and are staring at the lion.

'Will you and Barry be hearing the pitter patter of tiny feet any time soon?' Suzie repeats, one eyebrow raised.

'Yes, now that you're married, will the stork be planning a trip round your way, eh?'

Amanda's head is tilted to the side.

'What? No!' I laugh. It's a touch on the hysterical side – high pitched like a hyena.

'Not a chance!' I wave the idea away with my hand.

They nod, but their eyes are still glued to my belly which bulges against the waistband of my jeans. I might have to slip into the loo and pop a couple of buttons to relieve the tension. Either that or I could invest in a pair of elastic wasted trousers like mum got from the Family Album shopping catalogue. They only come in beige, but they'd do until I work off those few extra holiday kilos.

'No, I mean... what... this?' I motion to my muffin top.

'Nah. I've probably put on a few ...honeymoon pounds. Everyone does that. You know, starving skinny Minnie before the wedding and then boom! All you can eat holiday, ha-ha!'

'Ah well, I'm sure you'll have news soon.' Amanda smiles sweetly.

'Me? News? No! I mean, I've an elderly cat and a very hectic social life. That's enough for anyone!'

I swallow my annoyance. The only news I want to discuss is the news of the century: my wedding was the best wedding in history (celebrity or otherwise). The only occasion I want to connect 'pitter patter' and 'feet' in the same sentence is to describe my French-pedicure toes on the tropical white sands of Mexico! I only want to talk about the stork if he is making delivery of our deluxe wedding album from our award winning photographer.

'Anyway,' I break the uncomfortable silence. 'Let me grab the snaps. Suzie, you didn't get much of a glance this morning…'

Suzie and Amanda's internal phone lines are both ringing simultaneously. They have been saved by the bell, and scuttle off like schoolgirls caught in the corridor during class time.

Draining the dregs of my cappuccino, I considered the idea. *Me, a mummy?*

Nah! I quickly push the thought away. I mean…

1. I have a geriatric cat called Jessie to think of. The elderly feline could die any day now. It's touch and go. The vet says that he's about twelve, and definitely 'getting on'. That's about one hundred in human years. He prescribed medication for cataracts and said that it's

normal that he sleeps a lot during the day. This may have been code for 'brace yourself for moggy heaven'. He might have been breaking it to me gently, who knows? He may have been sending me a telepathic message about pet cremation. Poor Jess is bloody ancient and has to have his food mashed up now. He needs me!

2. My digital recorder TV box thing is full to the brim with four weeks of back to back episodes of 'Dr Phil', 'Home and Away' and 'Neighbours'. It will take my full concentration to get through that kind of backlog, but I'm committed to the task at hand. A baby would throw off my entire schedule.

3. I've put on a shed load of weight from the honeymoon and need to get rid of it pronto. It's not my fault. I had starved myself and attended Zumba classes before the wedding. With the help of industrial strength corseting, I had then squeezed into a size ten Vera Wang wedding dress. Breathing deeply and /or consuming food on the big day was, naturally, not an option, but it was so worth it. It now feels like all of my clothes have shrunk in the wash. The weight gain is obviously a lot more than I'd realized, judging by my colleagues' reaction. I will need to hire a sexy Lycra clad fitness trainer in tight shorts to get me back in shape.

4. I don't get overly excited about babies. Sorry, I know that's not very politically correct of me to admit out loud, but there you go. Look, I don't hate them. I don't love them. I'm somewhere lukewarm in the middle. To me, kids are a bit like rice pudding – I could take it or leave it, but I'm not in a desperate, heart palpitating rush to have one. Then again, chocolate rice pudding is quite nice.

5. I'm not good with babies. Or kids. Or teenagers. Or short people. The Great Poonami of 2003 is still ringing in my ears. You know those maternal women that are described as 'natural' with children? They smile a lot? Yeah, that's not me. I don't do it on purpose, I promise! I'm just awkward and babies cry a lot in my presence. It's uncomfortable and they want their mummies back.

There, that's five good reasons. I'm so good at making executive decisions. Perhaps I should ask for a promotion. Harry's office door is closed, so I'll ask him later.

I dial Karen's number for a girlie chin wag. I'm dying to tell her about the honeymoon. She has three kids now, so the furthest she gets is probably her local Tesco. Perhaps she's dead jealous of me because of my jet setting glamorous life. Oh, I do hope so!

'Hey, Karen, I'm back. So much to tell you. It was pure bliss. Very exclusive. We're talking five star treatment all the way!'

It's hard for her to hear me, because there are three kids squawking in the background, but I plough on.

'Did I mention that Pierce Brosnan got married there? Wall to wall celebrities, it was. No riff raff. The sister of your one out of 'Hollyoaks' was there. She had a boob job last year –'

'Now that you're married,' Karen coos, 'I bet you'll want to start a family now. Hashtag Broody Newlywed! Am I right?'

I've lost my train of thought. It was something about the Michelin star gourmet chef at our tropical report.

'Eh, not really, Karen. Not for a while. Anyway, it had this award winning golf resort. Not that I play golf, but you know…if you were into golf, it was the best…'

'So, no news then?'

I roll my eyes. 'News?'

One of the babies has just thrown up all over her shoulder, and she has to go. It's four o'clock and I'm exhausted, so I slip out of work. If I stay in the office any later than four, I feel like I'll break out in a rash. It's like I have a genuine allergic reaction to work. I will Google it later, it could be a real thing, like 'Office phobia' or something. I tell Harry that I'm off to buy stamps and that it can't wait. I'm sure he won't notice if I don't come back.

Four

When I get home from work, I want to turn and run in the opposite direction. I want to hide far, far away and never come back. The house is like a pig sty, and I'm far too tired to tackle it, so I go to plan B.

Since Barry and I landed on Saturday, my BFF slash head bridesmaid Emer has been asking me to call in. It will be great to see her, because I've missed her terribly. Also, her bridesmaid duties didn't end when I said 'I do'. Au contraire. Her most pressing post-wedding duty is to inspect each and every honeymoon photo in detail. She should then ask a lot of soul searching questions about the glorious holiday during said inspection. Above all, she has to listen to every long winded story and anecdote involving my Mexican paradise escape, with an expression of sheer delight on her face.

Oh, and in case you were wondering, additional post-wedding bridesmaid duties include, but are not limited to:

a.Help the bride (AKA me) to short-list photos for my wedding album. My dress shall look so very stunning in every heartbreakingly beautiful photo, it will be so hard to choose the best. Emer might cry as she remembers the magical day. She can make a scrapbook of her memories if she likes. We can cut out the photos where Barry looks red eyed, or isn't smiling properly, as per my instructions.

b. Assist in the dry cleaning of my couture bridal gown. When I say assist, I guess I just mean oversee the whole damn thing. It's a dull task and I'm busy. Also, Emer is loaded and it costs a lot.

c. Coach me, over large glasses of wine, to write thank you notes. Apparently it's rude not to thank people for wedding gifts, even if they did only give you a measly toaster. I had two Karaoke machines (one for upstairs and one for downstairs, obviously) on the wedding gift list and didn't even get one! Isn't it enough that these people enjoyed the best day of their lives without having to write to them individually and thank them? Apparently not. By the way, my handwriting is sloppy when I'm drinking wine; it's probably best if I just delegate the whole thing to Emer.

d. Tell me that I am not, in fact, fat. Rather, I am just back to a normal, all be it non-bridal but perfectly acceptable, size. Everyone goes crazy on nachos and Pina Coladas on honeymoon. No-one can maintain the weight they were when they first got married. It's unrealistic. Also, I need to hear that I am pretty on a regular basis and that Barry is lucky to have me. Being a bridesmaid is a lifelong commitment, I'll have you know.

At first, I find it odd of Emer to insist that I come to her house, since I'm the one who is literally only just back from a long-haul Trans-Atlantic flight and am yet to unpack. Then I consider what a state the house is in, so I agree to go to hers instead.

Emer and husband David live close by in Leopardstown. However, while Barry and I live in a three bed semi-detached, Emer lives in more of what you'd call a mansion. Think MTV cribs, and you're in the right ball park. It's got five bedrooms (ahem, all en-suite), and a gym (that helps to maintain Emers perfect teeny tiny figure) and a conservatory (that's posh for extension.) The lounge has a bar with three different types of vodka. The house even has gates and an intercom, so handy for keeping pushy door-to-door salesmen out. There are matching Mercedes (brand new S class, as if you have to ask) parked in the perfect cobbled driveway which divides a perfect manicured lawn. It's nice. You know, if you're into perfection.

'Oh my God, hi!' Emer squeals as she greets me at the front door. 'You look great! Fab tan. Listen, excuse the state of the place. Svetlana is on a day off. Come in!'

The place is sickeningly pristine. At any minute, the doorbell could ring with a journalist from 'Good Housekeeping' to interview Emer about her art collection. There's not a plumped designer cushion out of place. A massive gold mirror adorns a large entrance hall as she leads me into the grey marble kitchen. It's been recently remodelled, but the last one looked absolutely fine to me. Apparently, it was hideous and out dated and had to go pronto, along with the hideous dining room table that I thought was lovely.

'So! Tell me all about it!' Emer smiles.

I breathe a sigh of relief. Finally! Someone to revel in every minute detail! Emer is standing at a marble island in the middle of the kitchen. Her kitten heels click-clack on the porcelain cream tiles, as she readies the Nespresso machine and gets the mini coffee cups organised.

'Emer, it was heaven. I mean total bliss. So exclusive. I can see why Pierse Brosnan goes there. Loads of other celebrities too, for that matter. Oh, and the spa! You'd have loved it!'

Thank God I can count on Emer. I root in my handbag for the snaps. We sit in what Emer calls the relaxation room, which is basically like a lounge but fancier. It has three two-seater cream leather couches and a marble coffee table in the middle. I think she does yoga in it. There are wall to wall books with titles like 'The Seven Steps to Success' and 'The Power Inside'.

I notice that Emer has only brought in one coffee for me, and none for herself. It must be part of whatever no-caffeine / no-dairy/ no-wheat/ no-fun detox thing she's on now.

'Here.' I fan out the photos on the glass topped table. 'This is our hotel room. Well, it was more of a suite, really. Look at the little rose petals on the bed!'

'Cute,' she replies.

'Ah, now. Look at this one. That's Fernando, our head waiter. Served a very good Marguerita. We bonded. And there's Barry making a show of himself on a sun lounger. State of him.'

'Gorgeous.'

I can't put my finger on it. She's not as excited as I'd anticipated. I was banking on more hand flapping, and as much eyebrow raising as the Botox would allow.

'And here's me having my hair puffed by Consuela at the hotel spa. And here's me buying a case of tequila from the locals. Such a beautiful, ancient culture...'

'Hmm...'

There it is again, that non-committal nod. She is being so... *meh!* Where is my 'wow' reaction? Where are the little shrieks of excitement and clapping of hands? Where is the streak of jealousy I was hoping for? I know that Emer gets to stay in the top hotels, both on business and pleasure. She has travelled the world and has a salary that would make your eyes water. Is the resort not impressive enough for her? She's my best friend and chief bridesmaid, she could at least fake it!

'And here's me being abducted by aliens from Mars. Such a lovely gang of extra-terrestrials. So polite. And here's me being interrogated by nasty Al Qaeda men in Afghanistan…boo to those awful, bearded meanies!'

'Lovely,' Emer is staring into space.

'Eh, hello? Emer! You're not even looking at the photos! Look, I know you have been to Mexico, like, millions of times, but …'

'Sorry, pet. Sorry. No, they're great. It's just… sorry.'

It's weird, Emer looks tired, and I don't think I've ever seen her look so pale. Perhaps the new detox diet is too intense, or she has one of those yukky flus. It better not be catching, I'm already on a verbal warning for sick leave at work. It'd be awful if I actually became sick for real and had to call Harry. Isn't life ironic? Just to be sure, I move away a few centimetres.

'Sorry. No, it's just that something amazing has happened,' she smiles and leans in closer to me on the couch.

'Oh?'

I pray.

Dear Jesus,

Ah come on! Not another promotion for Emer. Please! Honest to goodness, the woman is already rolling in it.

David too. Could you not splash the cash in my direction for a change?

Amen.

'We're pregnant!' Emer clamps her hand over her mouth.

'We?' I blink.

'David and I. Pregnant! Can you believe it?'

I stifle a snigger as I imagine David with a protruding belly.

'Oh my God, Emer. Wow. That's… that's so…'

'I know, it's amazing.'

'Oh my God.'

'As you know, we've been trying for, like, months.'

This is news to me. She must have told me, but as this piece of information didn't relate to 'The Wedding of the Century', I must have filtered it out. You can understand why I was a tad distracted.

'Wow!' It's all I can say, over and over. I never had Emer down as the maternal type. She seems far too busy and successful.

'So, when are you…?'

'Due? Early January. A New Year's baby. I'm three months gone.'

I do the maths.

'Three months, you said?'

'Yeah,' she beams.

Good God. By my swift calculations, she was preggers not only on my wedding day but leading up to it. She was pregnant on my hen weekend to Monart. She could have jeopardized the entire celebrations! She could have been vomiting into my lily of the valley bridal bouquet, stealing the attention from my good self. She could have been fainting while the photographer was trying to line us up for the wedding shots. She could have been ripping the seams on the designer pink silk Diane Von Furstenburg couture bridesmaid's gown with matching pink silk headband!

'Oh, Rebecca,' Emers thin hands clutches mine. 'It's been such a long road. I just can't believe it. I didn't want to tell anyone until the three months had passed. You know, just in case...'

She's welling up, now, and I'm just smiling and nodding, processing it all.

'Long road...' I mimic.

I've absolutely no memory of hearing about this. All I know is, it's going to be pretty hard to steer the conversation back to me and my honeymoon now.

'The endless ovulation kits, medical appointments, negative pregnancy tests...,' a tear plops onto her knee.

There's flip all opportunity now to tell her about the Michelin star dining under the Mexican stars. There's an ice cube's chance in hell of getting around to the photo of me drinking champagne in the hot tub. My amusing anecdotes have been heartlessly hijacked.

'Wow.'

And where did this sudden baby obsession come from, I wonder? It's like she has had a personality transplant in the four weeks since we have seen each other. I mean, yes, she would admire other people's babies from time to time. Of course! And yes, she talked about one day she and her husband having a mini David and a little Emer. But I didn't think she meant it! I thought she was joking! I remember snorting with laughter when she told me. Emer does power suits and power lunches. She throws dinner parties and flies to New York for conferences. I can't picture her as the apron and slippers kind.

'And we had even made an appointment at...' her voice is hushed even though it's just the two of us in the house. There's not an Eastern European housekeeper within earshot. '...the Glow Fertility clinic... for tests.'

'No!'

'Really,' she nods. 'Really. But then it just... happened!'

'Well, you look good.' I offer.

'Oh do you think? I'm struggling to hide the bulge already! Thank God for empire line tops is all I can say. Here, look at this.'

Emer lifts her top and rubs her stomach.

'What?'

'There. Look!'

'Where?'

'There. I feel like a whale! The baby is the size of a walnut now. I've been reading up about it in my pregnancy books. I'll have to get maternity trousers soon. Either that or start wearing a size ten.'

Emer laughs at the thoughts of, God forbid, moving up from a size eight to a size ten. It's hardly portly. I, on the other hand, would sell my granny for the chance to wear a size ten. Judging by my recent weight gain, I'll be lucky if I see a size twelve again before I die.

Emer is a jammy cow in the looks department. Her body would make you sick, really. Her belly looks completely washboard flat to me. If I had a stomach like that, I would outright refuse to wear anything other than belly tops, even in December.

'Oh, and I've had to tone down the high heels,' she giggles excitedly. 'No more six-inchers for me. Three-inch heels only now. For safety reasons. Wouldn't want to fall over. That'd be awful.'

'Awful,' I deadpan.

'So now you understand why I didn't drink champagne at your wedding! Or cosmos on the hen night!'

I connect the dots. Come to think of it, she was a bit tame on the hen night. I distinctly remember, before passing out blind drunk, that she was decidedly sober and sensible that evening. She didn't perform the Macarena with me. Or the Time Warp. She outright refused to assist me stuff a banana down the stripper's shorts. She didn't even try to catch me when I decided to launch myself at her when the DJ played the Dirty Dancing soundtrack. I just landed on the floor. Don't worry, though, I didn't feel a thing. Pam broke my fall.

Also, I caught Emer yawning a couple of times, and she was in bed by midnight.

Pam, her co-bridesmaid, had complained that Emer ordering a Virgin Mojito at a wedding was definitely dull and very much frowned upon, and I had shushed her. And now that Emer has mentioned it, I did notice that there was orange juice in her champers flute as we did the cheers at the head table during the wedding speeches. I had just assumed that there was a double vodka in there. I'd guessed that, like everyone else, she was taking advantage of the free bar. Sure, I was too busy lining up the shots to notice otherwise. I thought she was taking her bridesmaid's duties seriously! I thought she was staying clear headed in order to get through the speech with elegance and charm! I was tricked.

'So, I've found this fab little place near Trinity College that does darling designer maternity wear. All French labels, of course. "Le Jolie Maman" it's called. Very classy. The great thing is that I get to buy a whole new wardrobe!' she thrills.

'Great.'

I can't imagine anything duller than buying stretchy maternity clothes, even if they are French.

'Sure, I'll be bursting out of this stuff in no time. Like the Incredible Hulk. I'm sure people will start to notice.'

'Emer, will you stop! Sure, you look as skinny as ever.'

'Thanks. I mean, I'm tired but that's normal. It should lift soon. I've cut down to a twelve-hour day at work.'

'Wow. Just the twelve hours, then.' My guilty mind flashes to my four o'clock exit stage-left from my office.

Emer's cut in hours, you must understand, is down from a fourteen-hour day. I kid you not. Like I said, she's super successful.

'Thankfully, I got none of that awful morning sickness you hear about. Between you and me, I think a lot of that is in people's minds. Positive mental attitude, and all that. Once you have a healthy diet, the rest should be plain sailing. I'm on this organic wheat grass shot every morning.'

Emer has whipped up a snack for us in the kitchen and is lowering it onto the coffee table. Thank God! I'm absolutely famished, and it's been ages since lunch. I could murder some biscuits or one of those fancy French pastries she always has, right about now.

'Oh...'

There is celery, actual raw celery, on the plate in front of me. There is a very real possibility that I may gag. Next to the celery, there are thinly chopped raw carrots. These are flanked by some cherry tomatoes. In the middle, there is a weird hummus type paste dip thing.

'Bon appetite!' Emer lays a jug of cucumber and mint infused still water on the table next to the crudités. There are green things literally floating in the jug. There's not even a glass of wine on the go. What is the meaning of all this?

'So, my consultant in Holles Street says...'

I glaze over. Emer is my BFF, my go-to-gal, my gossip partner. Now she has become a pregnancy bore. I didn't see the wrecking ball coming, and now it has bowled me over, leaving shards of broken glass and dust in its wake. It looks like Pam and I are the only ones left. We're the only bastions of fun remaining on this planet. Everyone else has signed up to the Parenting Club. It's like a cult – it takes all of your money and it becomes the only topic that you can ever talk about for the rest of your exhausted, puke-splashed life. Well, fine! Take Emer. Take everyone. I'm in no rush to join the club.

After I shuffle a carrot around in the grey paste, I sniff it and put it back on the plate. I'm trying to pretend that the iced water is a vodka tonic, but I can't swallow it. It's healthy and therefore like poison to my digestive system. You see, I physically crave grease, salt and alcohol. This muck has none of those ingredients.

'I'd better get going. I need to get the dinner on. Poor Barry will be starving by now.' I shove the honeymoon snaps back into my purse. The photos are feeling rejected and unloved. They will probably require intensive counselling to work through their issues, and you can't blame them.

'Ah. Look at you! Mrs. Devoted Wife getting the dinner on for her hard working husband. That's great. Give him my love.'

I couldn't give a flying flip about Barry's rumbling tummy. If he's lucky, I'll throw a few cold, half eaten chips and a battered sausage at him after I stop off at the chipper on the way home. Besides, he should be making dinner for me, not the other way around. Anyway, this is the only exit strategy I can think of before the boredom and hunger combination leads me to gnaw my own arm off.

We air kiss goodbye at the hall door.

'Ah, Rebecca, it'll be you and Barry next, eh?' Emer rubs her teeny tummy as she smiles.

'Hmm. Yeah. We'll see.'

It's official. Everyone is ganging up on me. I'm a victim of bullying.

'Oh! And, listen if you don't mind, pet...,' Emer's brow creases ever so slightly. 'Don't tell Pam, OK? I'll be seeing her later in the week. She and the boyfriend, Doug, are really hitting it off these days. They've moved in together and everything.'

I drive home at top speed. What is all this, a conspiracy? I'm surrounded by baby lovers. It's as if aliens have landed in the night and inserted a baby obsession chip that is lodged deep within the brains of the majority of the population. Well, they won't get me! I'll sleep with one eye open.

The order for my kebab and chips along with Barry's battered sausage will take just a few minutes, and it'll be just the ticket to cheer me up. You must understand – I'm under enormous stress, so the diet will commence tomorrow. Don't you start, alright?

I dial Barry and tell him the news about Emer.

'Oh, that's great! When is she due?'

'Dunno. Next year. OK. Gotta go.'

I hang up. This is going to make Barry even more broody, now.

I dial Pam's number.

'Hey! Welcome back!' she answers.

'Hi. Thanks. It was fab. Pierce Brosnan stays there. No riff raff. Five stars all the way. Anyway! Listen to this!'

'Yeah?'

'Emer's pregnant. Just told me.'

I pause for reaction.

'What?! Flip sake! No way!'

'Oh, God. You're not supposed to know. Oops. Act surprised when she tells you later in the week. Yeah?'

'Yeah. Is she OK? Freaking out?'

'No. It's mad. I think they... planned it.'

'What?!'

'Yeah, she said that they were actually trying for a baby for some time. Never pictured her with a baby before, you know?'

'Oh, man. Her life is over. I mean, she'll be up to her designer earrings in nappies and bottles. Can you imagine it?'

'Do you really think so, Pam?'

'Of course. Oh man. Poor Emer.'

'Yeah. You're probably right.'

'God, you're not pregnant too are you?'

Pam once described kids as noisy, whiney things. A well know Pam-ism is that she once said that she'd rather be trampled to death at a Justin Bieber concert than give birth to a baby.

I laugh. 'Eh no! God, no rush on that one, Pam. Emer will be a great mum, of course. The best,' I back pedal. When I play this conversation back in my head later, I will be extradited from all blame.

'Yeah. Defo.'

'Ah, and think of all the cool baby gear she'll be shelling out for. All designer clobber, I bet.'

'Yeah, only the best. Anyway, that's her out of action for the Saturday nights at the Ice Bar for a while, then. Another one bites the dust, eh?'

'Yeah, I guess, Pam.'

'So, anyway! Are you free for a quickie cocktail or three? Douggie and I were going to pop down the local for a few.'

'Ooh, I'd love to, but...'

I'm scrambling for an excuse. Don't get me wrong – there's nothing I fancy more than showing Pam the honeymoon snaps over a few cocktails and then maybe a bit of robot dancing at 'Howl at the Moon' 80s night afterwards. But lately she and Douggie are joined at the hip. It's like they are conjoined twins awaiting an operation, now. I can't remember the last time I saw her on her own. He goes everywhere with her. I couldn't even dance with her at my wedding reception to 'our song' without him right there beside us, smiling constantly. The irony is that our song is 'I Think We're Alone Now' by Tiffany. Not only is it a classic 80s song (I defy anyone to tell me they dislike it), it's a girlie song. I'm sure he's a nice guy and all that, but I would prefer Pam all to myself.

'Douggie and I are just settled onto the couch and there's an Indian takeaway on its way over. But we could meet you down the pub later?'

'No, thanks chick, I'm…just out with the work gang at the moment. Lots of people here. Bit of a session kicking off, actually. There's talk of Club 92. As a matter of fact…'

'Salt and vinegar, love? Love? Love? Salt and vinegar on the chips, love?'

The greasy woman behind the counter will not be shushed.

'Fine! Yes, loads please.' I thrust a twenty Euro note at her.

'Call you tomorrow, Pam.'

Back in the car, I dip into the brown paper bag. The grease has soaked through the bag, and the soggy chips are literally dripping. The vinegar is stinging my nostrils and it's divine. Absolutely divine! Don't get me wrong, the food in Mexico was amazing. I mean, they put melted cheese and sour cream on most things. What's not to like? But you can't beat an old chipper.

I think about Emer, and the walnut sized baby growing inside her. I think about mum waiting to hold a grandchild in her arms. I think about Barry beaming at me on the flight home, describing the long dark eyelashes of the baby at the top of the plane.

'Please God,' I say aloud. 'I'm not ready. I'm just not ready.'

Five

Ah. Welcome, Barry. How was the honeymoon?'

It's six o'clock on Tuesday, and Barry has called to see his mum after work. He's in no rush to get home. Since landing on Saturday, it's like living inside an episode of 'Hoarders'. There is stuff literally everywhere. Open, gaping suitcases litter the bedroom floors. Dirty clothes are scattered along the landing, as if a laundry bomb went off. All of the wedding gifts have been opened, and are piled about the place, wrapping paper littering the bedrooms. Rebecca is claiming 'post-wedding fatigue' and refuses to clean or tidy. Dishes that were piled in the sink before the wedding remain un-tackled. Breakfast cereal sticks to ceramic bowls like cement.

Before work this morning, Barry got stuck in with a bottle of Fairy washing-up liquid and some serious elbow grease. He had moved clothes from the kitchen floor to the washing machine, and emptied the bins. Still, there is much left to tackle. The bed sheets need to be changed, and the carpet is crying out for a Hoover. There's absolutely nothing to eat, apart from a can of tuna fish that has been there since 2012, and some bread that is seriously past its sell by date and looking slightly on the mouldy side. He'll enjoy a quick chat with his mum and then push a trolley around Tesco, before collapsing into bed.

Hopefully, Rebecca will be in better form when he arrives home. This morning, she insisted that she was suffering from a severe case of delayed jet lag, and was an hour late to work. She claimed that siestas should form part of her day now. She refuses to get up until her body clock adjusts and might call in sick from work for the rest of the week. On Saturday, after they had landed, Barry had dragged all of Rebecca's suitcases upstairs and she had then emptied the contents all over the bedroom and landing floor before crumpling into bed for the weekend.

'Grand, mum, grand.'

'So,' Margaret pours the tea and produces a pack of Custard Creams. 'Tell all.'

'Ah, it was lovely.'

'That's a great tan you got. Brown as a berry, you are. How was it? Any photos?'

'Yeah. Weather was great. Rebecca will show you some shots at the weekend I'm sure. Lovely place.'

'Great stuff.'

'Absolutely smashed, though. The honeymoon cost a packet!'

Barry dunks a custard cream into his tea.

'Oh, really?'

Barry feels guilty. Rebecca's dad and his own dad had coughed up a pretty sum for the wedding. The honeymoon has cost Barry all of his savings.

'Ah, sure you know Rebecca. Let's just say that she might be singly responsible for the end of any recession in Mexico.'

Margaret laughs and Barry can't help but grin.

'I'm not joking. We had to buy two additional suitcases for the way back. Designer ones, don't you know.

Bloody Louis Vuitton, if I'm pronouncing that correctly. So that's four suitcases in total, right?'

'Four? Ah, God.'

'Well, yeah. She took two with us. I just took hand luggage because there was no room for any of my stuff. I crammed a couple of pairs of shorts, flip flops and two shirts into a pull along. One of the suitcases was purely for her shoes. One to match each outfit. I counted seven pink ones alone. She says that one is coral and the other is bubble-gum. Another is lavender and another is rose. Oh, and I forgot – one was dusty pink. Apparently that's important.'

'Ah, stop.'

'Seriously,' Barry smiles. 'The other case was for clothes. Dresses of every variety. Pink ones, flowery ones... Oh, and large hats, too. And a giant vanity case. Then there were various sunglasses...'

Margaret is in hysterics now. 'Go on.'

'So four suitcases to check in on the way back, right? Then there's the extra cost at the check-in desk to get them onto the flight. That's not cheap.'

'But wait, what were the extra cases for? Souvenirs?'

'Pretty much. She pretty much has a lifetime supply of sarongs and bracelets in every available colour.'

'Ah, goodness!'

'That's not the best bit. Get this. She also shipped home ...' Barry is laughing now.

'What? What did she ship home?' Margaret has her hands over her mouth.

'A couple of crates of...' Barry can hardly get the words out. 'Mexican Tequila. Premium stuff. The ones with the worms swimming in the bottle. I said 'Rebecca! You can get Tequila at home. I saw it in O'Brien's off license. Anyway, you don't even drink tequila. You hate the stuff. Makes you sick!'

Margaret is wiping a tear from the corner of her eye. 'Stop!'

'She said she was planning a Mexican themed newlywed party. Shots of Tequila and Tequila sunrises. She can show everyone the honeymoon photos.'

'Ah, no.'

'Honestly, mum. There's enough booze making its way across the Atlantic Ocean in those crates to drown Pancho Villa. Oh, I dunno.'

'Hilarious.'

'Ask me about the phone calls. Ask me!'

'Go on,' Margaret smirks.

'Honestly, mum. I'm dreading my bloody phone bill. Rebecca rang home to speak to her mum every day!' Barry smiles. 'Every day!'

'Oh dear! And was the hotel pure luxury? Five stars, wasn't it?'

'Eh yeah – five star prices, too. Talk about a whopping bill at check out. I'll need another holiday just to get over it. The hotel brochure said that room service was available twenty four hours, so Rebecca decided to put this to the test.'

'She didn't!'

'She did. Several times. She said she wanted to prove a point. 'Chef should whip up a chocolate fudge cake at three in the morning if it took her fancy', she said. Honestly, she set her alarm clock and everything. Said she was starving from all the wedding dieting she'd been on. And don't get me started on the mini bar. There was nothing mini about the prices. A tin of those macadamia nuts cost all of ten US dollars. Ten!'

'Yes, the mini bar is always steep. Especially the alcohol. Was the service good?'

'Unfortunately, it was excellent.' Barry's face creases with laughter as Margaret's eyebrows knit together.

'What do you mean?'

'Rebecca took it upon herself to tip heavily. She said that celebrities stay at the hotel all the time, so it's expected. Seriously, she splashed enough pesos at our head waiter Fernando to put his great grandchildren through college.'

'Ah sure, she's gas.'

'I know. Ah, but we had a great time, and it was exactly what Rebecca dreamt of. Sure, a couple of frugal months should set us straight. We'll start saving again.'

'Good man. More tea?'

Six

It's Friday morning. My muscles ache and my head throbs. I'm like a marathon runner at the end of a particularly gruelling run. You know, if I was into running. God forbid!

This week has been tougher than usual, and I'm shattered. It's a combination of:

1. Completing a *full five day week* at work. That's five consecutive days – Monday all the way through to Friday, without collapsing, or calling in sick or faking a rare tropical illness. It's been absolutely ages since I did a full week. In fact, it might be a first.

2. Catching up on the work I missed while on holidays. Emails take a while to delete and letters take time to shred.

3. Adjusting to Greenwich Mean Time after three weeks in a Mexican time zone, most of which was spent in a tequila induced coma.

4. Jet lag. Yes, I am still suffering. No, I am not over that yet.

5. Realising, with a bone crushing reality that chills me to my very core that the wedding is in fact over. Done. Forever. I'll have to wait another ten years until I can convince Barry to renew our vows on a beach in Hawaii. Or The Maldives. Maybe we could do both.

Home time looms like a finish line in the distance. I can see the red ribbon and I'm staggering, but I don't know if I'm going to make it. My throat is sore. I've spent most of the week calling my nearest and dearest to dissect the wedding and conduct a detailed breakdown of the fabulous honeymoon.

There's a horrid screeching sound coming from the reception desk behind me. It's highly irritating. For a minute, I entertain the idea that perhaps I'm hallucinating from being overworked.

'What...what's that annoying noise?' I turn to Judy.

It's three o'clock, and Judy is smirking at her desk. It's probably because we had two glasses of wine with our lunch, it being LLF (Liquid Lunch Friday) and all.

'Ugh,' she responds. 'It's Belinda and her brats.'

I swivel round on my chair to have a good gawp.

Ah, Belinda! Where do I start? Back in 2009, Belinda started working here as a Human Resources administrator (that's posh for secretary). Anyway, she had a baby, like, years ago, and has not been back to work since. Brendan came from a temping agency to cover her maternity leave and he's still here. Before the next baby was born, she was off sick. Something to do with a bad back, I heard. Then there was another baby, and another baby, a career break, another illness, and now another baby. She is still off work, but rumour has it she's still on the payroll. Jammy wagon!

Suzie at the reception desk is cradling what looks like a miniature old man in a blue blanket.

'How gorgeous!' she squeals. 'Oh, he's precious. How old is he now?'

'Just six weeks,' replies Belinda.

Belinda was always a little on the chubby side. At least I can blame my recently expanded waistline on a Mexican honeymoon buffet. She is dressed in head to toe floral, which is making me nauseous. Her other children are flanking her, and are suspiciously quiet and well behaved.

'And the kids are getting so big!' Suzie continues her fan-club adorations. 'And what are their names, again?'

Suzie is being far too perky for my liking. Where was her enthusiasm when I was showing my honeymoon snaps? They were much cuter!

'So, baby Elijah is six weeks old. And this is Abel, he's two. Abraham is four…'

Judy and I snigger. It doesn't take much to set us off on a Friday afternoon, in fairness. Also, the wine helps.

'… And of course, Jeremiah is six.'

They have identical freckles, matching asymmetrical home haircuts and are all wearing grey trousers with braces. I jiggle my fingers on an imaginary whistle and toot-toot, like Captain Von Trapp. Judy salutes me and clicks her heels together. Then she sings 'the hills are alive, with the sound of music,' and I swear, she is absolutely choking on the laughter. We cunningly disguise the laughing fit for a coughing attack. I slap her on the back and then perform the Heimlich manoeuvre while trying not to wet myself.

'Girls, you remember Belinda?'

Suzie is all serious, now. She's just like the mean head mistress who glared at me for laughing in mass when the priest was talking about The Madonna (to which I whispered 'Papa Don't Preach' and nudged my best pal in the ribs. It ended in detention.)

Suzie's big serious head just makes Judy and I worse.

'Nice to see you again,' I compose myself and wipe away the laughter tears that stream down my face.

'Eh, hi kids,' Judy has recovered herself, and has resumed the ability to speak.

'So, when are you back to work, Belinda?'

I manage to keep a straight face. I can't help but ask, I'm dying to know what magic she will weave in order to stay home for another couple of years. Another career break, perhaps? A life threatening illness? Another baby? I mean, you've got to admire this woman and her work dodging ways. Seven years! She must have watched every episode of Dr Phil ever made!

'Well, as you know, the maternity leave is a year. And then...'

'A year? I'm sorry, but did you say a *year*? As in... twelve months?'

This is news to me. I need to know more.

'Yes, well...if you take the statutory twenty six weeks, which is fully paid here at the company... and then you can apply for the statutory unpaid maternity leave. Then there's parental leave. Oh, and of course I'll have accumulated annual leave....'

I'm having a Eureka moment, here. A working knowledge of Human Resources policies has clearly been in Belinda's favour. I nod furiously as she talks. It's like a crash course in pure genius. She's Professor

Evil and I'm her willing student, learning from her cunning plans to take over the world. I stare at her in disbelief. *How was I not aware of this scam before?*

'I might apply for a career break after that. Or go part-time. You know, for more of a work life balance. Who knows?'

My jaw drops. After almost a decade off, she'll go part time. Classic! I must ask her if she teaches private classes. Where is my notepad? I feel like I should be writing this stuff down.

'Of course, I'm busier than ever at home. Boys keep you busy!'

The children smile shyly. The little rotund one clings to her floral skirt. He reminds me of the little pot-bellied pig we used to visit on the farm when I was young, I think we called him Paddy. I suppose the little boys are cute. You know, if you like red hair and sticky out ears.

Of course, I think, having kids hanging off you all day is the huge catch to all of this time off. I'm about to ask her how she keeps them quiet when her soap operas are on, but I'm interrupted.

'Rebecca is just back from honeymoon. Hoping for a baby soon herself, aren't you?' Suzie elbows me in the jelly belly.

'What? No!'

'Oh? Well, then. Here, have a cuddle. Get a whiff of that baby smell.'

Before I can protest, the infant is passed to me and I'm holding him awkwardly – like an offensive cat turd I've discovered in the lounge and wrapped in kitchen paper.

The only baby smell I can get is a combination of sour milk and the stench of a lost youth. Up close, I can't help but think that his little face looks squashed, and there are bracelets of fat around his wrists. I fear that I may in fact be breaking out in hives as I stand here. Of course, the baby starts screaming as soon as he is in my reluctant arms. I shuffle him about desperately until Belinda removes him from me.

'Oh, thank goodness!'

Harry emerges from his office and gives Belinda a jolly welcome.

'Ah, Belinda. Hi boys. Great to see you all. Congratulations on the new baby. Please, come and join us for some cake in the canteen. I think we have a few little gifts also. After you.'

Harry follows us to the canteen where the staff have assembled.

Cake? Gifts? Belinda gets to stay at home baking flipping fairy buns for donkey's years and then gets serenaded in the canteen? I'm starting to think that Belinda might be on to something here! She might, in fact, be the smartest woman I have ever met.

We shuffle into the crowded canteen. Belinda has also brought a cake, and it's lush. I've decided, her new nick name shall be 'bun–in-the-oven-Belinda.' Judy will explode when I tell her. I'm so witty!

I've wolfed two large slices of each cake for comparative reasons. Oh, and to welcome the new baby and all that jazz. Judy has scoffed a miniature baby made out of blue icing, plus the word 'Elijah' in swirly blue icing, despite the hang dog looks she's getting from the six-year-old. "I saw it first," Judy whispers to me, 'so he can just flip right off. His mammy can make him another one when they get home. Sure, what else have they got to do with their spare time? There are only so many Lego towers they can build. Anyway, making more icing will give them a nice little project to do together.'

My trousers are really starting to dig into me, now. I'm going to have to pop the top button for sure.

'So! Belinda. Just a few small tokens to welcome the baby,' Harry passes a gift bag to Belinda. 'It's from all of us.'

Everyone claps. Except me, my hands are full with another slice of cake. I remember there was a whip round on Monday and then Harry asked me to pop out and choose something, which I completely forgot about.

The bag has 'It's a boy!' written across it, and someone has crossed out 'a' and inserted 'another' in black marker. The bag contains a couple of preppy outfits in teeny sizes. Everyone says 'ahh' when Belinda opens them up.

Half an hour later, Belinda and her offspring have toddled off and everyone is back at their desks click clacking away on their keyboards again.

My mobile buzzes. It's Karen again. No doubt she's calling to hear more about the five star honeymoon. What a pal.

After half an hour of my exotic tales, she butts in. She starts off by telling me how great the kids are doing, but then breaks down. Through sobs, she reveals how she and Frank are drifting. Between the mortgage, the crèche and the price of nappies, Frank's salary is not cutting the proverbial mustard. They're struggling financially, their marriage is being affected, and are in desperate need of a date night. The problem is that she has no babysitter. She's stuck, and she really needs my help.

Karen has been a good friend, and agreeing to babysit is the least I can do for her. Besides, I reason as I polish off the few remaining pastry crumbs that are scattered over my keyboard, I've nothing else planned this Saturday night. Barry is going to a conference followed by a client dinner. Mum and dad, who seem to have a better social life than me, are going to some gala charity thing. Pam and Douggie are loved up on the couch ordering takeaways. Emer is pregnant and taking it easy.

'So, what do you think?' Karen asks.

This could make for a very interesting experiment. All of this talk of pregnancy and maternity leave has me thinking. Much as I hate to admit it, I need to know if I'm mummy material or not.

There's silence on the line for a moment.

'OK,' I agree. 'I'll do it.'

Karen breathes a sigh of relief. I need to put 'the ghost of babysitting past' to the back of my mind where it belongs. I need to try again.

Seven

I'm parked outside Karen's three bed semi in Stillorgan. I can think of the following reasons to turn the car around right this very minute.

History has a habit of repeating itself. I'm no better prepared than I was more than thirteen years ago, standing outside the posh pad in Killiney, pressing the buzzer for the gates to open.

I'm gagging for a gin and tonic. Drinking hard liquor whilst in locum parentis is probably frowned upon. Shame, really, I'd be much more fun.

I should be at home applying fake tan and straightening my hair in advance of some cocktail party or other, not playing Mother Teresa to these kids.

I'm not Mary Poppins. I don't know the words to 'Spoon full of sugar.'

I'm probably missing something good on the telly.

Then again, I'm sure there are many reasons to march right in there and babysit the hell out of these kids. OK, I can only think of two. Karen needs my help, and Barry is going to ask me about having a baby again soon. I need to put myself to the test.

There's a scooter strewn across the driveway. It occurs to me as I ring the doorbell that I know very little about these potential monsters. They could be psychopaths in training for all I know. It's not Karen's fault that I'm unprepared. Over the years, she has prattled on and on about them. Daily, she upload pictures of them on Facebook. While I wait, I have a quick word with God.

Sweet Jesus, don't let them be like something from 'Supernanny'. I don't have Jo Frost's patience. I've seen enough episodes to know that I'm not cut out for tantrums and wailing. Also, if this turns out to be anything like the great babysitting disaster of 2003, I'll never ever do this again.

I know you can work miracles!

Rebecca.

Karen answers the door and greets me with a hug. She promptly ushers me into the kitchen. Two babies squirm in high chairs, their dinner painted all over their faces as they bang their chubby fists on plastic trays.

I give myself a pep talk.

Now, don't panic! They're just kids. Kids don't bite, do they? Well, OK, they do. But I mean, what's the worst that can happen? Apart, that is, from dropping one of them on their heads, and ending up in casualty explaining the concussion. Just... go in there and knock 'em dead. Well, metaphorically speaking.

Pep talks were never really my strong point. Still, I can't be fabulous at everything. That wouldn't be fair, now would it?

'Hey, Becks,' Frank waves hello as he rinses out baby bottles at the sink. 'Great wedding, thanks again, we had a ball.'

'Hey, Frank.'

'This,' beams Karen, 'is little Frankie.'

She points to the dribbling tot on the left. There's more beige mush on his face than, I would wage, is in his chubby mouth. He wears a blue striped vest, revealing his fat knees. I haven't seen them since they were born just before Christmas.

'And this', she points to an identical child in an identical high chair, 'is Alfie.'

Alfie, like his brother, is also caked in dinner. Frank has abandoned bottle duty, and wipes their faces with a tea towel as they howl their protest.

'They're great,' I smile, hoping that Karen doesn't detect the panic, rising like bile, in my throat.

They look like they're old enough to crawl now, but what would I know? I'm not exactly the baby whisperer, last time I checked.

'Now,' Karen is suddenly all business, and pointing to a white board mounted on the kitchen wall. 'After their tea, it's pyjamas, bottles and then bed.'

The timetable lists feeding, changing, play dates and Gymboree classes.

'And here', she points to the baby changing unit in the downstairs bathroom.

'This is all the stuff you might need: nappies, wipes, creams, nappy sacks, cotton balls, bibs, formula, spare bottles, sterilising fluid, vests....' Her voice trails off.

My head is spinning. How much stuff does a baby need in order to have a fresh bum? I don't even know what a nappy sack is!

'Now, the really important bit,' she eyeballs me.

Perhaps she's sensing my total, overwhelming desire to jump into the next passing taxi and collapse into tears. Once, at university, over my sixth pint of cheap cider, I told her about the Terrible Awful babysitting night form hell.

'Don't mix up the milk.'

'OK...'

I have reached information saturation point I'm really just blinking, now. It's like the tap is still running, but the water is overflowing form the cup.

'Alfie is allergic to dairy, so he gets soya.'

'OK. That's fine. Just one question. Which one is Alfie again?'

Karen and Frank exchange a look. I can read their minds. They're debating whether the moron standing in front of them is in fact capable of keeping their darlings alive for the duration of their date. Their desperation for a night out wins.

'This is Alfie. This is Frankie.'

'OK, Karen. Got it.'

I haven't got it. I repeat, I haven't got it. Send help! Send wine!

'Mummy!'

A curly haired girl in a pink dress leaps into the kitchen.

'Mummy. Who dat lady?'

She eyes me suspiciously as she clings to her mum's skirt.

'Ah, another one,' I laugh nervously. I'd been so terrified of the two babies that I'd momentarily forgotten that there were was another child.

Right! Well, that's it, then. A three to one ratio means that I'm well and truly outnumbered.

'Do you remember Becky?'

She child shakes her head shyly. There's absolutely no chance that she remembers me – she was still in nappies when I last saw her.

'Katie, tell Becky how old you are now.'

'Four and a half,' Katie lisps.

'Yes, the half is very important!' Karen smiles.

'Nice to see you again, Katie.'

I stretch out my hand to shake, as if this is a business meeting. Like I said, I'm rubbish with kids.

Little by little, Katie's grip on her mum's skirt loosens and after five minutes, she announces that we are now best friends. This is mainly due to the fact that I'm wearing pink, and pink is her absolute favourite colour. Next is purple and red. See? I was paying attention. Also, I brought sweeties. Her mum probably doesn't let her have sweets, but I need all the ammunition I can get. To top it off, I have lied to a little girl's face and said that yes, I do in fact still like playing with Barbie dollies.

Katie pulls me by the arm towards the living room to show me her dolls.

'Wow, it looks like you two will get on like a house on fire,' Karen grins.

'Yeah, but... listen, Karen...' I feebly shake my head.

I'm planning my exit route out the living room window. This is a mistake. It has been overly ambitious on my part. What had I been thinking? It's like going to the animal rescue centre just to have a wee look about, and coming home with an entire litter of pups. I should know, I've been volunteering at one for years, now, and I have to try not to adopt all of them and bring them all home at the end of my shift. If it weren't for Jess, I'd have done it by now! I should have eased myself into this whole baby experiment thing. Maybe I could have just visited. Briefly. Placing three vulnerable tots into my inexperienced hands is absolutely bonkers. Somebody should call social services!

'Thanks, Becks,' Karen interrupts.

She backs away and reaches for her jacket on the banisters. Frank is already gathering his car keys and opening the front door. 'Bye,' he calls. Karen hugs Katie and leans over the twins to kiss the tops of their heads.

'Back soon. Be good for Rebecca!' she calls as she rushes out the door.

We're alone. It's just me, three kids and a box of Barbie dolls. I have a sinking feeling that Karen and Frank might never be coming back. I don't blame them.

Katie is staring at me. 'Now we haf to pway more games,' she instructs.

'Nice try, Katie,' I smile. 'The timetable says pyjamas are next. Let's get you dressed for bed.'

She shows me where her pink Barbie pyjamas are laid out, and I help her undress.

'Alvie and Fwankie haf to wear deese baby ones,' she lisps. Her little chatter is getting cuter by the minute. I find myself actually smiling. Not the kind of pretend smiling that you have to do when your boss thinks he's cracking a joke, but a real grin.

'OK, we can play Barbies for a bit longer, if you like.'

Alfie and Frankie watch us from their highchairs. Don't tell anyone, but it's been so long since I've held a Barbie, that I'm secretly enjoying myself. It reminds me of Anna and the hours we spent under the stairs. I've gone for the posh spice style bob Barbie with a business suit. She's bossing the temps about and telling Cindy to hold her calls. Katie's laugh is infectious. 'You're silly,' she lisps.

Its seven now, so according to the timetable, the little ones will be in bed soon. It'll be great to pack them off to bed. I mean, so far they're adorable, but there's an hour long 'Coronation Street' special starting at eight, and I'll be damned if I'm going to miss it. According to the 'RTE Guide', Sally and Martin will be romantically reunited, and it's an episode not to be missed. Surely, the three amigos here will all be in the land of nod by then.

'Right. Let's get these two boys out of their stinky poo clothes, eh?'

'Stinky poo. Stinky poo. Stinky poo', Katie parrots.

I'm probably not meant to be teaching the little one vulgar expressions. Karen might not be best pleased.

'Oh, crap. Don't say stinky poo, OK?'

'Crap. Crap. Crap.'

Yikes. I'm sure she'll have forgotten that little word by the time Karen gets home. Surely kids don't remember things like that. In fact, they're probably like goldfish with three second memories, aren't they? Everyone knows that.

'Right, then. Let's get Alfie and Frankie into their pyjamas next.'

Lifting the little puddings out of their high chairs and onto the living room rug is an ordeal in itself. For starters, they squirm and laugh and their dirty vests make them slippery. Secondly, they crawl away in opposite directions like this is a game. This is much to Katie's amusement.

'Mammy dwesses Fwankie first', she informs me.

'Ah. Right. And how can you tell them apart?'

'Well...' Katie thinks, 'dey are not umdentical. Dat's Fwankie.'

The kid is right, they're not identical. It's subtle, but Frankie is definitely chubbier than Alfie. I make a grab for him.

'Come back here, Frankie!'

Wrestling Frankie is starting to feel like a Japanese game show, and I feel like I should be wearing a sumo wrestler outfit. I manage to remove the soiled vest from his wriggling body and Katie puts the ponging items into the laundry basket for me. She's turning into quite the little helper.

Frankie looks a little red in the face. Then the smell hits me. There's no avoiding it. For the second time in my life, I'm going to have to change a nappy.

'Fwankie is weally stinky', laughs Katie.

She's right. There's something disgusting under my acrylic nails. A quick spritz of Chanel No. 5 in the air masks the pong temporarily.

'Hold this bag while I vomit,' I instruct Katie.

'Vomit, vomit, vomit,' she giggles.

Getting a moving baby into a vest and sleep suit is not as easy as it looks. Soon, Frankie is powdery fresh, but Alfie is absolutely honking. It will be *De Ja Poo* all over again.

I did it! The two babies are clean and dressed. I'm about to text Barry to tell him that I'm a natural, but according to the timetable, the next activity is bottles. Thankfully, Karen and Frank had the good sense to label the bottles 'Alfie' and 'Frankie'. Perhaps they sensed the high likelihood that I would poison their beloved offspring by mixing up the milk, resulting in an emergency trip to Crumlin children's hospital. Again, Katie helps me to identify which tot is which.

I prop them up against a cushion on opposite sides of the couch. They happily glug-glug their nine ounces of milk. I shove a 'Beauty and The Beast' cartoon into the DVD player. Soon, Katie is mesmerised: Disney has a trance like effect for the very young.

Lifting the two fat lumps up the stairs is a cardio workout all on its own. I balance one on each hip. As I lie them down in their matching cots, they suck on the remaining ounces of milk. Their eyes grow heavy.

I click on the musical lullaby, and it projects stars onto the ceiling. Hopefully the babies won't need new nappies on my shift. I'd hate to have to crush some diarrhoea tablets into their milk and insert a wine cork up their respective bottoms until their mother comes home. I have my limits.

Alfie …or then again it might be Frankie, whinges and tosses a bit and the other one gurgles. I hold my breath. Should I rock them? Sing to them? Pat them? Ignore them?

Their breathing has become rhythmic, so I back very slowly out the door. This is the tricky bit. I've seen it in movies. This is the part where one false move on a squeaky floorboard will land me be back at square one.

I creep downstairs. Katie is still glued to the TV screen, as the Princess marries a hideous beast with the promise of living happily ever after in his castle.

'Disney has a lot to answer for,' I tell Katie. 'I mean, the girl is a total knockout, right? Killer body. She could have done a lot better for herself. The Beast is ugly and grumpy.'

'Gwumpy,' she giggles.

'You know, Katie, they should make a sequel. 'Beauty and the Beast 2.' Beauty gives up her promising PR career, and slaves over a hot stove until Beast comes back from his boring solicitor's firm and then picks his nose in front of the telly. Then the Beast bullies Beauty into having hairy babies. She's taken for granted 'til death do them part.'

'Picks his nose,' she laughs.

Katie climbs the stairs after the cartoon. Her bedroom is like a flamingo has exploded all over the place – pink duvet cover, pink light shade, pink canopy, pink curtains clashing with pink wallpaper. Even her toothbrush is pink. I like her style.

Not surprisingly, Katie wants a story involving some princess marrying some handsome prince and being rescued from her life of drudgery. She asks for another story and I agree. I defy anyone to look into those big caramel brown eyes and say no. The girl is playing me like a pro, and I'm way out of my depth when it comes to negotiating with little girls.

Eight

By half past eight, I'm bunched. I've already missed half of my 'Coronation Street' special. I kiss Katie on the forehead and turn out the light.

On the couch, I congratulate myself and turn on the telly. I have three kids asleep and everyone fooled. Maybe I'll be a super mummy one day, after all. A warm fuzzy feeling creeps over me. Then I discover the blob of baby vomit on my shoulder, and a silver line of snot like a snail's trail down my pink cashmere cardigan. I wouldn't mind, but it's a dry-clean only garment! I click on the TV and daydream.

Barry and I are terrific at the whole parenting thing. In fact, I've written a book on parenting, I'm so good at it. It's called 'How to be an awesome parent, just like me.' I tell my friends that they should totally buy it. Having children has brought Barry and I closer together as a couple. We give advice to friends whose children are unruly. We're a bit like Dr Phil and Robin – except better looking. Our kids are tucked up in bed. 'The earlier the better' is our motto. They'll be well rested for their advanced maths and violin lessons tomorrow. My little blonde girl is a musical prodigy like her mother, and my little blonde boy is a pro at junior rugby. They wear designer pyjamas and keep their bedroom tidy.

We slip down stairs, where Barry has prepared us a gourmet meal. It was no trouble, he insists. It's the least he can do to reward such an excellent wife and mother. We sip expensive wine, and picture what our little darlings will be like when they are older. 'Perhaps they'll be the next Brian O'Driscoll or Amy Huberman', Barry muses. The children sleep peacefully in their beds all through the night until, at a civilised time the next morning, they get the breakfast started. Because I'm such a safety conscious parent, they know how to operate the fire extinguisher if the sausages burn. They serve us Nespresso's and croissants in bed. 'What a lovely mummy you are', they smile, revealing perfectly straight, white teeth.

The Filipino nanny arrives and whisks the terrific two off for some organic roasted asparagus and goat cheese. Kids eat goat's cheese and asparagus, don't they? Barry and I laugh and praise each other, clinking our crystal goblets in appreciation.

My beautiful fantasy is interrupted by my rumbling tummy. Since I'm well and truly shattered, I'm just dying to ring in a celebratory pizza. It'll be a well-earned reward after all of my exertions. I dial Dominos. I have the number off by heart.

'Hello, Dominos pizza.'

'Maurice? It's Rebecca. Yeah, I'm gonna need the Becky Special.'

'OK.'

'Oh, and a garlic bread. Mmm. And some of those melty cheese strip things. It's been a tough week. Throw in a Ben and Jerry's, yeah?'

I add in a diet Coke just to balance out the calories. In case you're wondering, a Becky Special is basically a large pizza with ham, pepperoni, chicken, pineapple, extra cheese, chilli flakes and garlic. It repeats on me like a hell fire, and is laden with calories, but who cares. The diet will start tomorrow, when I'm not juggling three kiddies. Besides, I've been weightlifting today – those babies weigh a tonne each. The pineapple will be one of my five a day. Sadly, the bottle of red wine that goes so well with the Becky special will have to wait until I'm off duty. You know, because I'm so responsible, and all.

'Coronation Street' is turned up full blast. I missed the fist fight at the Rovers Return, and Steve McDonald is about to propose to Sarah Platt again. I'm not going to miss that!

'Oh no!'

Dread forms in the pit of my stomach. I can hear crying from upstairs. I race up the stairs and discover one of the babies standing up in his cot, crying. I'm not going to lie, I still don't know which one is which. His face is wet with tears, while the other sleeps peacefully.

I lift the little one into my arms and sit in a rocking chair. I've no idea what to do, I'm in completely in over my head. History is repeating itself, and this has been a huge mistake.

'Shush Alfie... I mean Frankie. Look, I'm going to call you Fralfie, get used to it. Shush, now, or you'll wake your brother!'

He won't stop crying. I'm dealing with a mini terrorist here. I start rocking back and forth on the chair and humming. Before I know it, I'm singing a little lullaby. Never underestimate the soothing qualities of 'Right Said Fred.'

'I'm too sexy for my shirt, too sexy for my shirt, so sexy it hurts. And I'm too sexy for Milan, too sexy for Milan, New York and Japan. And I'm too sexy for your party, too sexy for your party. No way I'm disco dancing...'

It worked! Fralfie's little heart beats against mine. His breathing is deep, and when I sneak him back into the cot, he doesn't move. I stand in the doorway for a minute, watching the rise and fall of his chest, and the little curl of his hand.

I tip toe down the stairs just as the pizza arrives. It's just all go! I resume the foetal position on the couch, and shove the pizza into my mouth, slice by delicious slice. I just about have enough strength to polish off the cheese strips and garlic bread.

A text comes in from Barry.

Hi baby, how R U getting on?

I text straight back.

Easy! Piece of cake.

That reminds me. I think I saw some cake at the back of the fridge.

How odd. I've a stabbing pain in my ribs. It's either the pizza doing a repeat performance (damn those extra chilli flakes, they are so deliciously awful) or a life threatening illness. Perhaps it's an acidic ulcer. Or a rare contagious disease! Perhaps I have merely months to live. The front page headline will read *'beautiful bride dies while dedicating her life to others.'*

I roll over to Google my symptoms on my IPhone, a giant ball of wind escapes, and the pain vanishes. Thank goodness for that! I get stuck into the ice-cream. All of the grub is making me sleepy. I decide to rest my heavy eyelids for just a second. There's no fighting it – I slip into a food coma.

Karen and Frank swan home at midnight. Loved up and tipsy, they sway into the living room. I deliver a brief synopsis of the evening: the house is still standing, the children are still breathing. No fires or fights broke out in their absence.

'Thanks, doll,' Karen slurs as I reach for my keys. When she hugs me, she whispers into my ear 'knew you could do it.'

I make a sharp exit stage left before she discovers:

1.The poor job I've done tidying the mush splashed highchairs.

2. The depleted fridge stocks plus cardboard pizza boxes protruding from the recycling bin.

3. The botched pyjama dressing efforts on her loved ones.

4. Her three year old's new vocabulary.

If I'm lucky, she'll be so annoyed that she won't ask me to babysit ever again. I'm an evil genius, really. Hurtling down the M50 towards my sanctuary of calm, my life of normality beckons. The house is quiet and the Egyptian cotton sheets are cool. Barry is not yet home, so I do a starfish impression in the bed.

Nine

Instead of my usual Sunday lie-in of eleven o'clock, I've pushed it to a respectable noon. I'm factoring in my exhaustion from my baby juggling act last night. Also, Barry is not up yet to make my breakfast.

Driving down the Wicklow N11 motorway to the animal shelter, I can't wait to see my little fur babies once again. I've been volunteering here every Sunday for the last few years, and it's the only thing I'm truly good at. It's been over a month since I last visited, between the wedding and honeymoon, and I'm eager to get stuck in.

'Welcome back!' Tammie greets me from the reception desk. 'We've missed you!'

The amount of change in just one month is crazy. One of my favourites, a Jack Russel named Teddy, has been re-homed, and after almost a year in residence, Pedro the terrified sheepdog has finally found a match.

'Hey, come and help me sort out the cats, Becky,' Tammie calls.

There's lots to do in the cat shelter, between feeding and mucking out. There's a tabby cat, no more than two by my guess, who's just had a litter of kittens. They're teeny, and haven't opened their eyes yet. I find myself staring at the way the kittens nuzzle into their mother. Their tiny cries are diminished as the mother licks them.

Once I'm home, I swap the mucky wellington boots and tracksuit for pyjamas and slippers. The evening passes with percolated coffee and reading the newspaper. Well, when I say newspaper, I mean the fashion and lifestyle supplement. I might have a bath with some Epsom salts and apply some replenishing eye cream to feel human again. I can practically feel those eye bags creeping up. I might open a bottle of wine. OK, the wine is already open. Whatever! Don't judge!

'So, how did it go last night?' Barry peeps over the top of the 'Irish Times' newspaper.

'Fine,' I yawn. 'I mean, I think I'm still on Karen's Christmas card list.'

'Oh yeah?' Barry is only pretending to read the sports page. He's dying to know if the woman he just married is a potential mummy candidate, or whether he's been duped.

'Yeah. I mean, the kids are still all present and accounted for, ha-ha.'

'Uh-huh? And were the kids good for you?'

This is code for: did you find the kids cute and do you want to have one? Honestly, I'm not being paranoid. We have skirted around the issue for years. If I gush about how fabulous they were, it'll fan the flames of hope. If I tell him they were horrid, he'll think he married a monster.

'Yeah. They were fine.'

Barry and I are enjoying a glass of Pinot Grigio and a pasta Carbonara with garlic bread.

'Great. So... Do you think we should just go for it, then?'

I splutter my wine.

'Eh, pardon? *Just go for it?!*'

He makes it sound like we're simply making a decision about buying a new car. We can't just kick the tyres and haggle. This requires a bit more consideration!

'Yeah, Becky. I mean, why not?'

'Wow, I dunno, Barry. We're only just back from honeymoon. And babies are expensive, you know!'

Appealing to his frugal nature is the best procrastination tool in the mechanic's box right now.

'True...'

As I mop up the Carbonara sauce with the garlic bread, I ponder what my life would be like in Karen's shoes. For starters, my shoes would not be quite the designer kitten heels I cherish, but frumpy flats. The baby-drains would more than likely dispose of any disposable income, and I'd be forced to buy my shoes from Primark. I shudder at the thought.

'And, I mean, there'd be no more of these leisurely pasta dinners with good wine. It would be all...chicken nuggets, chips and indigestion. You know Joyce from college? Her kids don't eat anything that isn't beige, and she has to cut up their food all the time.

'Yeah, sure I don't mind that.'

I forgot. Barry likes beige food, too.

'And you can wave goodbye to any fancy holidays once a baby arrives, Barry. It'd be Costa del Bray if you're lucky. Travelling with kids is a nightmare.'

Barry nods and pretends to read an article about Brian O'Driscoll.

'And another thing,' I'm on a roll now. 'You might not still fancy me if I got fat.'

OK, so we've established that I'm not currently what you would describe as skinny. Piling on the pregnancy pounds on top of the honeymoon pounds would not be a wise move.

'Of course I would, baby. I love you just how you are.'

Wrong answer!

Barry is meant to tell me I'm skinny and gorgeous *now*, and that he'll pay for liposuction and/or a personal trainer post-baby if so desired. Honestly, he's so clueless!

'And of course', I finish off Barry's garlic bread – too many carbohydrates are not good for him.

'I think we would be exhausted all the time. You know how I get cranky if I don't get my ten hours a night.'

We have avoided the icy waters for so long, but we're dipping our toes into the waters of possibilities, now. What will my relationship with Barry look like if we take the proverbial plunge? Will we happily glide like a family of ducks, quack quacking all in a row?

'We won't be exhausted all the time, Becky. The disturbed sleep won't last forever!'

Barry has certainly given this some thought. I can see the swimming goggles and the plastic cap behind his back. He's ready to jump into the choppy seas below, and he's trying to push me onto the plank. I'm not sure I'm ready. My hair might get wet!

'Hmm,' I step away from the port side of the boat and into the nice dry cabin. 'But some people are cursed with kids who start the day at ungodly hours. Sorca's little one wakes at five o'clock in the morning! It's not even bright out, then!'

I make a good point. Surely Barry will not be a barrel of laughs if he is wrecked from changing nappies and rocking a baby through the night. I assume that he'll be on night duties if I'm stuck at home all day. Surely that's how it works, isn't it?

'OK,' Barry looks deflated. 'Maybe it's too soon after the honeymoon.'

Curse Barry and his boyish charm. He looks like a schoolboy dejected from the sweetie shop. I throw him a bone.

'No, it's just... look, I do want a baby, too. I promise I'll think about it.'

His eyes are glued to mine. Hope registers.

'Really?'

'Yeah. I suppose having a baby would be nice...'

Stating that having a baby 'would be nice' is the first glimmer of interest I've shown to date in the baby department.

'Oh yeah?'

'Yeah, I could wangle at least a year off work for starters.'

'Well, that's not a real reason to have a baby, Becky!'

'Of course not, silly!'

I don't mention the other little bonus points I dreamt up last night:

a.Shopping guilt-free for baby clothes in a poncy French store, joint credit card at the ready.

b. Pushing a designer Bugaboo buggy (I've heard from Emer that this is the most expensive and therefore must be the best) with one hand and quaffing a takeaway cappuccino in the other, dressed in skinny jeans as I leisurely stroll through Dundrum Town Centre. It looks far more leisurely than an eight hour day at the office.

c. Hiring a personal trainer to help me shift those dreaded love handles and post-baby bulges. We'll pump iron to trendy uplifting backing tracks mixed by cool Ibiza DJ's that I'm not cool enough to have heard before, but will pretend I know intimately. We'll admire ourselves in gym mirrors, sculpted eyebrows raised. I'll call him 'Sven' and he shall be blonde, with a medium amount of muscles (enough to take him seriously, but not too much to intimidate me. It's a delicate balance. Ditto the tan.) We will flirt harmlessly. There might even be bottom slapping and arm touching involved in his motivational pep talks, but only in an encouraging/ platonic/ I'm-not- going-to–make–a–pass kind of way. Otherwise, it might be unprofessional.

d. Purchasing one of those designer nappy changing bags in Mamas & Papas. I saw Kate Middleton with one in last week's edition of 'OK!' magazine. There's enough room for nappies *and* a bottle of wine, those things are quite roomy.

e. Meeting my gal pals in Harvey Nichols café whilst comparing purchases from Baby Gap and House of Fraser. The little cherub (I'm toying with the name Kate for a girl and Wills for a boy, no idea where the inspiration came from) will sleep whilst I decide between the skinny fries or the baked potato. Babies sleep all day when they're little, you see.

f. Catching up on my yoga while the tot bounces in one of those bouncy chair thingies for most of the afternoon. Every mummy needs some 'me time'.

g. Watching back-to-back, uninterrupted episodes of 'The Real Housewives of Orange County'. I could plump cushions and arrange flowers while I watch, transformed into a domestic goddess. I might even learn to cook. Then again… it doesn't take much to set off our new smoke detector, so it might not be the best time.

I'm staring into space, picturing a steamy clinch between myself and personal trainer Sven in the gym locker room. I'm sweaty, but in a sexy way. He wants me desperately. He's only human, after all. I touch his rippling muscles as he presses me up against the cool metal lockers, his hot breath on my neck. 'I can't, Sven. I'm married now. Little Kate is waiting for me at nursery. I'll always remember you, Sven. What we had was special. Be strong. You'll find someone else, in time.' I have to let him down gently, you know? I wouldn't want to break his heart.

'That's great that you're giving a baby some thought, Becks.'

'What? Oh, yes…'

Barry has a broad smile on his stubbly face, hope sparking in his eyes. Perhaps now is the right time to bring up the subject of diamonds. Don't worry, I'll be subtle as usual. Like I always say: slowly, slowly catchy monkey.

'Now,' I fan myself. It's suddenly hot in here. 'You do know that you'd have to buy me an eternity ring if we have a baby, don't you, Barry?'

'A what? Ah, no. Didn't I just buy you an engagement ring and then a wedding ring? You must be joking. Tell me you're joking!'

'I never joke when it comes to expensive jewellery, Barry.' It's true. There are some things that are sacrosanct.

I pronounce 'Barry' like it's a horrid word. You know, so he can see that I mean business. My face is like a slapped bum. He needs to understand that this aspect is non-negotiable. A large eternity ring is not too much to ask, when you think about it. One of the temps who used to work in my office blatantly paraded her obscene 'thanks for having my child' rock in my face every time she was reaching for a file. I swear she was doing it on purpose, trying to outdo my engagement ring. No doubt she was trying to make me feel barren and childless. I could trump her in the diamond department, no problem. That would really shut her up.

'Anyway, more wine?'

This is Barry's 'subtle as a Katie Price boob job' attempt at changing the subject. It's fine. I'm not worried. I have it all worked out. You see, after pushing out one of Barry's babies, the guilt will be too much for him to bear, and he will cave. He'll see the woman he so desperately loves in pure agony, and when he is mopping my brow, I'll close my eyes a bit squinty, cough in a feeble way and then say 'I'm moving towards the light...I can see Jesus...donate my body to science...my darling...but tell them my liver is pickled like a gherkin and not to donate that bit...farewell..' I'll figure out a way of making the machines beep a bit. You know, really stir him up, like in 'Days Of Our Lives.'

Then Barry will say 'No! Move away from the light. Stay with me! Nurse!' all kind of dramatic, like. He might even press a panic button and thump the walls in terror at the thought of losing me. It will be so romantic. Then I'll make a miraculous recovery, and open one eye. Barry will mop my brow and feed me ice chips, or whatever it is that men do in delivery rooms. The close call (plus how radiant I look after bringing our cherished baby into the world) will confirm to him how much I should have the very best in life. He will feel compelled to make haste to the nearest designer jewellery store (thankfully, Holles Street hospital is within walking distance from 'Rocks' on Grafton Street) and demand a bespoke and ridiculously large diamond ring. Next to the Great Wall of China, it will be something else you can see from space. Honestly, I will deserve no less if I go through with the whole ordeal. Perhaps a large Ruby would settle the score – I hear Colleen Rooney has a blinder.

By ten o'clock, I've devoured the contents of the biscuit tin. The emotional anguish of my impending decision is to blame. In bed, I replay the image of the dribbling baby in my arms and remember the softness of his skin. When I close my eyes, I can feel his sweet breath in my hair, and his chubby face nestled into mine. I recall how we rocked back and forth on the chair as I sang. I picture how his rounded bottom was whooshed up on my chest and how his legs curled underneath my arm.

There was no rash breaking out on my skin. There was no perspiration pricking my forehead. There was no urge to call Karen and hand him back. This must be the maternal instinct you hear about. Perhaps it was there all along. It must have been buried deep, deep down under fear and selfishness and an intense compulsion to shop, and now it is here, knocking at the door. Pesky oestrogen!

Barry wakes me up at seven o'clock in the morning. A totally insane hour of the day, if you ask me. The hour is even more obnoxious as it is Monday. He's bashing around in the kitchen below our bedroom, clattering cutlery and clinking tea cups. So inconsiderate! A whole week of dreaded work stretches out in front of me. It might as well be a prison life sentence. All work and no play makes Rebecca a dull girl.

A thought pops into my head.

If I had a baby…

'Good morning, sunshine.'

Barry is standing over me, wearing a pair of skimpy black y-fronts and carrying a breakfast tray.

'Aw. How nice.'

Barry has poured the milk first and then added the Coco Pops. The strawberry pop tart has been dunked in the toaster twice and is slightly burned – just how I like it. I deduct points, however, as he has not put enough sugar in my tea.

I decide that the time is now. Carpe Diem, and all that. By the way, that's Latin for 'you should, like, *totally* go for it'. I clear my throat.

'I have a very important announcement to make.'

I wipe the sleep from my eyes and smooth down my hair. I want to look good for this earth shattering revelation.

'Drum roll, please. OK, Barry, it's finally happened. I think I want a baby!'

I watch closely for his reaction, so I can tell all my girlfriends in great detail, over champagne cocktails. Perhaps he will cover his face and cry a manly cry. Perhaps he will be so utterly grateful to me that he will choke on his indebted sobs and thank God in heaven for his dutiful, selfless wife.

'Barry?'

'That's great, baby cakes.'

Barry places the tray on the bed. He whistles off to the bathroom, rudely leaving the en-suite door open. There's a tinkling sound.

'Eh, hello? A baby! As in, a little wrinkled, crying, pink thing? I thought you were desperate for one.'

This is quite an announcement I have just made. Where's the fanfare? Where's the wailing and proclamation of love? A few red roses and an off the cuff sonnet wouldn't go astray, surely? Would it be too much to ask that you call everyone in your phone book and maybe lean out of the bedroom window to proclaim to all in the cul de sac that I, Rebecca Jane Browne Costello, shall henceforth bear your child?

Barry senses my disappointment as he re-enters the room.

'I am! Look, it's just that... this might take a while. Some couples have to try for ages. I'm thirty eight and you're thirty two. I just don't want you to get your hopes up, that's all.'

'Eh, thirty one', I correct. I refuse to let him age me so. 'Anyway, what are you trying to say? I'm hardly old! There's nothing wrong with my bits and pieces, thank you very much. I'm sure my ovaries are just as high functioning as anyone else's. Better, probably.'

My arms are crossed in a huff. How dare he insinuate that my reproductive capacity is below par?

'Maybe your fishing tackle is not up to scratch! Ever think of that, eh?'

'Look, Becks. It's great that you want a baby. I knew you'd feel ready once we were married.'

Barry hops back into bed and the bed frame creaks. His skin is hot against mine.

'Eh, what are you doing? Get up. You're going to be late for work. And shave, will you, or they'll think you're a homeless person. And buy bigger pants. Far too skimpy. We're not naturists. Move over, you're making me spill my Coco Pops.'

'I'm staying home, Becks. Day off in lieu of the weekend conference.'

'Huh! Well for some.'

There's an ice cube's chance in hell that I'm slaving away in an office now, when my lump of a husband lies in bed all day.

'Mmm,' he rolls over.

'Right, then. You can do some jobs around the house. I have a list. Call in sick for me, will you? Pleeeeease?'

Sometimes, Barry needs a good dig in the ribs to motivate him. It's not working now, he has already started snoring.

'Barry! Go on! Tell them I've a toothache. Anything. We can spend the day together…'

The puppy dog eyes always get him. He taps in the office number as I scoff the brekkie.

We're like John Lennon and Yoko Ono staying in bed all day. Except, instead of campaigning for world peace, we're talking about the possibility of having babies. After much debate, we have agreed to the following terms and conditions. Firstly, we will wait six months until the New Year before trying for a baby. There's no rush. I'll continue to party like it's 1999. Secondly, after said party time, when it's all out of my system and I don't feel cheated from my youth, I will then stop taking the pill. This will be like taking a safety net away from an acrobat, and then making her totter on a rope at nosebleed inducing height. I spent most of my adult life terrified that the pill would fail, and now here I am talking about not taking it. Anyway, like Barry said, it'll probably take ages to get up the duff. Finally, I'm going to start looking after Numero Uno. No, no. Not the unborn baby, silly. Me! If I'm going to be 'with child' in the near future, then it's about time I started looking after myself. No more overdoing it at the office lifting heavy files and making coffee for that balding, wretched man. No more babysitting for college chums who wish to rekindle their romance with exhausted husbands. I'm officially from this day forward, suiting myself. Yes, I added this bit in, myself.

News flash: love-ins are over-rated. It's boring staying in bed all day, and I'm desperate for a wee. I don't know how Yoko held it for so long!

'So...', Barry pulls me in close, his stubble tickles my face.

'Let's start practising.

Ten

'Hi, Jackie. Nice lunch?'

Barry smiles at the receptionist and continues towards his office. He parks his briefcase neatly underneath his tidy desk and shuffles the mouse until the computer screen lights up and his log in details appear. There are no new emails. There are no urgent messages scribbled on post-it pads on his desk. The only missed calls are from Rebecca, followed by a text asking him to stop off for some chips on his way home.

Having a day off yesterday to recover from the conference was great, but he had spent the afternoon doing laundry and getting the house back in order. Rebecca had spent it glued to 'Dr Phil' and shouting at the telly.

His three o'clock client has cancelled again. A quick flick through his diary confirms that the only task for the day is simply paperwork – expenses, returns and so on. Frankly, he would rather not. He surfs the web for a bit of soduko to kill the afternoon.

His phone beeps with an internal call. It's his boss, Nigel.

'Ah, Barry. You're back from lunch. Good stuff. Pop into my office for a chat, will you?'

'Eh, OK. Now?'

'Now.'

The phone clicks.

How odd.

Nigel probably wants to dissect the conference and analyse everything to death. Barry is not surprised. The conference was a last ditch attempt to link them with a few more contacts, in the hopes that this will eventually drum up more business. In the last couple of years, the amount of corporate clients has fallen significantly thanks to the economic downturn, and private clients are twice the time investment with half of the return. Drawing up wills with dithering elderly clients after they've had a health scare, and representing separated women in the family law court is time consuming and not exactly something you can bill heavily for. Corporate clients are where the big bucks are, but these are few and far between.

'Ah, Barry, come in', Nigel motions to an empty seat opposite his desk.

'Thank you.'

'You remember Arthur?'

'Yes. Hello.'

A tense silence follows as Barry wracks his brains, trying to understand why he is here.

Of course Barry remembers Arthur. How could he forget? He often wishes that he could forget Arthur and the stomach-clenching discomfort of their last encounter. Former colleague Shelley had resigned last year after the Bangkok conference, and during her exit interview, she had exaggerated her brief encounter with Barry during the trip – hence the necessity for Arthur's presence. Cue a wrapping on Barry's knuckles for fraternising with a work colleague, a mortified apology and a genuine promise that it will absolutely positively never happen again. The whole thing was excruciating.

Barry knew damn well that he had made a major mistake and it had nearly cost him his relationship with Rebecca. He didn't need everyone in the office viewing his dirty laundry, to boot. The irony was that while Nigel's crony, Arthur, was berating Barry, Nigel himself was having a jolly old time with Shelley.

'Good to see you again', Arthur unbuttons his jacket and gives Barry a firm handshake.

Barry's squashed fingers throb as he plasters on a false smile.

'And you.'

Barry can feel the sweat patches forming on his blue shirt. Almost a year has passed since the unfortunate incident where he ended up passed out drunk in bed next to Shelley. Although nothing had happened, it was still a lapse in judgement on his part. Too much booze and ten thousand miles between himself and Rebecca were to blame. He had filed the entire episode under C for cringe, boxed the memory in an airtight plastic box, wrapped it in heavy chains and a padlock, and placed it in the dusty cellar of his mind. Now, perhaps someone wants to unearth the box and exhume the contents, like a stinking, decaying body.

Barry directs his gaze at Nigel. He cannot seem to catch his eyes, as they are cast downward. Nigel shuffles some papers nervously and clears his throat.

What the hell is going on?

Bad news is coming, and Barry knows it. This is a recipe for disaster. The mathematical formula is well known.

Arthur + being called into Nigel's office = shit about to hit the fan.

'So, thank you for coming in, Barry.'

Nigel speaks in a meek voice, casting sideward glances at Arthur.

'As you know, business has been a little… slow, shall we say.'

Barry's shoulders drop a smidge – not enough to detect with the naked eye, but enough to note his relief that this conversation has nothing to do with Shelley. He exhales for the first time in a full minute. Yes, business is slow. There's nothing new here. This conversation has been re-hashed over and over. Many a brainstorm has taken place in this very office. But the presence of Arthur is still a worry.

'Uh huh. But the conference went great,' Barry lies. 'Really great. Things are picking up, surely.'

Barry is grasping at straws. He thinks about his diary for the week ahead. He has one probate on Wednesday, and one will and testament on Friday. Big whoop! He supposes that he must have been in denial about how slow things have been. Yesterday, he didn't delve too deeply into the fact that Nigel had given him a day off after the conference. He thought he was being decent to an employee who worked over the weekend.

Hindsight screams at Barry. *He can spare you for the day! Maybe he can spare you for good!*

Barry thinks back to the year before last, with his sixteen hour days and his Christmas bonus. How things have changed.

'And of course', Barry realises the gravity of the situation. 'It's the summer, so...'

Times are hard, Barry gets it. Business has been a bit slow, sure. The Nagasaki account in Thailand has fallen through, fair enough. But surely things will get better! Surely he and Nigel will dream up another hair brained scheme to lure in more clients. More schmoozing at business dinners, perhaps. A membership with a networking circle, possibly. An advert in the national papers, maybe.

'We have noticed the decline in your work schedule for some time now.'

'Look, Nigel...'

Nigel's hands are clasped, and he shakes his head. It's like trying to sell an oxygen mask to someone who is already resolved to drowning. Nigel, he realises, is waving a little white flag and sinking deep, deep under the waves.

Barry looks at Nigel's little weasel face. He notices the dark circles around his eyes and the shadow of stubble on his shrunken jaw. He will make Nigel see sense, here. He will talk him out of the path he is about to follow. He will make him understand, scream at him to grab onto the buoyancy ring, put on his life jacket and swim the heck to shore.

'Nigel. If this has *anything* to do with the unfortunate event of last year, let me reassure you one hundred percent that...'

'No, Barry. It's not just you. It's everyone. We are all struggling. Financially speaking, things are... not good. Our accountant spelled it out yesterday.'

Barry's mouth opens and closes like a fish blowing bubbles. He's a solicitor, he argues for a living. He was captain of the debating club in Blackrock College. He was a respected speaker at the Historical and Philosophical Society in Trinity College Dublin. He will not go down without a fight.

But the words don't come. How can he argue with the facts? The entire company has struck an iceberg, and the water is gushing up from the lower decks faster than you can bail it out with a bucket over the starboard bow. There are no more life jackets.

Nigel is silent, so Arthur interjects.

'So, you see, Barry. The company will effectively be going into liquidation. Nigel will operate as a sole trader. I'll be helping him with the transition, as such. It will be roughly three months in total. We thought it best to give staff as much notice as possible. We will be calling everyone in one by one. So, we wanted to start with you, as one of the more senior staff members. We really value your service to date and would appreciate your discretion in this matter. It's all highly sensitive information, as you can understand. Confidential.'

'I...' Barry attempts.

A wind has suddenly whipped up, rocking the lifeboat that he's clinging to. The boon flies across the mast and hits him in the face, leaving him reeling. He stumbles to regain his balance as his teeth skitter across the deck. He is seasick and disoriented.

'Of course', Arthur continues as Nigel remains mute, 'there will be a generous redundancy package on offer. Statutory plus one month per year worked. Should keep you going for a while. I'm sure you'll be absolutely snapped up, fine solicitor like yourself. Nigel here will furnish you with an excellent reference, naturally... we wish you the very best of luck...'

Arthur's voice trails off.

From the lifeboat, he can see that the ship has already submerged into the Atlantic. The distress flare has already been fired. It's a done deal.

Barry nods mutely, absorbing as much of the information as he can until his shocked brain screams 'no more!' He manages to replay the highlights on a loop: *three months, redundancy, good luck.*

He nods again, like a toy bulldog that you sometimes see through the rear window of a granny's Ford Fiesta.

'OK.'

It's all he can say. What else do you say when your ears are still ringing from the bombshell that has exploded without warning?

'Sorry,' Nigel offers.

Arthur is crushing his hand again with his rough finger clampers. He is rubbing salt into the recently exposed wound. Nigel is limply clasping his hand with a cold, clammy, waxy hand. Barry backs out of the room.

Since there are no appointments to cancel, he decides to leave. Right then and there at two-thirty-five on a sunny Tuesday afternoon. He can't meet Jackie's eyes as he slinks past the reception desk. Photographs of her grown up children and young grandchildren decorate her desk. She will be next, of course, to be tipped out into the freezing, churning waters. It's best to let her enjoy the last few minutes in ignorant bliss.

Barry must have been walking for hours, as it's now six o'clock. He can put the inevitable off no longer. He must go home and break the redundancy news to Rebecca. So much for their baby talk! That's the end of the six month plan – six years, more like.

Barry stops off at Libero's takeaway in Deansgrange, and orders a Donor kebab for Rebecca. It will help to ease the blow.

'On second thoughts', he calls across the counter.

'Better add in a batter sausage, some onion rings and a portion of garlic and cheese fries.'

Eleven

It's five o'clock as I slam the car door shut. I'm still in my work clothes, but I keep a pair of runners in the boot of my car which will do nicely. At the entrance to Dun Laoghaire Pier, I can see that Emer, punctual as ever, has already arrived. Her small bump protrudes from her Lycra jogging pants.

'Hi, sweets.'

'Hey, chicken. Wow, look at you!'

We air kiss hello and walk past the band stand. Emer walks at quite a pace and talks at the same speed. I'm winded, but trying desperately not to let it show. My cheeks have taken on a pink glow and there's a slight rasping in my chest. Still, I must keep up. Losing to a pregnant woman would be mortifying, even for me.

By the time we're halfway up the pier, Emer has updated me on her pregnancy news, and I'm struggling to disguise my hyperventilating. As she is past the three month mark, the cat is out of the proverbial bag. She has announced the news at work, despite being up to her tonsils in some merger or other. There's talk of getting two people to replace her because she is just so fabulous. She has had her twelve week scan. All on target with the baby, and she is in great health.

'Never felt better,' she declares as I pick up the pace to catch her. 'I have so much energy now, it's unbelievable. I wake at six and I'm finished in the gym by seven thirty. I'm thinking of running the Dublin marathon in October.'

Oh, yes. Did I mention that Emer runs? Yeah, pretty sickening isn't it? Like everything in her overachieving life, she's good at it. OK, she's bloody great at it. It's no surprise that she's so skinny.

'Oh? Is that safe?'

'Absolutely, my personal trainer says I'm at the peak of my physical fitness, and the consultant said it's fine. Did I tell you about my consultant? She's the best. An absolute doll.'

Of course she's the best. She's probably responsible for delivering the babies of Ireland's most powerful couples. You probably need a six-figure salary just to get past her receptionist.

'That's great.'

Emer shares her fears regarding Dave. Although a model husband, she frets that he will be rubbish at getting home before the baby goes to bed. Between you and me, the man is a total workaholic.

'And will he be any good at nappies?' I joke.

'No idea. But sure, the nanny will do all of that. Speaking of nannies, I've started interviewing for the position already. Nightmare! Totally unsuitable people so far. One woman was even cheeky enough to point out that she can't work *Wednesdays*. Can you imagine? What am I meant to do with that? I told the agency to send someone more committed.'

'Sorry, so …you've started interviewing already?'

'Well, yes. I won't be off for long, and I'll need to start the person right away.'

At the tip of the pier, we pause. The sun is hot on our faces and I push the sunglasses up onto the bridge of my nose. This is the most exercise I've had in months, apart form my cocktail fuelled rendition of 'Footloose' in Club 92 in June. That certainly got the old blood pumping. We turn back for the return journey.

'Well! It looks like Barry and I will be joining the club soon. We've decided to go for it!'

'Really?', her forehead crumples briefly. The Botox must be wearing off.

'Yes, really!' I bristle.

'Oh?'

'Yes, well we're married now, ready to take things to the next level.'

It feels like I'm justifying my decision to her. Why do I need to convince her? Or is it me who still needs convincing?

'I mean, we'll wait a few months. Probably til the New Year at least. Then we'll start trying. No mad rush.'

'Well, that's great, Rebecca. Fingers crossed. Keep me up to date.'

I spy an ice cream van in the distance. I'm so exhausted that I'm not sure I can make the journey, but I battle on. I'd absolutely mill a large '99 with extra syrup. Emer has to dash. She's late for a Pilate's class. She might pop into the Advanced Spinning class afterwards. I watch her walk briskly away.

I'm feeling a little queasy. Maybe it's because eating a '99 after a power walk isn't a clever idea, or maybe it's because Emer's hesitation still haunts me. Is it such a joke to entertain the idea of me being a mum? Can my best friend in the whole world not picture it?

Barry's already home by the time I get back. My thighs are like jelly, but the whiff of salt and vinegar chips revives me as I stagger into the living room. Barry greets me with a large glass of tequila. I down it in one, and he refills my glass.

'Salut!' he cheers. 'Look what arrived today from Mexico. Bernie next door nearly had heart failure accepting the delivery.'

Barry points to the two crates in the dining room. There's enough booze in the house to throw Charlie Sheen a bachelor party. It looks like Barry has had a couple already, and I join him on the couch.

'Hi. Everything OK?'

'Fine, Becky. Sit down, I got us a chipper.'

'Nice one. I met Emer for a walk, I'm famished.'

'Mmm.'

Barry pours another tequila. The bottle is already half gone, and he seems distracted.

Once the meal is finished, I let the exhaustion wash over me. The last couple of nights, Barry has had to nudge me awake at nine o'clock, halfway through an episode of 'Love/ Hate'.

'I'm so tired this last week. I just feel …drained.'

'Mmm.'

'Barry! You're not listening! I said I'm exhausted. And it's only seven thirty. Like, seriously *shagged tired*. I'm tired, like, in my *bones*. I could barely keep up with pregger McGreggers during the walk. I yawned my way all through work. I wouldn't mind, but I've been in bed every night this week at nine. Barry!'

'Sorry. Yeah, you look tired.'

'Eh, pardon?'

I can literally feel my blood boiling. Perhaps this will be how World War Three starts. I wonder if I hold a pillow over Barry's fat head in the dead of the night, if I can blame it on PMT. Come to think of it, I've had PMT for a whole week now, and still no period. It's annoying, because (if you must know, nosy parker) my body is usually precise like a Swiss clock. It's the only thing about me that's punctual.

'Anyway, listen, Becks, I had a pretty rough day today myself to be honest.'

Trust Barry to change the subject to himself when I'm in need of his sympathy and attention. I rub my tummy. Something is not sitting right. It might have been the grease on the onion rings that did it, or it could have been the cheese on the garlic fries. Either way, I feel like I'm swaying on a cruise ship after too many Mojitos. If I lean over the edge, I'll vomit onto the holiday makers on lower deck.

'Really? Yeah. Barry, get me an antacid, will you? And bring the pudding bowl. I think I'm going to hurl.'

'Ok, but listen, I need to fill you in on something.'

I look at Barry like he has two alien heads sewn onto his body.

'Flip sake, Barry. I'm sick! Quick! And bring me a glass of iced water, too.'

Barry runs off, but he's not fast enough. I've splattered the cream carpet. Then I see the lumps swirling in it and go again. Then I get the wretched stink and go again. Finally, as Barry arrives back with the pudding bowl and medicine, I have nothing left. I'm like a limp rag washed up on the shore. He races back to get the rubber gloves and paper towels.

'Take a note', I demand from a foetal position on the couch, as if I'm the solicitor and he is the office assistant.

'We are going to sue those charlatans at the chipper. I've got food poisoning.'

By leaning on the banisters, I make my way up the stairs and into bed. It takes all my strength. When Barry finishes the clean up job, he follows up with the water, a cup of tea and pudding bowl for any repeat episodes.

'Thanks', I simper.

Good old Barry is great in a crisis. Also, he makes a good cup of tea. He's a keeper.

'You wanted to tell me something, love?'

'That's OK, Becky. It can wait until tomorrow.'

'OK,' I murmur, and fall into a deep sleep.

By morning, I'm still feeling like a limp lettuce leaf. I don't think I've been this tired since the 'New Kids On

The Block' reunion concert in 2005, when I got a little hysterical during 'Cover Girl' and consumed a few too many cans of Ritz. I haven't been sick through the night, but I'm feeling rough.

'Barry', I call feebly. 'Call work. Tell them I'm sick. Like, *really sick* this time. Possibly dying, and in need of urgent hospitalisation. Probably out for the rest of the week. Tell them I've been cruelly poisoned and that I'll be battling the chipper through the courts for justice. Tell them you'll be representing me, and that you won't rest 'til I get what I deserve. Then call the chipper. Rattle their cage. Tell them to either see us in court or else settle now. A lifetime supply of chips would suffice.'

My stomach heaves at the thought of chips.

'Are you sure you won't have some breakfast before I go? You probably just have a vomiting bug, baby. Or a flu. I feel fine, and I ate the same thing. Or maybe it was the tequila. I don't think it suits you. Maybe you shouldn't have any more of it.'

'How absolutely dare you!' I roll over.

'Right then. Call you later.'

The stairs creak and the door closes heavily. Poor Barry, I'll have to make it up to him later.

At ten o'clock, I make my way downstairs. Even with gravity on my side, the stairs nearly wipe me out. Maybe my usual pick me up will do the trick: a heavily buttered croissant with cream and jam. I take the plate and a cup of sugary tea upstairs. It's like I'm wearing lead boots. Under the covers, I reach for my IPad and enter 'celebrity hot gossip' into the search engine.

The tea tastes funny, and I can't face the croissant. The thoughts of the cream makes me wretch. Later, a Danish pastry smells off. When I wake again at lunchtime, I try my luck with a deep fried waffle and beans – a classic that never fails. I can barely look at it.

For the first time in the history of Rebecca Costello Browne, I can't face food. I have missed two meals today, and threw up the one from yesterday. My stomach must be going into deep shock. Like a Drill Sergeant, it does a daily roll call and discovers the omissions in disbelief.

'Dinner?'

'Sir, no, sir! Contents lost, sir.'

'Breakfast?'

'Sir, no Sir! Declined.'

'Brunch? Mid morning snack? Lunch?'

'Sir, no Sir. Soldier is negatory for food, sir.'

This is *so* not like me. I mean, I've heard of the overly eager office types sometimes working through lunch. Well, not me. I've a hearty appetite and I'm proud of it. My blood sugar would dip if I did that. I'd faint or scream or cry.

Barry is home from work at five o'clock – a new record for him. Perhaps he's very concerned for my health. Well, he should be. I'm now fully convinced that I'm suffering from a rare, tropical disease. Like bird flu... or swine flu... or some kind of flu involving animals that's life threatening and contagious. As he climbs the stairs, I visualise a quarantine tent surrounding our house and scientists in gas masks, like those nasty geeky science men who took poor ET and hooked him up to all those blinking, beeping machines. Barry will be like Elliot, banging on the glass of my incubator and looking at resurrecting geranium plants! God, what if I die? I haven't had my roots done!

'How are you feeling, baby?'

'Yuk. Tired. I've stopped vomiting, but I feel queasy as hell. And hungry. All at the same time.'

'Oh, no. Poor Becks.'

'God, you don't think I've got, like Ebola, do you? I Googled it. God, I'd be in all the newspapers.'

'No, Becks. You haven't been to sub Saharan Africa recently, now, have you? Highly unlikely.'

Barry is mocking me. He once told me that he thinks that I have hypochondriac tendencies. Once I looked up the word 'hypochondriac' in the dictionary, I was most insulted and denied it completely. He'll be sorry when he starts to feel as rough as I do, I've probably passed the plague-like disease onto him.

'Anyway, I'll be back in a sec. I need the loo again.'

On the loo, I enter the symptoms into my 'Net Doc' app on my IPhone: lethargy, low appetite, frequent urination and nausea. I've clicked on the 'diagnose me now' button, and the results are in. Are you ready? Brace yourself. I'm suffering with either:

1. A rare type of disease of the bladder and/or lymph nodes. Sweet Jesus. If I don't make it, tell Barry I favour the white coffins with red velvet lining and a moving bagpipe rendition of 'Amazing Grace'. There should be flattering photographs of me on a loop, projected onto a

large screen, flanked by a dozen white roses. Tell him I'll be insulted if the entire congregation doesn't cry. Anyone not wearing black should be excluded without question. Period.

2. A peptic ulcer. Sounds awful, but it would mean some serious time off work.

3. Pregnant.

A penny drops as Barry rubs my tummy. Cold sweat breaks out on my forehead.

'Oh, Barry, you don't think I could be …like, preggers, do you?'

'Nah.'

'It's just… there's something else. I'm a tad… late.'

I can hear the second hand on the clock ticking, as if it's the same decibel level of a chainsaw. That's probably not a good sign.

'How late, exactly?'

'A smidge.'

'How much is a smidge?'

'Like, a few days? Well, a week really…'

'Nah, you couldn't be…', repeats Barry unconvincingly.

Oh sweet Jesus Christ who is seated at the right hand of the father and will ascend into heaven on the third day. It's so obvious now. Why hadn't I seen it before? Flip. Flip. Flip. Flippety Flippin' flip. This is not good.

My eyes are closed and I'm giving myself a damn good talking to.

OK, OK. Calm down. Calm the flip down!

I know I said I wanted a baby. But it was a lovely glossy dream for a few months or years down the line. Not now! I think of the case of Tequila downstairs. The sweet, booze soaked little drunken worm in the bottom is smirking at me, making my stomach flip. Being late wasn't even on my radar. I have other things on my mind. Like, arranging the honeymoon photos and losing a stone. Also, I'm still on Mexican time and reacclimatising!

Barry sits on the end of the bed.

'So, let me tell you about work…I have to tell you-'

'Barry! Not now! I'm feeling totally pants, here. Will you just pop out to the chemist and get me a pregnancy test. Seriously. I think I need to do one. Just to be sure. Thanks, baby.'

Barry doesn't tell me I'm being silly. He doesn't dissuade me. He silently reaches for his car keys.

'And just buy the most expensive one, OK? Buy two of them.'

Fifteen minutes later, Barry is back. I take the paper bag from his hands.

'Seriously, Barry. This had better not be positive.'

'Relax, Rebecca. It'll be fine.'

I have the stick-like pregnancy test out of the cardboard box and have skimmed the instructions in a flash. Here's the Becky Guide To Pregnancy Tests::

1. Wee on the stick. Duh!

2. Repeat the following mantra on a loop: *no line = good, pink line = bad!*

3. Close your eyes and pray like the clappers. Bother the bejaysus out of St. Anthony, St. Jude and anyone else who will listen. Tell them you promise to go to mass every week if the result is in your favour. Don't worry, they're gullible and will believe you.

4. When two minutes and your entire patience has passed, open one eye, kind of sneaky-like.

5. If there's no pink line, resume breathing. Call all of your friends and laugh about it. Have a glass of Sauvignon Blanc. If there is a pink line, go to instruction six.

6. Descend into a blind, frantic, rabid-animal-trapped-in-a-cage style panic.

Thankfully, I've never gotten to stage six, and I'm praying harder than I've ever done in my whole life that today won't be the day I'll see what it feels like.

It turns out that it's hard to pee on demand. That's ironic, because I've needed the loo every half hour today, but now it's not happening. Perhaps my bladder is shy, listening to Barry shuffle outside our tastefully decorated en-suite. I send him off for water and then hear the trickle.

'Baby? How you getting on? Baby?'

Barry's pacing on the other side of the door like a demented, incarcerated tiger.

'Shush, Barry.'

Through a slit in my left eye, I take a peep. The two minutes have not passed, but I'm in danger of passing out from holding my breath.

There, in all its glory is a very clear, very definite and very smug pink line. I do the next test. It's the same.

'Ah, damn!

Twelve

I think the appropriate cliché to use in such a situation goes a little something like this: *be careful what you wish for, because it might come true.*

When I close my eyes, I see the pink line. It's mocking me. I can see it laughing and clinking tequila shot glasses with all of the discarded pregnancy tests from my twenties.

'We finally got ya!' they cheer in unison.

Naturally, Barry said all of the right things last night, as I cried and blew snot into a ragged tissue. 'Yes, it's a little ahead of plan. Yes, we were going to wait a few months and then try. Yes, we are literally just back from a honeymoon, and a bit broke. But it will be grand, baby. We're married now. We love each other and have a roof over our heads. Life is precious.'

He was comforting, supportive and wise. I believe the exact words I muttered before turning over to sleep were 'get stuffed'.

It's all so easy for him to say.

a.He has always wanted a baby. He's far broodier than me. He probably schemed the whole thing. Perhaps he switched my pill for Tic Tacs whilst on honeymoon. I was so out of it, I can't be sure.

b. His ass will not swell to the size of a giant watermelon. Mine will.

c. He will not be forced into ridiculously comfortable but highly unfashionable stretchy maternity trousers (although he's sporting a bit of a belly these days, if you ask me. However, I'm not one to criticise, so I won't say anything.)

d. He will not have to push an infant's head through something the size of a Cheerio. Ouch. I'm not ready to talk about that bit yet.

Before Barry goes to work in the morning, he leans over and plants a kiss on my forehead.

'Love you, baby. Call you later. It's going to be great!'

I mumble a profanity and roll over. After a few minutes of staring at the ceiling, I venture down the stairs to retrieve the sick-day-essential-kit:

1.A hot water bottle. Yes, I realise that it's August. No, I have not lost my marbles. I am queasy and crampy and tired and fed up, so shush.

2. Sugary tea and some ice-cream. It's all I can manage for breakfast. Who cares?

3. The latest copy of 'Hello!' Magazine. It's the one with the hunky Danish Prince, and the new Royal Baby.

4. The remote control.

'Desperate Housewives' is on the telly. It's a repeat, so I don't have to engage my brain. Brie is having an affair with a neighbour and Gaby is being her usual backstabbing bitchy self. Classic stuff.

After a lunchtime snooze, I've perked up slightly. Don't laugh, but I've sent a text to mum, and she's on her way. I need her. Yes, smarty-pants, I know I'm in my thirties now, but my mum is the best when I'm not well.

'Ah, you poor chicken,' she struggles through the front door with three full shopping bags from Marks & Spencers.

'Just stopped off and picked you up a few bits in Marks.'

As she unpacks the bags at the kitchen counter, I switch the kettle on.

She has brought an impressive array of treats. My mummy is the best.

'So, you've a bit of a tummy bug?' she quizzes me as she loads up the fridge.

I stall. I've promised Barry that I'll wait until we're all together at the weekend to tell the news to family. There was talk of swearing on dead grannies' graves.

'Yeah. Feel pretty rough. Like a hangover, but without the booze.'

'Gosh. Hope you didn't pick up anything in Mexico. Like dysentery. Or Lyme disease. Or typhoid! They have dirty water there, you know. Oh, God, you didn't drink the water, did you? And those mosquitoes carry terrible diseases. That's why you need shots. Did you get shots?'

She speaks in a hushed voice, in case Amnesty International are hiding behind the curtains, waiting to correct her political incorrectness.

'Mum, it was a five star hotel. I told you. Anyway, I didn't drink the water, I drank the cocktails.'

'Oh, good. Thank God. Much safer. But these places are very poor. Terrible sanitation. I saw a documentary on South America. There were these people in slum cities. God help them.'

'OK. Well, it's just a tummy bug. I'm grand.'

Mum has that look on her face. It's the same face she wore when I was five and told her that it wasn't me but my younger brother, Ian, who had in fact put the green Playdough in the washing machine before the whites were loaded. She can see right through me.

'Anyway, how are you, mum?'

Mum can smell my attempt to steer the conversation and is having none of it.

'You're looking quite flushed, pet.'

'Am I?' My hand subconsciously reaches for my cheeks.

'Yes. Definitely flushed.'

'Ah no, I'm fine. I hear there's a big twist coming in 'Corrie'.'

Mum doesn't take the bait to discuss our favourite soap opera.

'Rebecca, will I put some lunch on? Do you think you could face some soup and dippy bread?'

'No, no. Just a cup of tea. I could take it back to bed.'

I try not to yawn but the urge overpowers me.

'A slice of cake, even?'

She's testing me, now. She knows I would normally have ripped the cake packet open and devoured two slices by now.

'Maybe later...'

She's smirking, arms folded.

'Oh my Goodness. You're pregnant, aren't you?'

I think about my promise to Barry. I've got to be as watertight as a duck's backside. I've got to lock the secret up like Fort Knox and throw the key over the razor sharp six foot fence.

'What? No! Don't be ridiculous.'

Then again, I consider, *if anyone were to guess my news – an older, nosy relative who brings me treats from Marks & Spencer, for example – keeping a secret would be beyond my control. To deny the fact when someone guesses would in fact be lying, and therefore wrong. I would be a blameless victim.*

'Well, maybe...'

I'm a terrible liar, always have been. Especially when it comes to mum. I'm warning you now, don't tell me a secret, I can't keep it. Even as a teenager, when the whiff of cider was reeking from me, I couldn't pretend to be sober. Any half assed attempts to cover up were always rumbled, so why bother? Mum knows me too well.

The details come flooding out. I can't help it. I'm so relieved to be able to talk about it.

'Oh my God, Rebecca! Finally! A honeymoon baby!'

Mum's arms are around me, squeezing me tight.

'We just found out last night. I did a test. Well, two of them. I promised Barry we'd wait until the weekend before telling anyone.'

'But sure, I'm your mum, I don't count. How far along are you?'

'It's early. I don't know. A few weeks, I guess. Haven't even been to the doctor yet.'

'Ah, love. I couldn't be happier. No wonder you're not feeling well. I've been doing my Tuesday Novenas to St. Anthony. I'll be a granny! Oh, but I don't want to be called granny. Or nana. Maybe Glam-ma. That's kind of fun, isn't it? Because, I'm not old or anything. But sure, we can think of something. Oh, wait 'til I tell dad!'

'But mum, listen... I'm not... I don't know how I feel.'

Tears are pricking my lids, threatening to spill out.

'What, love?'

'It's just a bit... soon, you know?'

I swallow hard, trying to push the tears back down.

'Don't be silly, it's great news.'

'I suppose. I just thought I'd have more time to, you know...enjoy myself.'

Mum laughs.

'Rebecca, for goodness sake. You'll still be able to enjoy yourself! And listen, Barry must be thrilled!'

'He is. We are. It's just... I don't know. Maybe we're not ready.'

'Let me tell you something, Rebecca. No-one is ever ready. Not really. Sure, your dad and I were totally unprepared when we had you. Living in a one-bedroom flat in Rathmines. We didn't even have a car! You'll be fine.'

'Ok.'

We sit on the couch with some sugary tea.

'I'll have to get my crotchet needles out and get cracking on some baby blankets. There was a lovely pattern in 'Woman's Way' the other day.'

I smile. Mum is soaking up her new role as grandmother already.

'Oh, and speaking of babies and all that,' mum puts down her tea. 'You'll never guess what. You know Lorraine?'

'Who? No.'

'Lorraine! *Lorraine* Lorraine!'

'Mum...'

'You know. *Lorraine.*'

'Oh, yeah.'

I haven't got a clue to whom she is referring, but trust me, it's better to play along and save time. Otherwise, it'll be precious hours lost that you'll never get back.

''Lumpy Leggings Lorraine', your dad calls her. Jean's daughter. From number twenty six? Well, between you and me... herself and Dylan broke up. It's all off. They were only married five years. Can you imagine? And after all of the money her poor dad spent on the wedding! It cost them a bomb, apparently. There were fireworks and everything at it. But if you ask me, the food wasn't up to much. Not a patch on yours.'

'Of course not. Anyway...'

'Well, anyway. They've got this massive pad down in Arklow. Four bedrooms, it has. And two baths.'

'And...'

You have to hurry mum to the point. Believe me, it's a skill – a bit like a sheepdog rounding up the little fluffy lambs and nudging them through the farm gates to safety. Otherwise, she'll meander through meadows all day and the lambs will be drawing a pension before she has finished drawing breath. Honestly, she can talk and talk all day. Thank goodness I'm not like that, eh?

'And, well, they bought that house to fill it with babies. That young one was pushing dollies in a pram since she was five. A real natural mother, she was. Couldn't wait to get married and start a family.'

I remember her clearly now. When Bean Ni Murchu went around the classroom in second class and asked us all what we would like to be when we leave school, the response was pretty standard. Sinead wanted to be a hairdresser (a rather dull, unambitious girl, at best. Last time I saw her, she was looking bedraggled in a tracksuit at a bus stop. I presume her hairdressing dreams were unfulfilled, judging by her inch long black roots.) Jenny wanted to be a vet (good luck to you with those grades, love. Last I heard, she was a dog groomer specialising in Bichon Frises. Sad.) Tara wanted to be a teacher (she not only became a teacher, but is teaching in my old school) I said 'pop star'. You know, because I'm such a good singer, and was born to perform. I had potential. I had charisma. I had a certain *je ne sais quoi*. I had private lessons at 'Mrs. Higgins Stage School'.

But Lorraine was different. She said that she wanted to be a mammy. I sniggered when she said that. Then I nudged Jenny. 'Yes, yes', Bean Ni Murchu grew impatient. 'Great. But what do you want to have as a job? *As a career*? What about a doctor or a dentist …or a dancer?' I'm not sure why Bean Ni Murchu was only mentioning occupations that begin with the letter D. Lorraine looked that teacher square in the face. 'I want to be a mammy', she repeated.

Mum has opened a packet of custard creams, and I gag.

'So…?'

'So! She can't have babies, Rebecca. So devastating. Something wrong with her…'

Mum covers her mouth as she whispers. 'Ovaries'

'Oh?'

'Mmm. Her mother told me. In confidence. They tried the VHF, and everything.'

'IVF, mum.'

'Yes, the VHF. No luck. Five grand a pop. Three attempts. Tore them apart. The woman is a wreck.'

I think mum secretly loves the drama of it all.

'Who, Lorraine?'

'No! Well, yes, Lorraine obviously. But her mother, Jean, is crushed. It was her only chance at grandchildren. You see, she only has one other daughter and it turns out she's...one of *them*.'

Mums eyes widen and she nods.

'One of what? Circus performers? In a cult?'

It's so much fun taking the you-know-what out of mum. It takes my mind off wanting to vomit into her lap.

'No! She's a *lesbian*. Not much chance of Jean becoming a granny any day soon, then.'

I yawn. Other people's problems are so tiresome.

'Right. Finish your tea, Rebecca, and get yourself back up those stairs and under the covers. When I was expecting you and Ian, I felt like death warmed up. Honestly, I couldn't keep anything down for the first few weeks.'

My face must look crumpled, because mum starts to back pedal.

'Well, I mean it wasn't that bad, you know? Passed quickly enough. Right, then. I'll bring the tea up. And I'll just run the hover around. Might get the duster out, too. Few cobwebs over there. And how are you fixed for ironing? Sure, I'll just give the place a quick going over.'

'Thanks, mum.'

Thirteen

It's been a gruelling week for Barry. Receiving the bad news at work on Tuesday and making it through to Friday has been slow and painful like pulling teeth.

Understandably, everyone at the firm is in bad form. The receptionist went home in tears after the bombshell of her redundancy was dropped on Wednesday, and has called in sick for the rest of the week. I mean, you've got to feel sorry for the woman. She was the last one to know. Her husband is out of work with a bad back, and they re-mortgaged the house to fund her son's art gallery which is failing miserably. The reception desk is now unmanned. Not that the phone needs to be answered these days, anyway. It hardly rings. He had spied the receptionist doing crosswords on more than one occasion over the last few months.

These days, Nigel is either hiding in his office with the door closed, or is out at a meeting. The rat is clearly unable to face anyone. The office is like a ghost town in the Wild West. All the place needs now are a few tumbleweeds to sweep past and for everyone to start wearing Stetsons and chaps to complete the look.

Anyway, it's Friday afternoon. Not long until he and Rebecca can start telling their parents about the baby. He feels a stab of guilt at the thought of Rebecca. She still hasn't got a clue about the looming redundancy. He has tried to tell her a few times, but he couldn't, as she's been so unwell. He will have to hold off. Just for a little while. Just until they are at the three-month mark and they have the all clear that everything is going to plan. Rebecca has enough to concentrate on, now. It's best not to worry her. If anything ever happened to the baby, he would carry the guilt forever.

Besides, Barry can fix this. All he needs to do is click another job in the next three months before this job runs out. Sure, that's loads of time. He's highly qualified and he has great experience. He can slip out of here for interviews whenever he feels like it. He can tell Nigel he's off to meet a client. He owes him nothing at this point. He can negotiate an impressive package at the new job, and maybe even a company car. He should have done it years ago, this place has been circling the drains for ages now.

Barry decides to spend the rest of the afternoon polishing his CV. When another job arises, he can tell Rebecca the whole story, and then she won't have to worry.

A light bulb flickers on above his head. Hey! Wasn't his old college mate Stephen telling him about his new role in some recruitment company or other? Yes, he mentioned it at the wedding. 'Headhunted', he'd said. 'To a major agency', he'd boasted. Perfect!

Barry searches through the contact list on his IPhone and hears the ring tone.

'Stephen? Hi, mate, it's Barry. Yeah, we got back from honeymoon a couple of weeks ago. Amazing, man. Yeah. Listen, I need to call in a favour...'

Fourteen

This morning, I tried to go to work. Honestly, I did. It's Friday, so I thought that if I could just scrape myself in for one day, I'd be a hero. The girls in the office are probably missing me tons by now, and Harry is probably feeling like a little lost puppy without me there to run silly errands and photocopy stuff for him. Also, Judy and I have a mini Candy Crush tournament on Fridays. I'm not competitive or anything – it's just that I don't like anyone else winning, that's all.

Oh, and just a wee footnote. It's nothing, really. It's just that I'm on thin ice with the old sick leave policy of late. No big deal. I just have to make sure that it's all certified sick leave from now on. No more duvet days to catch up on Netflix for me. But sure, I'll go to Dr Logan and get him to scribble something illegible on a cert to keep Harry happy. Problem solved.

Yesterday, there was no way I was going to work. I got up, retched in the shower and went back to bed. At least I tried. This morning didn't go well either. There I was, showered, dressed and in the car. I was dead late, but better late than never, right? I even got as far as starting the engine and putting my seat belt on. See how I had good intentions? My stomach lurched, but I pushed on, thinking only of others. Well, I got as far as the end of the estate and was about to turn onto the M50 when I got the queasy feeling again. I vomited all over my lap. Looking back, I'd made the following mistakes:

1. I had chosen a lie in over breakfast. It was ten o'clock when I left, and I had to get my skates on. Morning sickness is worst with an empty stomach. Lesson learned.

2. In full-on martyr mode, I'd fed the cat. Now, this is Barry's job. I'm making a baby from scratch and have enough to do. However, the selfish sod was very distracted for some reason this morning, and left without feeding Jessie. The poor moggie was meowing all over the shop. Well, I couldn't ignore my little pussy cat pal, so I fed him quickly. See how my maternal instinct is kicking in? Yeah, well, it turns out that spooning kitty chum chunks into a bowl is enough to stir the nausea to new heights. I won't be making that mistake again.

3. In typical gallant fashion, I'd chucked a black bag of rubbish into the purple wheelie bin on my way down the driveway. This is more evidence that Barry is very forgetful this week, I don't know where his head is at these days. The pungent whiff of the bin, stuffed with takeaway leftovers, coupled with the heat was enough to leave me gagging.

Next thing you know, I'm projectile vomiting all over my new black trousers (the good ones that are a size too big, and allow for bloating.) Honestly, it was like a scene from The Exorcist. This is a new low. I mean, it's one thing to be feeling as rough as a bear's backside, but to actually throw up all over yourself while driving? Awful. I think people should start calling it 'morning-noon-and-flipping-night sickness' and start a helpline for sufferers. It's the pits

There was nothing for it, but to go back to bed – but not before I scooped myself a large portion of Haagen-Dazs. You know, to line the tummy and all that, seeing as it's the only thing that stays down these days.

I think that I've made a discovery. This must be how Alexander Graham Bell felt when he discovered the

IPhone. Or when Thomas Edison invented Facebook. I could win a Nobel Peace Prize for this. I could change the lives of pregnant women all over the world. The discovery is both fabulous and horrifying at the same time. You see, as I've mentioned, I am nauseous as the day is long. From the moment I open my eyes until I close them at night, my stomach is churning. I've tried ginger biscuits, ginger tea, nettle tea, peppermint tea, dry crackers, rice crackers, ice pops and glucose sweets. Nothing helps. There is no escape. Until now...

I thought I was imagining it at first, but it's real. When I am actually eating, I am fine. The sickness lifts. Then, about ten minutes later, the nauseous sensation is back with a vengeance. The trick, it seems, it to keep eating. Then, everything is happy clappy again. If I wake up in the night, I just nibble on a selection of yummies on my bedside locker. There is an impressive array of chocolate chip cookies and Pringles for midnight munchies. I keep breakfast bars in the glove box of my car and wham bars in my purse.

And the horrifying but? If you are going to eat from morning 'til night, your ass is eventually going to be the size of a small country. I know what you're thinking. Eat celery. Eat lettuce leaves. Eat teeny tiny mouthfuls of air-filled cardboard–tasting rice cakes. No thanks! This baby, it seems, likes carbs and saturated fats. And plenty of them!

Fifteen

'How was your day, baby?'

Barry kisses me and then reaches into the kitchen drawer for the takeaway menus. He knows the drill by now: I cannot possibly cook for him, I'm far too unwell. He doesn't seem to mind. Funny, that.

'Fine. After the puking in the car episode, I tried to go shopping. All I could put in the trolley was ice-cream, chocolate, jellies and nachos. Everything else makes me gag.'

'Ah, baby. And where's the chocolate you bought?'

'Hmm? Oh...it's gone.'

As Barry completes the pizza takeaway order, I reach for the Pinot Grigio without fluttering an eyelash.

'Baby! You can't drink now. Remember?'

I can't help it. Reaching for the gargle in the evenings is a genuine involuntary reflex – like a knee-jerk reaction following a hammer blow to the lower leg. Seriously, you could stick me in a medical journal and everything!

'Yeah, but I was only going to have one, Barry. Flip sake!'

'I know, but the baby, Becks... You're not meant to.'

Barry's such a kill joy. Separating me from my glass of wine on a Friday night is like separating Pamela Anderson from her breast implants: it won't kill me, but I am far less bouncy fun without it.

'Actually, clever clogs,' I call to Barry from the kitchen as he sets the plates and cutlery on the coffee table in the sitting room.

'Yeah?' Barry collapses on the Lazy Boy recliner and switches on Netflix.

'I read my new book today. 'What to Expect When You're Expecting.' It says one small glass is fine.' I cough over the word small, so he won't hear it.

I've poured the wine into a very large glass, and filled it all the way up to the brim. I then take a generous swig from the bottle and put it back in the fridge, and slurp at the top of the glass so that it looks like a smaller measure before bringing it to the sitting room.

'See?' I raise the glass in the air. 'Just a little tiddly teeny baby one. That's fine.'

'Oh, OK. So, I'm dying to know. How did you get on? What did Dr Logan say? Everything alright?'

'Yeah, everything's fine. I'm about eight weeks gone. You must have knocked me up on the wedding night, or thereabouts,' I laugh.

'Around the time of the wedding? Wow!'

He will dine off that one for weeks, no doubt.

'Yeah, anyway, the baby is due on the seventeenth of March.'

'No way! Paddy's day! Oh, that's great. We can start telling everyone in a few weeks, then.'

'Yeah, cheers.'

I raise my glass, but it's empty. Without thinking, I stand up for another.

'Eh, baby, you can't have another one. Remember? I'll get you a nice sugary cup of tea. Yeah?'

'Fine!' I manage to reply without separating my teeth.

Barry returns with tea, biscuits and a bottle of beer on a tray.

'Eh, excuse me?'

'Hmm?' Barry doesn't look away from the telly. Ever since we subscribed to Netflix and he discovered 'Breaking Bad', it's like he is unreachable. If a fire broke out, I doubt he'd even notice.

'Beer, Barry? I don't bloody think so.'

Barry eventually tears his gaze away from the TV screen. He must be taking me seriously, because we were just at the bit where Walter White is mixing up a new batch of blue Crystal Meth and getting ready to shoot that big drug cartel war lord, and the dude with the moustache gets blown up and bits of him are splattered all over the ceiling. Oh, you haven't got to that bit yet? I've ruined the ending for you? Sorry.

'I mean it, Barry. If I can't drink, then you can't.'

Misery loves company. There's no way that I'm stuck on a one drink limit for nine long months while he's drinking his head off. I mean, I haven't been on a one drink limit since I was seventeen and my parents knew bloody well that I was drinking cider with the lads before the Rugby Club disco, but tried to teach me about drinking responsibly.

Barry stares at me. Ha! He wasn't expecting that. I have knocked the wind out of his sails, big style. Well, good! He'll probably lose stones and increase his life expectancy. He'll thank me for selflessly helping him get rid of his beer belly. He'll be a daddy soon, so it's for his own good.

'But… baby!'

'What? I'm bloody serious, Barry.'

I swipe the bottle of beer from his hands to show him that I'm one of those 'she who shall be obeyed' types, and stalk into the kitchen. My mind is made up on this one. I take a sneaky gulp or three of the beer, nearly choking on it. Then I pour the other half down the sink. It fizzes and froths as it circles the plug hole to its impending doom. What a waste.

'There, it's gone.'

'Ah, baby. You could at least have let me have one. Like you.'

'Ok, fine! We'll both limit ourselves to just one, right?'

Barry nods, and I get him a fresh beer from the fridge. We watch back-to-back episodes of 'Breaking Bad', tummies rumbling, waiting for the doorbell to ring. I can't concentrate. My mind keeps reverting back to all the booze in the house, begging to be drunk.

'Becks!' the tequila calls to me. 'Come party with us, Mexican style. Try us with lemonade! The bubbles will tickle your nose!'

The vodka is three quarters full. 'Why don't you love me anymore? Is it something I said? I didn't mean to give you a muzzy head last time.'

The wine sniggers. 'You know you can't resist me for long. We have history, you and I. Anyway, the bottle is open, now. I'll go off if you don't finish me.'

Even the half bottle of sherry at the back of the cupboard (next to the vanilla essence and other baking accoutrements that I ignore) jeers me. 'Admit it. You keep me here for dry spells. Break glass in case of emergency, that's what you said. You took a sneaky drop last Christmas while pretending to bake.'

The beer doesn't need to say anything. It's watching me, waiting for me to cave in.

The pizza order, along with all the trimmings, has arrived. Barry unpacks the cardboard boxes and unloads two large pizzas, wedges, cheese strips and chicken dippers. 'Here,' he passes me a large tub of Ben & Jerry's and a spoon. 'I thought you'd enjoy this.'

These days, I have an on-again off-again relationship with food. Sometimes I'm too ill to touch anything, other times I'm eating like a starved, flea-bitten dog. Today is a ravenous day. I haven't spoken for a five full minutes. All I'm missing is a nose bag to help get the food into me faster.

'That's good, baby. You're really getting stuck in, there. Will I finish your pizza crusts? Great to see you've got your appetite back. I was starting to worry!'

'If only I could wash it down with a cold beer,' I smile. The tea is just not doing it for me.

'Hey, maybe I'm having a proper pregnancy craving for alcohol,' I suggest.

Barry laughs.

'Seriously though, Barry. Pregnant women get cravings for mad things. Coal, I heard of once. Petrol was another. Some fruit cakes crave chalk. So, is it beyond the realms of possibility to crave alcohol?'

Barry's not convinced, but I'm going to Google it. There could be something in alcoholic drinks, like, subconsciously on a deeper level, that the baby needs. You know, nutrients, or stuff like that.

Barry is unable to move after the feeding frenzy and his eyelids are heavy, so I decide to go in for the kill.

'Oh, and another thing, Barry. I'll need a new car. Nothing flash, just something new and safe. You know, for the baby.'

'Your car is fine! Just get the windscreen wipers fixed, and send it for a service. I'm sure it'll pass the NCT this time.'

'Oh, fine. Fine.'

My arms are folded. That's woman code for 'I'm seriously annoyed with you.'

'What's wrong?'

'No, no it's fine.'

'Spill it, Becky.'

'No, not at all. If you want the mother of your child to drive around in a 2005 Volkswagen death trap, then that's perfectly fine. Good to know where I stand, that's all.'

'Baby, it's a Volkswagen Golf, and it's grand.'

'Grand? Grand, is it? Barry, it's a rust bucket!'

'Look, I'll swap you for the Jag. Happy now?'

'No, I am not *happy now*.'

I make a sound – it's a cross between a 'ppppppfft' and a 'humph'. Either way, it translates as properly ticked off.

'Well, I was thinking more along the lines of a yummy mummy mobile. David traded in Emer's convertible Mercedes for a brand new Nissan Qashquai. They come in pretty colours.'

There's an oh-so-subtle message here, along the lines of 'David loves Emer more than you love me.'

'The Jag is a lovely colour.'

'Barry, it's a wishy washy boring dishwater blue. Big whoop. And it doesn't have a good stereo. The baby needs a good stereo.'

'Okaaaay...'

Barry's laughing at me. The villain! This is completely unacceptable. I should have thrashed out the terms and conditions of this pregnancy before getting myself into this situation. Now, it's harder to negotiate. He's taking advantage of my vulnerable condition.

'Look, Barry. It's a science thing. You wouldn't understand. There's, like, a connection between maths and music. Don't you want her to have a high IQ? Look it up!'

'Baby, there's a link between classical music and maths. We can play him a bit of Mozart and Bach. I know what you're saying. Research shows that the baby can hear while in utero.'

'Hah! Bach! I don't think so. Britney Spears will be classical music one day in the future.'

Barry knows not to argue with me when it comes to Britney. Or Rhianna. Or Michael Bolton. Don't ask.

'And I'll need a sunroof. The jag doesn't have one.'

'Becks, we live in Dublin, you know? Rainy climate? What would you need a sunroof for?'

'Not for me!' It's hard to keep a straight face, so I pretend to watch the telly when we talk. 'For the baby!'

Barry is rolling his eyes like a petulant teenager.

'The baby,' he smiles.

'Yes. We don't want her overheating. I'm only being safety conscious.'

'Of course. Safety first.'

I hope for the sake of Barry's safety that was not sarcasm I detected. He's in so much trouble.

'Oh, and another thing. I've been reading up. I can't lift anything heavy. I saw it on mumschat.com.'

'Of course not. Absolutely no lifting. Just ask me if there's anything heavy, Becks.'

'Right. So, how much do you think the Hoover weighs?

'No idea...'

'Yeah. Probably about ten pounds. Best not to risk it. Lifting can affect the flesh around the lining of the womb. It could, like, rip and stuff.'

'OK, OK. Stop. Fine! Don't lift the Hoover.'

Got ya! Barry always squirms when I talk about blood and guts and stuff. It's how I got him to agree to buy our dining table and chairs in solid oak last year (at full price, and way above our budget.) He would have flitted about and pointed to hideous dining furniture on special offer, so I just told him that I had my period, had to go home and that the blood loss was making me feel faint. He went pale, and produced the credit card faster than you can say 'squeamish'.

On the downside, he'll most likely be a total pansy in the delivery room. The smelling salts will be out, by the looks of him. Once he doesn't distract the nurses from the main focus (AKA me) we will not fall out about it. Stand between me and an epidural at your peril, mate.

'Great that you're thinking so much about the baby, now. Are you feeling better about things? Getting your head around it all?'

'Eh, yeah. Suppose. Anyway, probably best if you Hoover for a while, then. Also, pushing a heavy trolley around Tesco might be taking a chance. And bending over to clean the bathroom. And stooping to load the dishwasher. Oh, and obviously the cooking. Very heavy, eh, saucepans.

Sixteen

Barry's parents Margaret and Patrick are expecting us. They haven't got a clue about our news, they think we're just meeting up for brunch and a catch up. Barry is like a child on Christmas morning. He can't wait to tell them about the baby. We have a bet going as to how long he can hold it in once he presses their doorbell. My money is on two minutes.

The heavenly whiff of the Hicks sausages and rashers hits me as soon as I get through the front door. The fried eggs are crackling on the pan and there's a pot of fresh coffee on the go. I can literally smell everything these days. It's ridiculous. It's like having a new superpower; except it's a lame power and I don't get to fight crime or wear either a cape or red boots. They would call me 'Pregger Girl' and I'd have a large P on the belly part of my costume. The down side of this heightened sense is that anything even slightly stinky has me bent over into a wastepaper basket, which is most unflattering.

The 'eat as much as you can so you don't feel sick' rule to avoid morning sickness is still very much in play. I daren't do anything to jeopardise things. The good news is that Margaret is great for the grub, so I've come to the right place. She and my own mum are what you would call 'feeders'. You know, they like to feed people and are constantly offering biscuits in between the meals they've prepared for you. It's a nurturing thing, I guess. Margaret likes to shop in Donneybrook Fair and always has these fancy-shmancy cheeses. Also, she makes her own chutneys and carrot cakes. They're to die for.

It's eleven o'clock and I've already had a three course breakfast in bed, courtesy of my doting husband: coco puffs, pop tarts and a cream cheese bagel. If I were to be reincarnated, I think I'd choose a hobbit for the next life. No, seriously, hear me out! They have three breakfasts, and I'm telling you, it's not to be sniffed at. Also, they stay at home relaxing a lot which looks cosy. Apart from the orcs and the fire breathing dragons lurking outside the Shire, it looks like a nice life. I do, however, object to having hairy toes, but I'm sure a few waxing strips could fix that bit.

During the brief car journey to the in-laws, I've consumed two breakfast bars. Margaret barely has time to serve me my full Irish breakfast and pour my tea before Barry is straight to the point of our visit. Honestly, can I not swallow my food in peace?

'We have news!' Barry is standing.

Why on earth he is standing, I cannot tell you. He's making such a song and dance about this. If there was a champagne glass in his hand, he'd be clinking it.

'Barry,' I hiss. 'Wait 'til I've finished my sausages!'

There are some croissants on the kitchen counter from the local bakery, and I know that Margaret has some of that Butlers Pantry jam that I like so much in the press. Margaret and Patrick exchange a look. There's a tense silence.

'Right. Fine, go on then.'

I squirt more organic ketchup on my plate. Barry clears his throat. It occurs to me that perhaps he has been practising the little speech in his head. That's so cute.

'Rebecca and I have some news. It's very exciting.'

I'm smiling like an absolute simpleton, but I've no idea why. I think that's what you're meant to do in these situations when announcements are being made about you. It didn't cover what to do during announcements in the pregnancy book, so I'm kind of making it up as I go along.

'Rebecca is…'

Barry can't get the words out, he's too choked up. Honestly, I have to do everything around here!

'I'm pregnant.'

Margaret's hand shoots straight to her mouth in surprise. Patrick slaps Barry on the back in congratulations.

'Well done,' Patrick offers me his hand. 'Fantastic news.'

I'm mortified. Now there will be no doubt in their minds that I've had actual proper sex with their son. How embarrassing!

'It's early days,' Barry has regained the power of speech. 'About nine weeks, did you say, Becky? Due in March.'

'Amazing. A little grandchild!' Margaret is on her feet hugging me.

Before I have a chance to ask for seconds, the plates are cleared and more coffee is served. Margaret produces a photo album. Barry and his dad grumble, but they are smiling. Let me tell you, the album is one of many. Margaret and I once spent an evening drinking wine and bonding as we went through about five of them when Barry and I were first dating. I nearly wet myself when I saw the dodgy seventies décor and the eighties home hair cuts.

I haven't seen this particular album before. It dates back to the late seventies when Barry was born. It's orange and brown striped and has a thick layer of dust. Margaret sits besides me at the dining table.

'Ah, would you look at him,' she coos. 'These ones are all from the year he was born. Such a gorgeous baby.'

A large baby with thundering white thighs lies bottom up on a white fur rug and I guffaw. I'm going to start calling Barry 'wonder boy' when we get home. His parents flipping idolise him, and have done since he graced their lives with his presence.

Margaret is in full on reminiscing mode. We're holding hands, which is slightly awkward. Still, I go along with it.

'Oh, and it was a tough labour with this one. Thirty-two hours, he was.'

'Thirty two?'

I gulp. Surely that can't be right. Perhaps Margaret is prone to bouts of exaggeration. Or forgetfulness. Maybe thirty-eight years of mothering Barry has clouded her memory. I'll read up later to see if this is even possible. Surely after a few hours of excruciating pain the nurses feel sorry for you in the hospital and help things along. I'm sure she's made a mistake.

'And I'll never forget how he kept me waiting. Two weeks late, he was. In absolutely no rush to get here.'

The lazy streak in Barry obviously goes back to when he was in the womb. Even in utero he was being a selfish sod! I'll have words with him about it. How could he treat his mother in such a way?

'Back then, they shaved you. You know, *down there*. And gave you an enema. In case you poohed yourself, dear.'

Oh, no. We have taken a wrong turn. We were happily making polite small talk over rashers and sausages in normal-Ville, and now we have stumbled into the twilight zone. It's a strange place where your mother-in-law holds your hand, and the stories about her private parts don't remain private. Here, polite and refined people from Dalkey say pooh. It's wrong, I tell you! I'm like Dorothy in 'The Wizard of Oz', desperately trying to get back to good old Kansas where people remain in black and white. I send Barry a signal with my eyes to rescue me, but he doesn't get it.

'Oh, but what a beaut! Look at him there, with his little podgy bottom.'

Margaret has flipped to the next page. In the photo, she's looking pale and worn out in a hospital gown with baby Barry in her arms.'

'Barry?,' I say, 'I never knew you had to be admitted to hospital when you were little?'

I use the word 'little' lightly. He looks about three months old (but, sure, what would I know) and let's just say that he's really filling that cotton sleep suit. I'd say the poppers are under immense strain.

'Eh, that's the day I was born, silly!' Barry laughs.

'Oh...'

It's like the blood is whooshing in my ears. I'm the last to get the memo. Everyone knew it but never mentioned it to me before. All the clues were there. The headline reads: *Local boy Barry Costello born a flipping whopper*.

'So...'

I can't say it. It's too awful.

'So...' I try again. 'You were a big baby, then?'

Margaret is laughing. That's not good.

'Big? Oh, Rebecca. He was huge. Did he never tell you? It's a funny story.'

'No, Margaret. He didn't.'

Margaret is wiping a laughter tear from her eye. Patrick is pushing air into his cheeks, pretending to be a fat baby. He looks like a balding hamster. This is awful. Everyone is sharing the joke but me. Ha-ha, Barry was a big baby. Hilarious! Now poor sad Rebecca is going to have to squeeze a large baby into the world. It's the probability of genetics. Excuse me if I won't join the raucous party, I've just been handed the bill, and it's a big one.

'So, eh, sorry...just to clarify. How big are we talking here?'

'Eleven pounds. Biggest on the ward, weren't you Barry love?'

Barry shakes his head to confirm it. Is that...? No, it couldn't be. Is that actual pride I can see on Barry's face? Being an overweight child is nothing to be proud of. It's not an achievement or anything. There are child obesity campaigns running now. There's no trophy given to the biggest one (like they do for prizewinning turnips at a country fair.) In fact, it's awful. Starting life as a fatty is disgraceful and should be banned. There should be petitions signed in protest regarding any baby crossing the ten pound threshold. I'm sure it would be for humanitarian purposes and such like.

'Eleven pounds,' I repeat it aloud and it sounds even worse than it did inside my racked brain.

Patrick whistles. 'What a bruiser, eh? Your poor mother.'

'Patrick!' Margaret scolds. 'Wasn't he worth it? And look at him now. An accomplished solicitor, about to be a daddy. Ah, look at this photo. Such a darling. Ah there he is in the bath. Oh, we can see your little Willy in that one, Barry! Ha-ha.'

'Mum!'

I don't even have the ability to snigger at her use of the words 'little' and 'willy' in the same sentence. Usually, I'd have some sarcastic innuendo by now. Something witty and cutting that would make everyone laugh. But I'm far too traumatised. There are tiny white stars forming on my eyes, and the room is spinning. Perhaps I'm about to have an out of body experience. Maybe I'll hyperventilate. I need a paper bag in which to inhale deeply, until I either pass out or this whole nightmare goes away.

Barry detects my panic. Finally! He took his bloody time about it.

'But, sure just because I was big, that doesn't mean that our baby will be big,' his eyes plead with his mother to corroborate his story.

'Well, who knows? I think babies are getting bigger these days. Probably something to do with MSG in our food. And bigger food portions. Now, Julie down the road... You know, Mrs. Baker's eldest? Her first was ten and a half pounds. Jack, they called him. Beautiful looking child.'

I shoot her a disbelieving look. The very minimum that the woman could do is to play along. We could all have a nice parlour game called 'denial' right about now. It would be jolly good fun. Let's all pretend that just because Barry was born of Frankenstein proportions, that Rebecca's baby will be a delicate wisp of a thing. A slip of a child! Lightning doesn't strike twice. Barry was just a freak accident. Maybe Margaret was smoking weed or dropping acid at the time. It's plausible – it was the late seventies! Maybe her dates were mixed up and Barry was way, way overdue. Maybe she has a Nordic Viking in her distant ancestry who made a once off visit to her offspring's DNA. Sure, it's occasions like this for which little white lies were invented to protect feelings and dignity and such.

Margaret is still smiling, oblivious to my inner turmoil. I turn to Barry. He's absorbed in a picture of himself, and laughing at what looks like a bowl of pudding on his head, dripping onto his fat face.

'I loved my food even then, eh?' Barry is enjoying the trip down memory lane.

'Some things never change, eh Becks?' he rubs his belly.

I look at Barry as if for the first time. His height and broad shoulders are what attracted me to him in the first place. Truth be told, I fancied him rotten when he stood up from his desk to shake my hand, and I took in the sheer size of him. He played rugby for Blackrock College, and I liked that about him. He's definitely not what you'd call fat. He is not muscular, either. He's just cuddly. He makes me feel petite when he stands next to me and puts his arms around me. I can wear heels when we go out. It never occurred to me that he was born looking like the Incredible Hulk!

'The doctor said that it would probably be best to bottle feed,' Margaret reveals.

'Of course!' we all nod enthusiastically.

The woman is a total saint, but everyone has their limits. Also, she looks recently exhumed in the photos. I think that Barry drained every shred of nutrients from her. In fairness to the poor woman, her intentions had been honourable. She had tried to breastfeed baby Barry on the hour every hour for two days straight, despite the exhaustion (and presumably the agony as this was pre-epidural days) and then had no choice but to give up. Even the sisters on the ward felt sorry for her and passed her a bottle of formula, saying that she would happily be excused from this impossible task of filling the unfillable void. He was a bottomless pit of an infant, and guzzled ten ounces in ten minutes. The woman deserves a medal or some kind of recognition. Despite her ordeal, she smiles lovingly at him in the photographs, the golden child.

'Ah, he was the most gorgeous baby.'

Margaret reaches for the box of Kleenex and gives her nose a good hard blow. I pray that we can skip through the rest of the photos quickly, so that I can go home and have a panic attack in private. I don't want my in-laws to think I'm inferior. I mean, I'm sure I could push an eleven pounder out if I wanted to. Right now, I just want those albums to go far, far away to the dustiest most remote part of the attic and for the hatch door to be shut and double bolted.

Margaret still has the floor, despite my efforts to change the topic of conversation to the current story line in 'Fair City'. It usually never fails.

'He was so handsome. With a head full of thick black hair! He looked like he had been styled at 'Vidal Sassoon'. Oh, and those broad shoulders!'

Patrick nods as Margaret leans into me. The rest of her story is for my ears only.

'That's why they needed the forceps, dear.'

My eyes widen.

Like most couples, Margaret and Patrick are unable to tell a story uninterrupted. One will always finish the other's sentence. It's Patrick's turn, now.

'The clothes we had brought to the hospital, you know the little vests with the poppers?'

'Baby grows, Patrick.'

'Yes, well, sure, they didn't fit. Too small.'

'Didn't fit!' Margaret claps her hands in delight. 'Too small!'

'Can you imagine?' Patrick continues. 'His little toes were peeping at the bottom of the baby grow.'

'So, Margaret sends me home for bigger clothes, so she does.'

I picture a young Margaret lovingly packing and repacking the little hats and vests and crocheting booties into the late evening.

'What a guzzler, eh?' Barry laughs.

My face remains like stone, the nervous smile has now completely disappeared. Why has Barry not mentioned this to me before? It's like me marrying someone and not revealing that I used to be a man. Or that I used to like Bros. A birth weight of eleven pounds is vital information. It's a deal breaker – like a secret gambling problem, or a penchant for wearing silk panties on your head while you howl at the moon.

If we were smart and had a prenuptial arrangement, it would have stated in the fine print that failure to disclose important information was in fact deceit. Our marriage would be null and void. He really should have told me. OK, maybe not on our first date, but certainly before we were married and started talking about babies! The sad reality is that I have been tricked into marrying this family of monsters.

'OK, Becks?' Barry smiles.

'Mmm. Fine.'

There was nothing in the wedding vows about marrying someone who was born half boy, half -mutant. I mean, there's 'til death do us part. Well, fine. It turns out that giving birth to Barry's baby might in fact kill me. I could die from the shock of it. Then there's something about for better or for worse. Well, Barry got off lightly on that one. I'm a sheer delight. Then there was something to do with sickness and health. I wasn't really listening. I was trying not to pass out from holding in my stomach in the designer dress. If I breathed too deeply, the bodice of the size ten dress would have given way. Think of tightly packed sausage meat, and you'll have the idea. Oh, and for richer or for poorer was there, too. But there was definitely nothing about marrying someone whose rugby player shoulders needed forceps to rip their way into this world bloody. No, I would have definitely remembered the priest talking about that. It would have livened things up for sure.

I'm reminded of the immortal words in that classic film 'The Snapper'. When Colm Meaney's character announces the baby's birth weight of seven pounds six ounces, the old man in the pub responds: is that a baby or a turkey?' Well, I'm no Sharon Curley and Barry is no Georgie Burgess, thank you very much. I'm determined to have a baby of normal proportions, thank you very much.

'And isn't it true,' Barry is ignoring my distress, 'that you had to put me on solids early?'

I sink lower into the chair, hoping the ground will swallow me up at any moment. Perhaps, like waking up in a cold sweat from a nightmare, I will discover that it was all a mistake. Barry was, in fact, a respectable seven pounds. There were no kryptonite enhanced genes, after all.

'Yes,' Margaret laughs heartily.

'You had your first Weetabix at four weeks old.'

According to Margaret, Barry went on to become a solid child. No surprises there, then. She confesses that she found it hard to keep the fridge stocked.

'As a teenager, he used to go through a sliced pan a day. And that was after a hearty dinner. Once, when he was three, he ate a man-sized shepherd's pie in one sitting'.

I had never really paid attention to his old photos before, but now I examine each one closely. After all, this is my only clue to how our baby will look. Thank God I was a beautiful, slim, blonde child. At least we have a fifty-fifty chance.

Hopefully, the large ear lobe gene the whole Costello family seem to have, will bypass the next generation. I'm not worried about it, though. Technology has advanced to such a degree since Barry's childhood, that a little nip and tuck could be arranged if the baby's ears were a bit asymmetrical. Emer knows a great cosmetic surgeon in the Beacon Clinic.

'Well, now. More tea, Rebecca? Will you have a biscuit with that?' asks Patrick.

'Yes, please.'

Truth be told, I could do with something stronger than tea. Barry smiles at me lovingly as the tea and biscuits arrive.

'Oh, Rebecca's eating for two now. Eating like a trucker already. Aren't you, baby?'

I turn to give Barry the evil eye, and say something cutting about how it is he who has been eating for two his whole life — since birth, according to the latest newsflash. But I can't get the words out. I'm transfixed. It has just occurred to me with alarming clarity and undeniable stomach lurching truth that Barry has a very large head. I'm staring at it. I didn't really think about it when he talked about how hats never seem to sit snugly upon his head. He had joked during our wedding preparations that the top hat he tried on in the dress hire shop got stuck on his head. In fact, if memory serves, he had to have another size shipped in especially. I didn't tease him. Not even a teeny bit. I had soothed him with the same fib that I tell myself when trying on Versace: Italian sizes are notoriously small. I had told him not to give it another thought.

'Just kidding, baby, great that you have the morning sickness under control. Been tough on you hasn't it, baby?'

That's more like it.

'Very tough,' I agree. 'Been off work and everything, Margaret.'

'You should stay off next week, too,' declares Barry. 'Don't want you overdoing it, baby.'

Good old Barry. I suppose it isn't his fault that he was born the size of a baby elephant, with a melon for a head.

Seventeen

'Tell me honestly, mum. Be harsh, OK? Have I piled on the weight already?'

'No!'

There's something forced about her exclamation. The phrase 'the lady doth protest too much' springs to mind. She changes the subject sharpish. It's a tactic I learned from her.

'So, darling, have you decided? Will you have your baby in Holles Street? Yourself and Ian were born there.'

I'm crashed on mum's sofa with a packet of Jaffa Cakes. The morning at the animal shelter really wiped me out, and I'm absolutely starving despite a huge pasta lunch. According to 'What to Expect When You're Expecting', the three month mark is where the baby's important organs are all forming, and there is a heartbeat and everything. I have another Jaffa cake – the baby probably needs the vitamin C.

The book also states that a pregnant woman should increase her calorific intake by a mere three hundred calories per day. It suggests that said calories might consist of a piece of wholemeal toast and a banana, followed by a glass of milk. It's preposterous. I consume three hundred calories while I'm deciding what to eat next. Damn it, I've consumed three hundred calories just lying in the bath!

'I don't know yet,' I admit.

'Well, you'll have to make your mind up, love. You'll need to book in for the scan and all that.'

'Yeah. Emer's going to Holles Street. Private, of course.'

'Of course,' mum's lips curl up at the side.

'Dave is splashing the cash big time. No expense spared with that pair. She's almost six months gone, now. Jammy cow still looks amazing.'

'I bet. Sure, they're loaded.'

'Loaded.'

Mum and I love a good gossip from time to time.

'They got the buggy already. It comes with everything. Are you ready for this? It cost more than dad spent on my first car. Remember Betsy the Toyota Starlet? Now, OK the car was a total banger, but still! Honestly, I think she said the buggy is made out of titanium. That'll come in handy if they go to space.'

'Ah, no! Goodness!'

'Yup. And you should see the clothes she has on her. Ah, mum. It'd make you sick. She has an entire new wardrobe from this fancy French maternity shop in town. 'Le Jolie Mama', I think it's called. Really pricey designer stuff. She's all, like, 'Isabella Oliver said that pink is in fashion this season.''

'Money to burn. In our day, you just wore a bigger size. Sure, you'll be treating yourself to a few new bits and pieces in a few weeks.'

'Yeah. Suppose. Clothes are getting very tight already.'

That's an understatement – today, the jeans were sprayed onto me. I struggled with the zip and then gave up. I've opted for a pair of grey tracksuit bottoms and a t-shirt.

'And does your friend, Pam, know?'

'Yeah. Met her for a coffee and a cream slice yesterday.'

'Ah. That's nice. Was she thrilled for you?'

'Yeah, I mean… kind of. She's not really into babies, so you know. Doesn't really get it.'

I wonder about the hospital. We will have to make our minds up soon enough.

'And Mount Carmel is closed now, isn't it?' mum reads my mind.

'Yeah.'

It's such a shame. Mount Carmel hospital used to be a haven for yummy mummies in waiting, especially those in the South County Dublin area. It was a shining beacon of loveliness in a sea of crowded wards and irritable, overworked staff. I'm pretty sure a few celebs popped a baby or two out there.

'Remember I stayed there for the toenail?'

Mum nods. I was only in for two nights, but I was hoping the doctor would push it to three. It was like a hotel, but without the swimming pool. They had a hairdresser on call and a flat screen telly in my room. The tea was served with a little paper doily underneath it. If I fancied more, all I had to do was dial zero for the operator and a fresh pot came right in, accompanied by a piece of pie.

It had comfort. It had class. And most importantly, it had absolutely no riff raff allowed. Sadly, the pesky recession hit and things went belly up when it was signed over to NAMA. It tried to stay afloat. It introduced affordable packages, basically opening its doors to all kinds of undesirables. That's never good. It's like the golf club allowing non-members – chaos ensues! Sure enough, it closed.

'Just go public,' dad puts in his two cents.

Mum and I stare at him in total disbelief. My jaw drops to cartoon-like proportions.

'Sure, what are we paying bloody taxes for? This government have a lot to answer for. Shower of bloody criminals, that's what. I heard on 'Joe Duffy' last week that they plan to…'

'Ah, Gerry, no. We're not going to talk about politics. So, go on, Rebecca.'

'Dad! Honestly!'

There's no way on this earth that I'm agreeing to go public. God help me, I would rather perish. I'm not a snob or anything. Far from it!

'Dad! Going public would be like…'

I try to explain to dad that to subject myself and my new-born infant to the hellish pit that is the public services would be suicide.

'I mean, I could contract some kind of life threatening disease. It's like a petri dish. They let absolutely anyone in.'

'That's why they call it public, Rebecca.'

Dad is trying to reason with me. Silly of him, isn't it?

'Gerry, will you stop winding her up, now. It's not good for her blood pressure. Never mind him, love. Now, what were you saying?'

'Dad!'

I can't drop it. Not now that the can of putrid stinking worms has been opened.

'It's hard enough having a baby. I don't need to sit in a queue for ten hours waiting to see a consultant, perched next to the world and its mother on some wooden bench! With no air conditioning! While a little person inside me kicks me in the spleen! I mean, that's fine for the general public. You know. Unemployed people, and that. People who have nothing better to do. I'll be fitting appointments in between my busy work schedule. Oh, and I hear that you have to wee into a plastic cup before appointments. Sure, I don't want people seeing my wee!'

Dad wearily shuffles off to read the paper in the sitting room. He can't argue with logic.

'Honestly, mum. What's he like?'

'Shush, now. Don't mind him, darling.'

'Sorry, mum. I think the penny has dropped about the pregnancy. Speaking of pennies, I have to spend one every flipping ten minutes. I've the bladder of a four year old girl.'

'You'll be grand.'

'I know, it's just…I've been reading up on these pregnancy sites, you know? There was some woman blogging about her birth experience in the public ward. She had to remove her heels and coat in order to be weighed in full view of everyone in the waiting room.'

'Goodness, imagine that!'

'I know!'

'Don't look at those websites any more, love.'

Mum is right. It's not good for my delicate, shredded nerves.

'Dead right. Anyway, when it's my turn, I won't be sharing a ward with some stranger. No way!'

As mum reminisces about Holles Street in the early eighties, I allow myself a glimpse at what the private clinic will be like.

There is a full array of pharmaceuticals available to me, as detailed in the glossy brochure that's just been handed to me by an upbeat nurse in a crisp white uniform. Her name is Gwen, but she lets me call her 'nursie', and we are new best friends. I peruse my options.

'Nursie? Yes, I think I'll have a gin a tonic to start, followed by the gas and air. Just for fun. And a shot of the pethidine served on the side. Good to try new things. '

'Good choice. An excellent vintage. And for the main course?'

'Oh, an epidural. Naturally!'

'Yes, madam. Straight away.'

She scuttles off the get the goodies ready. Mustn't leave me in pain, or anything. God forbid! Gosh, I wonder if they would bring some champagne into the delivery room. Not, of course, before the baby is born. Obviously! That would be inappropriate. Fun, but inappropriate. I should have asked.

Barry sips an Earl Grey in a comfortable leather chair and scans the sports page as I flick through 'Hello!' Magazine. Poor Brad is still traumatized after the divorce, I'm reading all about it.

'Happy, darling?'

'Super, darling. Super.'

'Jolly good.'

Oh, I seem to have coughed and the baby has arrived. How spiffing. Wow, isn't she pretty? And I didn't feel a thing. So convenient. And just in time for supper, too. Cook has been in. He's dashed sorry about the mix up. No fillet steaks left, he's afraid. Blasted nuisance. But the Fois Grois is pretty good. There is a full wine list. No trouble to pop down to the cellar and dust off a bottle or two.

I've been wheeled from the delivery room into my private bedroom, now. I'm not sure where the baby is. They are probably bathing and fluffing her up for me, maybe she's having her first up-do with a pretty pink bow. That's nice.

Aha! Here comes the supper now. Ooh, it's sumptuous. There was really no need for silver cutlery, I'm easy to please. Mustn't make a fuss over little old me, eh? And it's served with a selection of petit fours, too. How elegant! Here comes the dessert trolley. Oh, I couldn't possibly. Stuffed, I tell you. Then again, must keep the strength up. I've just had a baby, after all! It will be good soakage, too. See how I'm so responsible, now?

Oh, look. Sky Movies are showing some hilarious rom-coms this evening, and a nurse is waiting just outside the door to fulfil my every need. Oh, and the baby's needs too. I'm too shagged to think about that!

'Rebecca? Becky! Becky!'

'Hmm?'

'I said, it looks like you've made your mind up, then. Private it is. So that leaves Holles Street, the Rotunda or The Coombe'

'Mum, that's easy. Holles Street. No contest.'

'Ah, lovely. Is that because you and Ian were born there?'

'Eh, no mum. It's because the others are on the North side. Duh!'

Mum and I are so efficient. We've already decided on a consultant and have made a call. Once Barry and I see the baby on the ultrasound screen, it's going to feel very real indeed.

Eighteen

'Anyway,' mum passes me a cup of tea, 'Ian will be here soon. He's bringing Cindi.'

I roll my eyes. My little brother, Ian, and his on-again off-again girlfriend, Cindi, are not exactly top of my list of people I want to see. Ian is an eternal student and always hitting dad for cash. He's so immature. Himself and Cindi are forever having some kind of dramatic break up and then patching things up. I love soap operas, but when it's in your own family, it's just plain annoying.

I'm trying to scrape together enough energy to get my pregnant ass off the couch when I hear the doorbell.

'Ah, flip.'

'Alright, dad. Alright, mum.'

Ian has his arm around Cindi. Clearly, they're in the 'on-again' portion of the romance. They have just moved in together, but we will see how long that lasts. The two of them are just toxic for each other. No doubt it'll be merely weeks before one of them starts a row, and the other moves out. It's a bit tragic, really. If only they could take a leaf out of mine and Barry's book. We are excellent role models for them.

'Alright, sis,' Ian addresses me. 'Eh, mum told me your news. Congrats.'

This is the closest Ian gets to gushing declarations.

'Thanks Ian, just popping home now. Smell you later. Mum, I'll give you a buzz after Corrie, yeah?'

'Eh, well, wait a bit.' Ian and Cindi exchange a look.

Something is up. Ian is not the type to request the pleasure of my company for more than five minutes at a time. I smell a rat. He's either:

a. Looking for money. It's the safe bet.

b. Confessing some speeding ticket or overdue student fee – please refer to a) above.

c. Worried about his rent / car loan – please refer to a) above.

It's odd, though. He doesn't usually need Cindi here to back him up. It must be really bad. Maybe he has a serious gambling problem and the loan shark breaks thumbs. Or maybe he got fired from a job. Then again, he hasn't got one of those.

'Right, Ian. Let's have it.'

Sorry, but I'm not beating around the bush this time. He's looking to sponge some dosh from dad. What else could it be? That man-child will have the poor man bled dry. There will be nothing left for me to inherit!

'Eh, sorry?'

Ian is fooling no-one. I'm well aware of his scrounging ways. Been there, done that, dad's bought the t-shirt.

Cindi clears her throat. 'Eh, Ian and I are really glad we caught you all together as a family. We wanted to tell you all something.'

I'm on tenterhooks to hear what disaster is about to unfold, it's even more tense than EastEnders. I'll have to hang about for the cliff-hanger. Oh, and moral support, obviously.

'Yeah, Cindi and I have some news.'

Ian takes Cindi's hand.

Wait. Hang on there just a minute. It can't be!

Mum clutches dad's arm. 'Is it good news, Ian?'

'Yeah, mum. We're having a baby.'

'Oh my goodness,' mum manages.

I sit down. Well, it's more of a flop, really. It's like someone has taken a large sharp needle and popped the lovely cosy little bubble I was floating in, and now I'm falling to the earth from fifty thousand feet.

'What?'

Yes, I'm aware that I'm on my feet, now. A sudden burst of energy propelled me forward. Yes, I do realise that I'm shouting. That might be perceived as rude in some cultures, but here in the Democratic Republic of Rebecca, it's perfectly acceptable.

'But...' is all I can manage.

Ian and Cindi have stolen my limelight. They crept in the dead of night and snatched it from me. You see, it's been like this all of my life. Even my wedding day, the happiest day of my life, had to be shared with Barry! In school, another girl celebrated her birthday on the first of November. The inconsiderate, selfish girl! The teacher used to make us stand on plastic chairs in the classroom as the class crowed 'happy birthday to you, happy birthday to you, happy birthday dear RebeccaandLindaaaaaaa, happy birthday to you'. I couldn't even have a flipping birthday all to myself.

'I…'

Being pregnant is my one and only shot at having the attention on me. I was planning on milking it for the full nine months. After that, it will be 'baby this' and 'baby that'! But oh, no! I can't be the only pregnant one in this family. Cindi has to go and ruin it on me.

'Rebecca,' mum's eyes widen, begging me to be polite. 'Isn't that great news?'

'Yes, it's…'

I can't finish the sentence. My mind is attempting to answer the following questions:

1.Will I have to share my chief babysitter with Cindi? There's only one thing for it. Mum will simply have to choose a grandbaby. She will be like Meryl Streep in 'Sophie's Choice'. It's either my baby or Cindi's baby – she will need to pick a side. If she values peace and quiet, she will have to go with team Costello.

2.Which baby will be born first? The first grandchild is going to be the favourite, the one to inherit the family heirlooms and the silver pocket watches. Everyone knows that. If I have to bounce about all day on a pogo stick to push things along, then so be it. I refuse to be beaten.

3. Will Cindi's ass swell to irreversible proportions? Oh god, I do hope so!

'Oh, Rebecca!' Cindi is smiling. 'They'll be so close. Cousins!'

Cindi is despicable. It's possible that Cindi got pregnant just to annoy me. It's unlikely, I'll grant you, but possible. Also, she doesn't use deodorant. What kind of person does that? Says it's because of aerosols in the atmosphere or something lame like that. Eh, weird! Oh, and here's the best bit. She's a flipping vegetarian. She goes on about animal cruelty when I'm trying to enjoy a Big Mac. I mean, that's unforgivable!

Dad has regained the power of speech.

'Well done, son. Great news. Congratulations, Cindi.'

Well done? Well flipping done? Congratulations? Eh hello? What planet is this? Ian's accidentally knocked up his on-again/off-again girlfriend and you're actually happy about it? Well that's that, then. Ian will be tapping dad for money for the rest of his mature student days. Dad will be coughing up for nappies and bottles and whatever else it is that babies need.

'When are you due, Cindi?' mum fidgets with a tea towel.

There's more. The horror is not yet over. Ok, are you ready for this? Set your face to stun. Cindi's baby is due… I'm sorry, I can't say it. It's too awful. I need a stiff drink to get me through the rest of the day until I can crawl into bed, wake up twelve hours later and hope that it was all a bad dream. But oh, no! How can I forget? I am denied even that simple pleasure.

Ok, I will try again. I apologise in advance for my language, but I think you'll agree, it's justified. She is due on the same day as me. The same flippety flip day. There are three hundred and sixty five days in a calendar year. What are the odds of her not only being pregnant at the same time as me, but having the same due date? Don't answer that, smarty pants. It's a rhetorical question. I don't want an actual maths answer. What I want is a drink.

'I don't believe it!' mum cries.

She gives Cindi a kiss on her smug little face. Mum is such a traitor. She has snuck out of our tent and crossed over to the enemy's camp. She is one of them now, there's no going back.

'It's amazing,' mum gushes. 'Here I was, dying to be a granny, and now there are two grandchildren on the way. And both due St. Patrick's Day! We're in for a busy few months!'

'But...' Cindi stares at me. 'You're due on seventeenth of March as well? Oh my God, Rebecca! Two Paddies' Day babies!'

I'm being hugged. She is squeezing the air out of my lungs. Cindi seems to think that we are now best friends.

'Isn't this just awesome?'

'Awesome,' I deadpan.

I pretend to be overwhelmed with tiredness and slip out. Mum is too busy grilling Cindi to convince me to stay. As soon as I've sped home, I put a shaking key into the lock and scramble for the house phone. I dial Barry at work. It's weird, there is no answer. Maybe the receptionist is on a day off or something. I try his mobile.

'Hi, baby. Everything OK? Feeling OK?'

'Yes, yes. Fine. Anyway, get a load of this.'

I fill Barry in and wait for his words of disgust, so that I can agree with him whole-heartedly.

'Wow, that's gas.'

He's not playing ball. I'll have to call Pam if I want a suitable reaction.

'Gas? No, it's not gas, Barry. Don't you think it's so...'

'And she's due on the same day as us?'

'Yes, Barry. Exact same day. So, anyway – '

'Same day. That's gas.'

'Again, Barry, it's not gas. I'm sorry, but I think it's absolutely...'

'Ah. A little niece or nephew for us...'

Oh. A niece or nephew. I hadn't thought of it like that. I never had a burning desire to be a mum. We've covered that topic at great length. Now I'm pregnant. No need to rub it in my terrified face. I'll muddle through. However, I *did* fancy being an aunt. A cool one, though. The type of aunt who allows them to chew gum and buys them their first flagon of cheap vodka. One who provides a solid alibi when they say they are having an innocent sleep over at mine, but are instead knocking back cans of cider at the Rugby Club disco. The type of aunt who insists they are out with me shopping for chastity belts when they are in fact snogging someone on the back seat of the cinema. Isn't childhood precious?

I would absolutely rock as an aunt. I mean, really it's the perfect thing. You get to fill them full of sugar and caffeine and then hand them back. Then you get to criticise your sibling behind their backs for their poor parenting skills and pretend that you could do a much better job than them. It always sounded like fun to me.

'You must be thrilled for Ian,' Barry says.

'Thrilled? Not exactly, Barry. They are stealing our thunder. They are trying to beat us. What if her baby is born before ours? What if their baby is cuter?'

Barry says I'm being silly. He wouldn't understand. He has a foot in the enemy's camp, already. Well, I refuse to cross over. I'm going to stay right here on my high horse.

Nineteen

Ok, so you know how I like to make lists? Have a peep at these.

People who know about my pregnancy:

1. Mum and dad. Just as well, I need someone to cook and clean for me and mum is very discreet. Sure, she has loads of time on her hands since retirement. What else would she be doing with herself?

2. Barry's parents. However, all they've done so far is put the fear of God into me. Not helpful.

3. Pam and emer. As my bridesmaids, they have a life-long commitment to my happiness. Selfishly, Emer is even more preggers than me and excelling at it, like everything else in her overachieving life. Annoying! Pam is not interested in babies and only wants to talk about Doug. Super annoying!

4. Ian and Cindi. Also preggers. I'm still too upset to talk about this, try me again in six months.

5. The entire online community of the popular pregnancy website www.mypregnancy.com know the intimate details of my life and the melodrama that accompanies it. For anonymity purposes, I am @hotblonde1989. The hot blonde part is self-explanatory. Duh. The 1989 bit is to create the impression that I was born recently and am therefore young and trendy, call it poetic licence if you will. Sure, everyone lies on their on-line profile. I post every sixty minutes, it's my new obsession.

People who don't know about my pregnancy:

1. Harry the Horrible. However, I won't be able to hide the bulge forever. When I'm back to work, I'll be confessing to my bun in the oven. Frankly, I'm looking forward to the way his wrinkled face crumples at the thoughts of losing me for a year.

2. All of my wretched colleagues, whom I despise with a passion. They currently just think I'm overweight.

3. Mum's retirement biddies. Mum's chomping at the bit to tell them, so I called her last night to give her the go ahead. Last we spoke, she was considering hiring a plane and making a banner.

4. Judy, my work wife. She will be crushed, as she will be losing her Thursday night two-for-one cocktail at The Stags Head partner in crime. Well, newsflash: it's not all about her!

5. My old college buddies, most of whom have their own screaming brats by now. They'll be scheduling play-dates before the kid is born, no doubt.

Well, I'm officially three months pregnant today, and it's time to let the cat out of the bag. You see, my jeans don't fit, and I've got a serious muffin top going on. I don't want people squinting their eyes when they look at me, trying to answer the question 'is that woman pregnant or just plain fat?'

I haven't bought maternity trousers just yet. It's like giving in and going for a wee when you're out in the pub drinking pints. They call it 'breaking the seal'. Once you go once, you'll be going to the loo after every pint. Well, it's the same with maternity trousers − once you pack away your old clothes for stretchy elasticised maternity ones, there's just no going back.

Speaking of pints, I'm absolutely gagging for a cold one. Or a wine. Or a bandy. Or absolutely any flipping thing that contains a remote amount of alcohol. I'm still having a glass of wine some evenings, but Barry is watching me like a hawk, so it's impossible to sneak another one.

Dr Logan has been a wee pet with the good old sick certs. I've been off work for four weeks now, and managed to get through every single episode of 'Orange is the New Black'. Bliss! Every Monday, I've gone to the clinic, said I was still desperately nauseous, made a retching sound into my purse and reached for some tissues. Dr Logan then scribbled something vague on the cert like 'Mrs. Costello is suffering from a medical condition'. Sure, that could be absolutely anything. I just posted it to Harry on my way back to the car, blasted the stereo, stocked up on goodies and then resumed the foetal position on the couch. Easy!

That's why it's an absolute shock to the system to be going back to work today. I'm aiming to be in for around ten, so that I can reacclimatize myself.

'Good morning!' I sing song to Suzie at the reception desk. 'I'm back!'

I plonk down at my desk opposite Judy.

'Miss me, babes?'

'Hey! Becks! Oh my God! It's been, like, four weeks. How are you? I heard you had, like, a serious illness or something. What's up?'

A stab of guilt strikes. There's no point in lying. Might as well spill the beans straight away.

'Thanks, no I'm grand. I'm actually preggers. Yay!'

'Oh ...'

'Yeah, so I'll be off in six months' time.'

'Great. You could 'do a Belinda' and never come back. Nice one!'

'Yeah, sounds good.'

'Oh, listen, did you hear about...'

Judy's head has dropped mid-sentence, and she is pretending to type. Harry must be approaching.

'Ah, Rebecca. You're back. Step into my office, will you?'

Judy mouths 'Good luck.'

In Harry's office, my palms are sweaty. I rub them on my trousers.

'So, Rebecca. You've been absent for four weeks. Feeling better, I presume?'

There's no point in pulling at the band aid around the corners and slowly peeling it off at an excruciatingly slow pace. It needs to be ripped.

'Actually, Harry...'

Harry is the key jangling prison warden and I'm the downtrodden inmate. But that's OK. I found a way out of the life sentence. I figured it out. I'll be rid of him in just six teeny months. All I need to do is keep my head down for the rest of the prison sentence. You never know, maybe I will get out of jail early for good behaviour. I'm sure I could convince Dr Logan that I am unable to continue working further down the line. Perhaps I will be lucky enough to get preeclampsia, gestational diabetes, heartburn, swollen ankles or one of the many pregnancy complaints I've read up on. Fingers crossed.

'Yes, I'm feeling better now. But I wanted to...'

'How wonderful for you. As you can imagine, there's quite a lot to catch up on. We had to ask Judy to pick up some of your work. Now, in relation to all of this sick leave you've had, I must inform you that I'd be obliged to reveal the extent of your absenteeism in the event of you looking for a reference or applying for a promotion. Our HR policy states that...'

'That won't be necessary.'

'Pardon?'

'Writing a reference letter for me, if I were leaving or applying for a promotion, I mean. That won't be necessary. I'll be doing neither.'

'Right. I see. But...'

'I'm pregnant, Harry. Due in six months' time.'

Harry is puce. If I had a basketball in my possession, I would slam it into the net and yell 'slam dunk!' into his fat face. For now, a smirk is all I give away.

'Well, I... Well, congratulations.'

It's by far the most insincere congratulations I have ever had the misfortune of receiving in my entire life. I can read his mind. He is:

a. Mortified that I have used the word pregnant. For an old fart like him, this conjures up images of sex, swollen bellies and midwives boiling water and fetching clean towels.

b. Waiting for me to leave the room so that he can call one of his colleagues and complain about the fact that now I'm going to be an even more useless assistant than before, and that he will get absolutely flip all work out of me now.

c. Itching to find someone to replace me. He knows as well as I do that there is no way my sick leave record is going to improve now that I have a bun in the oven and all the career ambition of a dead rat. As soon as I leave, he will be flicking through his Filofax (this will tell you what age bracket he is in – only ancient people past their sell by date are still using one of those wretched things. He makes me Tippex out any colleagues who have either died or retired and type their names over the white bits. On an actual typewriter. Barbaric, I know!)

'So, Harry, I will consult with Brendan in HR around the maternity leave documentation and will, of course, give you adequate notice regarding antenatal appointments and so on. Speaking of which, I have one at three o'clock, so I'll need to leave at lunch-time today.'

'Right. Right. Fine. Yes. OK, then.'

The poor sad creature doesn't know what else to say. He picks up the telephone receiver, which is my cue to stand up and leave. I smile sweetly at him as I reach for his door handle and give it a good slam. Back at my desk, it's hard to shake the grin.

Judy is keen to talk about the latest crisis with her boyfriend. Or should I say boyfriends, plural? Seriously! She is dating so many people that I lose track. I think that's what you call hedging your bets. I wonder how she stops herself from calling out the wrong name at critical moments. Her phone never stops beeping, and she asks my opinion on every flipping microscopic thing. Her relationship rules are as follows:

Step 1: Ignore nice, reliable men who call when they say they will call, and offer to take you to fancy restaurants, open doors and behave in a mannerly fashion.

Step 2: Choose sleazy, untrustworthy men who borrow money from you, don't call you after they sleep with you, are still married to women who don't understand them, and have kids that they pay no maintenance for. They dress well, drive nice cars and have careers like pilots or doctors (or so they say until you rumble them).

Step 3: Jump when they call or text. Drop any existing plans with friends. Sleep with them on the first date.

Step 4: Analyse every detail of communication, or lack thereof, for every waking minute. Lie awake at night, annoy friends and work colleagues. Consult psychics, tarot readers and spoon benders.

Step 5: Repeat ad infinitum.

I'm clicking on various discussion boards on the pregnancy website, but Judy is not taking the hint. She wants my opinion. Should she text him? Should she not? Should she call him? Should she not? Should she wear heels on her date? Should she give her old fling Jake another shot? Should she give him the money for his grandmother's operation? Why hasn't he called?

What exactly did Tiernan mean in his latest email? Was the exclamation mark just punctuation or was he being sarcastic? Was he giving her the cold shoulder? Do I think Jacob's voicemail is broken? Do I believe that he is seeing someone else on the side? Do I think it's odd that he still sees his ex-wife for drinks?

Don't sweat it, though. I have a flawless system. It's a bit like those multiple choice maths quizzes, you know? You answer A, then B, then C and then D. Someone in my class at school worked out the pattern. Anyway, I only scraped a pass on an ordinary level maths paper, but it seems to work for this scenario. I say 'yes', then 'no', then 'maybe, it depends.' Then, just to throw her off the scent, I throw in something vague and mysterious like 'follow your heart' and 'what does your gut tell you?' Judy seems to find it helpful. I'm like a magic eight ball.

Honestly, though. I don't know how she managed to put one foot in front of the other while I was absent. Who did she bug for romance advice? Anyway, her problems are all so damn insignificant right now. I'm actually growing a live human being here. I don't need her dating dilemmas. Barry and I have our first scan in Holles Street today. We will be meeting our consultant for the first time, and I need to make a good impression.

'Sounds like you need to listen to those alarm bells, Judy. He sounds creepy.'

'Want anything in Burger King?'

Judy is hung-over to kingdom come, and depressed that some man or other has not texted her back. She says that the only cure is a large double bacon burger with fries and a diet coke. I say I'll have the same, and she is back in ten minutes with a brown paper bag for each of us. It's glorious. There are gherkins stuck in my teeth and some secret sauce dribbled on my chin. I don't care.

Suzie the receptionist passes my desk with an armful of documents and gives me a knowing smile. It looks like the word is out.

Twenty

Take it from me: meeting your obstetrics and gynaecology consultant for the first time is terrifying. You see, when I chose her, she seemed great. Then I found out that she has four children of her own, and now she's threatening.

At home, waiting for Barry, my mind is racing:

Did you know that sharks can smell fear? Or is that bees? Anyway, the consultant will get the whiff of terror from Barry and I for sure. What if she's one of those 'get over yourself, I've pushed out four babies already, it's easy' kinds? She could be of the opinion that woman in the third world pop them out in the paddy fields and continue on about their day, collecting rice or whatever it is they grow in poor, underdeveloped countries. She's less likely to keep the sick certs coming if that is her appalling attitude!

What are her thoughts on pain relief? If she says anything along the lines of 'you don't need pain medication, try deep breathing' or 'let's see how you get on' this will sadly be a nail in the coffin of our relationship. I shall stand up and walk out, even if I am naked from the waist down. I have principles, and I intend to stand by them. This is a free country and I choose drugs, and plenty of them. I shall be making my point very clear from the start.

Perhaps Barry and I could try a nice word association game to suss her out. I'll ask her to say the first word that pops into her mind when I say, for example, 'fluffy bunny'. Then we'll step it up to words like 'epidural'. If she answers correctly, I think we can do business. If not, it was nice knowing her.

What if she judges me? Even Vicki Pollard can see that I'm a novice when it comes to being a mum. I know absolutely nothing about babies – their wants, needs and how to birth them. She will take one look into my guilty eyes and see that this baby, although loved, is an unintended by-product of too many tequila shots on our wedding night. Will she be a party pooper? If she is the type that says that I am allowed zero fun for nine months, I will be shopping around for a new consultant. Simple as. Does she have cold hands? Think about it. What kind of pants should I wear to the appointment? I am deadly serious, don't snigger. I mean, white cotton granny briefs say 'I'm no fun', but a pink lacy thong says 'I'm lots of fun'. What kind of pants will portray the correct amount of fun? I settle on boring black cotton briefs. They say medium fun.

With a permanent marker, I mark the calendar with our important milestone.

Baby's first scan, 3PM. Holles Street.

Then I circle it and draw a little love heart. Barry will think that's cute. Maybe he'll buy me something pretty afterwards. I'll mention that I'm running low on perfume. Wouldn't it be fun to draw a little face on my belly? Ah, yeah. Just a little smiley mouth and eyes. My belly button is the nose. I'll rub it off before we go in, will you relax!

Barry's key is in the door, so I throw the black marker into the drawer.

'Hey, baby! All set?'

He places a bunch of flowers on the kitchen counter.

Barry and I have an argument in the car on the way in, which is not a good start. Barry doesn't know which turn is for Holles Street with this bloody one-way system, and doesn't have a sat nav. He hasn't brought enough change for the meter, and clampers are rampant around this area. He's breaking a fifty euro note in Centra buying pecan slices and large frothy cappuccinos.

He's back with the goodies and a fist full of change.

'You forgot the sugar for my coffee. What next? You'll forget to bring my bag to the delivery ward? You'll forget to tell the nurses to keep topping up my pain meds? Barry!'

'Will you relax, Becks?'

Barry sees straight through me. He knows it's the nerves jangling. I don't know anyone else who'd put up with me. Next thing you know, I'm crying and apologising. It's a hot day and the car is like a sauna. My arm pits are going into monsoon season, and I'm flapping at my face.

'Sorry. But what if she doesn't like me?'

'Who? The consultant? Don't be daft!'

Barry is the voice of reason. He says that it's not about me, it's about the health of our baby. Also, he says that we are paying her enough to be nice to us. He has a point, this is costing us a fortune.

We pass through the double doors and into the waiting room. The air conditioning greets us with a cold waft.

'Thank Goodness. Who knew Dublin in September could be so tropical?'

Barry has no idea what I'm talking about. He says it's my hormones. He's been reading up about it online.

There's a cappuccino maker in the waiting room. Barry has two. He says he deserves it, as he is putting this consultant's kid through college at these rates. My bladder is fit to burst when I've finished mine, but I've read that this is the best shot at getting a clear ultra sound. The latest 'Hello!' And 'Vogue' magazines are spread across a mahogany table. There are luxurious plants dotted about the room and plinky plonky music. There is no-one else in the waiting room.

I flip nervously through a recent edition of 'Hello!' Every celebrity seems to be either pregnant or showing off their new darling. Rod Stewart and his stunner of a wife have their arms around two blonde boys wearing matching Tommy Hilfiger V-neck sweaters. A swimsuit model sprawls on her Malibu sun terrace, her two week old baby 'Trojan' sleeps angelically in her arms. She wears an oyster coloured silk bikini and diamante stilettos, without even a hint of a stretch-mark. Her post-baby body is flaunted across seven pages and she has a different bikini on in each flattering shot, the baby an accessory in each picture. Her tanned skin glistens in the sun and she pouts in designer sunglasses. Her personal trainer describes her as dedicated and hard working. She has a new cook book and weight loss DVD coming out. I scoff. She probably has had speedy liposuction as soon as she'd pushed the baby out. Plus, I bet she has a secret surrogate mother stashed away in her Malibu mansion, paid an outrageous sum to stay quiet. No doubt there's some ferocious airbrushing going on in the magazine's editing department.

Either way, I feel like a total failure already.

'Dr Grainger is ready for you now,' the receptionist announces.

A slim woman in her early forties greets us. She is wearing a pale pink Chanel skirt suit and matching pink heels, and I instantly love her.

We kick off with the blood sample. Dr Grainger says it's best to get this out of the way. She passes the test with flying colours: I barely feel a thing. She uses the numbing gel to desensitise the area before inserting the needle. We're chatting away so much about Kate Middleton and the royal baby that I don't even notice the three vials that she has filled with dark burgundy blood. The woman is a pro.

'I believe in making the mother as comfortable as possible during her entire pregnancy, and especially during delivery. The less stressed the mother is, the better the outcome for baby. Have you any thoughts on pain relief during labour, at all?'

'I'd like the works. Everything going, legal or otherwise.'

She smiles.

I turn to give Barry the thumbs up, but he is sitting with his head in his hands. Turns out the blood test made him dizzy. Bless his lily livered socks. I mean, it's not even his arm that's being used as a pin cushion, or his flipping nether regions we are discussing stretching a child through, either. I rub his back and tell him with a smile that I'm expecting him to man up before March. He's absolutely mortified.

When Barry smiles back, I remember when we first met. Of course, he had far fewer grey hairs back then – the stress of living with a drama queen like me is probably accountable. How times have changed. I used to lie on top of bars in Ibiza, so that hunky men could do Sambuca shots out of my flat belly. Now here I am, lying on an examination table with my shirt rolled up to my bra, holding the hand of the man I love, wedding rings on fingers, chatting about our baby. I wouldn't have it any other way.

Barry is squinting at my stomach.

'Is that a smiley face on your tummy, Becks?'

'Yes. Yes, it is,' I manage to keep a straight face.

Dr Grainger stands beside me and slips on a pair of latex gloves.

'OK, then Rebecca. Right, well, let's just take a little look at you. No, no, Rebecca. You don't have to take your trousers off... you can keep your pants on.'

Barry is laughing as I scramble to zip up my trousers.

Dr Grainger squirts some cold jelly stuff on my stomach and rubs the wand over the area. A fuzzy black and white image appears on the screen. Barry squeezes my hand. Instantly, a whooshing noise dominates the room.

'Well, you can definitely hear the heartbeat, Rebecca! Sounds like a strong one!'

'Are you sure? Everything look OK?' Barry's eyebrows knit together.

'Does everything look... like, normal? In proportion?' I blurt. 'What about the head? Does it look big to you?'

I mean, it's worth asking. If the kid has a gigantic noggin, I'd like as much warning as possible.

'Everything looks fine. All good,' Dr Grainger laughs.

I start to breathe again. Fair play to Dr Grainger. I mean, it all looks like a fuzzy alien with vague arms and legs to me. If you squint and tilt your head to the side you can make out the shape of a baby. Kind of.

'And look. See that dark spot there? It's kind of pulsating? That's the heart. Everything looks great.'

'Ah, baby, look. He looks incredible. Like a little potato!' Barry's getting carried away and it's contagious.

'Potato? More like a jelly bean! But Barry, I don't know why you keep saying 'he'. She's a she. Am I right, Dr?'

'Well, we won't be able to tell the sex of the baby until, say, the twenty week scan. We'll also be able to see baby in more detail then.'

The tears come out of no-where.

'I'm sorry. So silly.'

'What's wrong, baby?' Barry grabs a tissue and passes it to me.

'I'm just so… relieved.'

'This is normal,' Dr Grainger reassures. 'It's very overwhelming to see the baby for the first time.'

'No. No, it's not that,' I wipe away the tears and blow my nose. 'I'm just so glad that she doesn't have a giant head.'

Twenty one

After his shower at seven o'clock, Barry had layered on two rounds of deodorant and selected a dry cleaned crisp white shirt, followed by a splash of expensive aftershave. His best navy Calvin Klein suit and silk tie were chosen for the day ahead.

It's only nine o'clock, and yet he is sweating profusely. He sits in the plush reception area of a law firm in Gallery Quay in Dublin's city centre. There are potted palm plants and copies of the 'Financial Times' and 'Law Society Gazette' arranged neatly on a metallic coffee table. Another man in his early forties is also waiting. Barry watches him. He's dressed in a charcoal suit, and has a leather document holder under his arm. Barry's competitor, no doubt. Well, this is war, and there can only be one victorious survivor and one bloodied and bruised body cast aside at the end of the day.

Failure is not an option for Barry, today. The scan of the baby on the monitor yesterday made that obvious. He allows himself a few minutes to break from rehearsing his interview statements in order to remember the image. It was blurry at first. But then, like a camera coming into focus, he could make out the profile. It was just a black and white grainy image, but something he will never forget. The whooshing sound of the heartbeat comes flooding back.

From inside his pocket, he pulls out the ream of twelve shots of the little guy. He rubs the shiny material with his thumb. Some of the images are a bit vague, but some are crystal clear – you can see the shape of the head and the little arms and legs. Barry thinks he can even make out the spine and eye sockets in one of the pictures. He folds them neatly and replaces them in his breast pocket.

The enemy in the Charcoal suit has to move over on the leather couch opposite. Another candidate in a grey pencil skirt and jacket has arrived with a resume and a briefcase. It's not one-to-one combat anymore. It's Barry against an army with war paint streaked across their eager faces.

Doubt creeps in. What good will he be if he can't provide for the baby? Babies need nappies and wipes and formula. Damn it, they need college funds and expensive orthodontic braces on their adolescent, crooked teeth. Rebecca's going to be out of work in less than six months, and then after the maternity leave they'll have crèche fees. This redundancy couldn't have come at a worse time. Normally, his pride would have prevented him from calling Stephen to ask a favour, but pride doesn't pay the mortgage.

Right on cue, a text comes in from Stephen.

Good luck, mate!

Luck, indeed. He's going to need it. This recession is supposed to be lifting. According to a recent economic survey, house sales have picked up, new jobs have been created and new car sales are on the up. Well, the new jobs must all be in technology or something, because this interview was the only one to materialise since his frantic job search began.

Another text comes in from Rebecca.

Have a nice day at work, daddy! ;)

Barry silences his phone. He feels guilt rise to the surface but pushes it down again. Hiding the redundancy from her is in the same category as his close call last year with Shelley. But he can fix this. When he gets this job, and make no bones about it, he will get this job, he will tell her the whole story. He will take her out for a slap up meal, somewhere that stocks good champagne, and they will laugh with relief.

'Mr Costello?' the receptionist interrupts his thoughts. 'They're ready for you in the board room. Please follow me.'

Barry straightens his tie and fingers his cufflinks – they are the ones engraved with 'B&R' from Rebecca last Christmas. The blood rushes in his ears, like the whooshing of the baby's heart.

'You can do this', he tells himself. *'Do it for Rebecca. Do it for our jellybean.'*

Twenty two

Monday mornings in late September are the absolute pits when it comes to getting out of bed. The weather has turned, so that you start buying cardigans and thick tights, all of the snotty kids are back to school, and the traffic is just yuk. For the last two weeks, I've been off work with a cold. Now, as you know, I'd usually soldier on. I'm not the type to let people down. However, before you cast the first stone, let me say in my defence that a pregnant woman can't take cold medication. I know, it's totally bonkers. Basically, even the pet shelter, something I look forward to every week, has had to take a backseat. I've been fighting this runny nose and sore throat with only honey and lemon tea and a box-set of 'The West Wing.' Last week, I finished the box set, the novelty of being home ran out and the cabin fever set in.

My sick cert, like Harry's patience, has now expired. I suppose I can't blame the man entirely. After the honeymoon, I was in work for a week, then had a month off with morning sickness, went back to work for a couple of hours, dropped my news like a skunk delivering a stink bomb, skipped off to my antenatal appointment and haven't been back since.

I would hit the snooze button again, but it's already nine o'clock. I have two black bin bags full to bursting point with all of the trousers and skirts that no longer zip up. It's time to face the truth- I have only two clothing options:

A pair of grey tracksuit bottoms. However, I've worn them every day this week. They are caked in snot and, well... cake, and are lying at the bottom of the laundry hamper in desperate need of a boil wash.

or… brace yourself, now…

Pyjamas. That's no good. If I wear pyjamas to the office, Harry will have me carted off to some nut house, and committed. Now on the plus side, it would be classified as additional sick leave, but it would be an atrocity against fashion and everything it stands for. It would be like admitting defeat.

I pick as much gunk as I can off the tracksuit bottoms. It will have to do. I can't be expected to fire on all cylinders between now and March. I mean, this is a life changing event that I'm going through. I'll have to take my foot off the pedal at work and set the motor to cruise control.

'So!', Suzie at reception is all over me like paparazzi on a well-rounded Kardashian bottom.

'Welcome back. And when are you due?'

The nosey cow is pumping me for details before I've even reached my desk.

'March.'

'Oh,' she looks disappointed. 'Not until then? I thought you were further along.'

'Did you, now? Why is that?'

A tense silence follows.

Say it, I dare her. *Say it! Say you thought I was about to give birth in just a few months. Say I'm Shamu the whale. Say it to my face.*

'Anyway, great news Rebecca.'

'Mmm, thanks.'

Harry is standing at my desk like a great, hulking buffoon. He looks at his watch.

'Rebecca, good morning. Or should I say good afternoon?'

He has a cheek. It's only eleven thirty five. There are twenty five minutes remaining until one can officially greet a person with 'Good afternoon'. Anyway, the tracksuit bottoms took a while to sponge clean. Plus, there was a long line at the deli counter.

'So. Have you recovered from your... what was it this time? Oh, yes... a cold.'

'Eh, a *serious* cold, yes. More like a 'flu, actually. Could have developed into pneumonia, if ... you know... Here's my cert.'

I cough quite close to his face. Harry examines the paper and folds it up again. It turns out that Dr Grainger is a wee doll with the sick certs, and she says that I'm to look after myself now. Who am I to disregard doctor's orders? I swivel my chair away from Harry, and lick the ketchup off a breakfast roll.

'Eating for two now, eh?' declares Harry as he plops a large folder on my desk. 'These invoices need inputting on the system.'

I try to say 'excuse me?' in a sarcastic tone, but my mouth is too full. I chew wildly so that I can hurry up and hit him with a sharp come back.

'Are you sure it's not twins in there, ha-ha?'

Judy smirks and Harry thinks he's hilarious for about one second, but I stomp all over his hilarity. I have a secret weapon that never fails. I give him 'The Death Stare'. This is not just any old glare I use if Barry has forgotten to put the bins out or if Harry asks me to do some photocopying. No sir! I keep 'The Death Stare', or TDS for short, reserved for certain situations. It's a cross between 'I'm going to stab you in the eye with a knitting needle while you sleep' and 'I am going to pull your teeth out one by one with a pliers while your family watches.' TDS has the desired effect, and Harry scuttles back to his office.

'Oh my God! Can you believe what that man just said to me, Judy? Seriously! Commenting on a pregnant woman's body is... is... harassment in the workplace! That's against EU law. And the law of... Human Resources. He's breaking the law!'

I recall that there is something in the anti-bullying and harassment policy about being mean to pregnant people. We are a vulnerable category or something.

'You're a witness, Judy. I'll be calling on you to take the stand on this one. Barry can represent me. He can wear his good suit, and everything.'

Judy has a vacant smile. She thinks I'm joking. Harry can well and truly shove it. He has just asked me to file something. He requested it by email, because he can't face me. He's not brave enough. Does he not realise that women in a delicate condition can't over exert themselves? And yet, he expects me to climb a step ladder (that's classified as working at height), reach into the filing cabinet (that's manual handling), retrieve the file and add some documents to it (that's operating a heavy load). I reply with haste.

To: Harry.OShea@PR_Solutions.ie

From: Rebecca.Costello@PR_Solutions.ie

Re: Filing request

Harry,

I don't think so!

Rebecca.

The man is such a Neanderthal. Next thing you know, he'll be asking me to just pop out of the second story window and give the glass a bit of an old scrub. Sure, why don't I clean his car while I'm at it?

'That man has no regard for my health and safety in the workplace.'

Judy doesn't hear me. She is texting ferociously – probably to one of her flings. I don't need her. I've drafted a stinker of an email to the Trade Union. I'm in a fighting kind of mood, now. This means war.

To: info@tradeunion.ie

From: Rebecca.costello@PR_Solutions.ie

Re: pig of a boss.

Status: urgent

Dear representative,

I wish to report my inhuman boss for endangering my foetus. Put me on the stand and I'll sing like a canary.

Yours sincerely,

Rebecca Costello

PS I have media experience and am happy to conduct press interviews.

When I say media experience, I mean I watch TV. Same thing. As I hit send, I imagine how I'll spend the financial settlement. It will no doubt be huge, setting an example across this fine land to other downtrodden employees and giving them courage to report their respective pigs of bosses. I'll start with quitting my job in dramatic, document flinging fashion. I'll need to make sure I'm standing close to a plug in fan with a stream of papers in my hand and a good audience for that. Next, I'll purchase a diesel guzzling Range Rover. Then I'll stay at home all day pruning roses or whatever. It's a flawless plan.

'Right! That's it!'

I am standing up with my handbag.

'Where are you going?' Judy looks up from her mobile phone.

'Lunch. Might never come back. So sick of this place.'

Judy glances at her watch. If she points out that it's only a quarter past twelve, I'll brain her.

I catch a glimpse of myself in the reflection of my car. I can't go another step in these hideous grey tracksuit bottoms. Besides, I haven't treated myself to anything since the honeymoon, which was a lifetime ago. Barry and I are married now, which means I can stop calling it 'his' credit card and start calling it 'our' credit card. My crippling debt is now his crippling debt, it's so romantic. I don't know why I didn't think of it earlier.

In Dundrum Town Centre, I practically have the whole maternity section of Next to myself. I drape various items over my arm. In the changing room, I wriggle out of the tracksuit bottoms and slide the maternity jeans up my legs. They fit like a dream. They even have this cool navy material stretchy bit that goes snugly over my tummy to support it. It's like a bra for your belly! Whoever invented this deserves a humanitarian award. I buy the jeans in five different shades. I also spot some formal trousers, a skirt and a few maternity tops. I might as well kit myself out here. The cashier charges three hundred euro to the credit card and puts the filthy tracksuit bottoms in the bin under the till.

'And another coffee, please.' Barry has joined me for lunch in Douglas and Kaldi café.

'Great to see you enjoying your food. Jellybean must be hungry, eh?'

It's hard to reply when you are cramming skinny fries in your mouth, so I just nod.

'It's like I have worms,' I finally manage. 'Just can't stop eating.'

Barry completely understands. If Mother Nature is telling me to super-size my burger meals or request extra hot chocolate sauce for my caramel sundae, then I should just go with it.

'Can't tell you how fab these new jeans are,' I explain as I load more creamy coleslaw high on top of my bagel. 'Everyone should own a pair!'

Twenty three

Barry checks his phone in the consultant's waiting room for the fifth time. The wallpaper on his screen is of the baby's last scan. There are no missed calls since he last looked. The interview was two weeks ago, and every day that passes without news is an invisible clamp around his chest, getting tighter and tighter. Hope is fading like a flickering candle. One puff of wind, and it will be diminished.

Yesterday, his friend Stephen had sent a text to say that there would be news soon. It isn't Stephen's decision, of course. He had just put Barry's CV into the right hands. He worked in an entirely different department and his hands were tied. Still, Stephen had heard over the water cooler that the competition for the job had been stiff and that there had seen about six candidates in total.

Since the text, the candle has been burning a little brighter. He can just about make out vague shapes in the distance, possibilities of what might be. There is still a chance. If he has nailed the interview, he'll be able to slip from one job to the other with no staring at the ceiling at midnight imagining the worst. The timing would be perfect.

It's four o'clock on a Friday. If he doesn't get a call in the next sixty minutes, the worry and dread will climb on his back and weigh heavily on his shoulders throughout the weekend. With only four weeks until Barry's job comes to and end, it's like waiting for the axe to fall.

'Stop checking your phone, Barry!'

'Sorry, Becks.'

'You're checking your work emails, aren't you? Tell them to leave you alone for the rest of the day. The twenty week scan is far more important.'

'Dr Grainger will see you now,' the receptionist interrupts.

Rebecca throws the magazine back down on the leather couch and claps her hands in excitement. Barry's phone vibrates. It's Stephen.

'Sorry, baby. It's work again. I've just got to take this. Go on ahead and I'll be right in. I'll turn my phone off after this.'

Rebecca mumbles something under her breath. Barry knows that she is far from impressed, but it's a necessary evil.

'Stephen, hi mate. Any update?'

'Yeah, Bar, just heard on the old grapevine. Sorry, it's not good news. Rumour has it that someone internal got the job. He's been here a while and was looking to move up the ladder. I heard they'll be writing to everyone else next week. Sorry, man.'

'Grand, Stephen. No worries, mate. I've a few other irons in the fire as they say. No hassle.'

'Alright, Bar. Sure, catch you for a pint soon, yeah?'

'Cheers, yeah. Thanks for that, mate. Better go, we're just here at the hospital.'

Barry returns his phone to his jeans pocket and pushes the sick feeling in his stomach lower and lower. He plasters on a smile, even though the invisible clamp is restricting his breathing. He can smell the wick smoking, but there is no longer a flame.

'Sorry, baby. Just the office on the phone, there. Hi, Dr Grainger, how are you?'

'Hi, Barry. Welcome. So! We're just going to take a peek at baby now, Rebecca.'

Dr Grainger applies the gel to Rebecca's belly which has grown a lot since their last visit. Rebecca is smiling, oblivious. Barry's stomach knots.

'Everything looks great, Rebecca. Just taking some measurements of the limbs, and taking a closer look at the heart. All looking good.'

Barry has to look again in case his mind is playing tricks on him. He thinks he can make out the baby's face. Rebecca squeezes his hand.

'Wow, Barry. Look at her little face!'

Barry wipes his eye with the palm of his hand.

'He's gorgeous, baby.'

'So, Rebecca tells me you both want to know the sex of the baby?' Dr Grainger asks. 'Well, sometimes it can be a bit tricky to see, but you're in luck today... if you're sure you both still want to know?'

Barry nods. He pictures a little pig tailed girl bouncing on his knee and a little freckle faced boy kicking a football. He knows he will love either equally.

'Well, I can't be one hundred percent certain...' Dr Grainger tilts her head to the side. 'But it looks like a little girl.'

Rebecca grins. 'Told you, Barry!'

Twenty four

Barry helps me up from the examination table and holds the main door open. I dial mum's number.

'It's a girl!'

We're standing on the pavement outside Holles Street with matching grins.

'Mum? Are you there? Mum?'

There's a high pitched sound and I realize that mum is sobbing.

'That's wonderful, darling,' she finally cries.

There's a fumbling sound as she passes the phone to dad.

'Great news, fairy. A little girl. Lovely stuff. We're delighted.'

Dad passes the phone back to mum, as she is clawing for more details.

'Now, did she check the heart? All going to plan?'

'Everything's fine. She was waving her little fists at us and everything. We got loads more scan pictures. We'll go to Barry's folks first and then come straight over to show you.'

Barry is still beaming as he turns the key in the ignition.

'A girl. Isn't it great, baby?'

'Yeah. Are you sure you're not a little… disappointed?'

'What? No!'

'It's just that you kept saying 'he'. Some guys only want boys. You know? Someone to kick a ball with and take to rugby matches. I know you wouldn't admit it out loud, but…'

'Baby, I'm thrilled. A little girl to bounce on her daddy's knee. I'm chuffed.'

Barry is not old-fashioned like those sheep farming muckers who only want boys so that they can take over the farm. To them, girls are only good for making the tea and require dowries. Thank heavens we live in Dublin where people are civilized! Also, Barry and I don't own any sheep.

'I'll just give Emer a quick ring before we get to your mums. Take the next exit, will you Barry?'

'Next Exit? But that's for Deansgrange. We need the Dalkey turn off.'

'Yeah, but there's a great chipper in Deansgrange and I'm famished. Oh, and so is she…'

I rub my belly with a smile.

'OK,' Barry agrees.

I have just realised that I now possess a certain power. All I have to do is rub my belly like a rusted golden lamp that has been found in the depths of a cave, and ask for anything my little heart desires. Then, poof! The genie appears.

'Yes, master?' the genie calls.

'Batter burger and garlic chips. Can of diet Coke. Side order of onion rings, please.'

Next, I have to say the magic words. No, no. Not Abracadabra! Not please! I say 'the baby wants it.' Faster than a Katie Price marriage breakup, my wish is granted. Magic, yes?

Now, the great thing is that the genie grants a lot more than three wishes. I can wish for a bowl of Sugar Puffs at three in the morning if I so desire. I might need to whine a bit, but he is not going to deny our baby food! And he doesn't just do food orders, either. Oh, no. He does foot rubs, dish washing and hovering. I just need to test my powers once we get home to see if there are limits. I mean I don't know, for example, if the magic would work on things like 'the baby really does want that new car we spoke about' – that might be pushing it. I will chance my arm the next time we are renting a movie. I could try 'the baby wants Jennifer Anniston, not Sylvester Stallone. The explosions and hand to hand combat frighten her.' It's worth a try.

The magic is very potent now, because the genie has just seen the baby on the monitor and is now imagining a little blonde angel dressed in a pink sleep suit. The only limitation is that the magic might wear off once the baby is actually born and I'm not pregnant any more. Best make the most of it.

'Eh, Barry?' I roll down the window and call after him.

'Sorry, forgot to say, can she please have a battered sausage too? Terrible craving for one. Terrible. Ta. Oh, and don't forget the curry sauce. Love you!'

I've time to kill, and a quick nod to the man upstairs is definitely in order.

Dear God,

Cheers, the baby looks great. Not a freaky mutant or two headed monster in sight. Phew! Actually, it looks kind of cute now. It looks like a real baby, stretching and kicking and everything on the screen.

I can stop saying 'it' now. I can start saying 'she'. Thanks a bunch for that, by the way. I didn't want to jinx things, and I didn't want to be greedy, but you must have read my mind. What on earth would I do with a little boy? I mean, I couldn't possibly amuse a boy. Girls are fine. Girls like pink things and sparkling things and play with Barbies. They wear pretty dresses with silk and satin bows. They care about hairstyles. Now, this is my area, I've got that covered. But boys on the other hand? They like cars and soldiers and dinosaurs. I don't know my T-rex from my ... see? I can't even name one other type of dinosaur. I'd be useless. Also, boys jump in puddles and muddy up their good clean trousers. Think of the laundry!

Gratefully yours,

Becks

Barry is taking ages with the grub, so I call Emer.

'Hey, Rebecca! How did it go? All well? Did you find out the sex? How are you feeling?'

'Hi! It went great. Barry cried. He had actual man-tears and everything.'

'Ah. Bless.'

'I know. Cuteness. Yeah, everything looks good. Really great.'

'Oh, fab, honey. And…?'

'And… it's a girl!'

I have to hold the phone away from my ear for about twenty seconds until the screeching has died down.

'Oh my God! A girl! Ah, honey, I'm thrilled for you. A girl! I'm a bit jealous of you to be honest.'

'What? Don't be daft! Boys are… lovely.'

Emer and David found out the sex of their baby a few months back and Emer is still struggling to accept that she will not be dressing the baby in pink or painting the nursery lavender.

'But sure, Emer, you can dress him in a little sailor suit and everything. That'd be gorgeous on him. Totally cute. And you can gel his hair all spiky when he's older. Kinda punk rock slash nautical style?'

'I know…it's fine. It'll be fine.' Emer sighs. It most definitely is not fine, but I'm not going to be a cow and point it out.

'And boys fashion has really come on over the years. It's not all just beige and blue anymore. There's green and brown too…' I search for words of comfort.

'Thanks, pet.'

'No probs.'

For a second, I flirt with the idea of training to become a counsellor. I am so good at helping people with their problems. I just wish sometimes they wouldn't go on about them so much, it's such a snore fest.

'Oh my God! I just thought of something, Rebecca. Oh, how cute!'

'What?'

'They can be boyfriend and girlfriend!'

'Oh my God, yes!'

'They will be best friends first.'

'Obvs.'

'And then they'll fall in love with each other. Then they shall be wed! We can be the mummies in law!'

It's an ingenious plan, and I agree to it on the spot. After all, I don't want my dainty princess to marry some ruffian. And Emer's tiny gentleman deserves a proper lady to be his wife, not some tart. Only the best for our little ones.

'I mean, we should let them pick the wedding venue, though. We don't want to be all mom-zilla on them.' I offer my pearls of wisdom to Emer.

'True.'

Emer has gone a bit quiet.

'All OK, mummy in law?'

'Yeah! I'm grand. I've a few… niggly pains again today. I'm sure it's nothing. Sure, I've a full three weeks to go.'

'Uh-huh. Hopefully nothing. Anyway, gotta dash. Barry's back from the chipper and then we're off to his folk's place. See you at preggers' yoga tomorrow. Ciao, babes.'

I don't call Pam. I hardly think she gives a flying flip if it's a boy or a girl I'm carrying. Barry's back and the salt and vinegar hits my nostrils in a welcome wave.

'Ah, thanks babe.'

'Anything for jellybean.'

Barry is being so attentive these days. We really are the perfect couple. Every song on the radio is about us. By the time we reach Dalkey, the chips are scoffed and we hide the paper bags in the wheelie bin outside the house.

'It's a girl!' Barry shouts when his mum opens the hall door.

'Can you believe it? A girl!'

'Wonderful, Barry, wonderful! Patrick! Get the kettle on. Come in, come in!'

We settle onto the couch and pass the scan pictures around. Barry is keen to explain each one in detail, pointing out tiny arms and legs.

'We got to see so much of her, she was kicking about the place, wasn't she Becks?'

'So!' Margaret passes me a sugary cup of tea as Patrick readies the biscuits. 'Have ye thought of names? You know, now that ye know you're having a girl.'

'We have absolutely no idea!' I confess.

'Jellybean is starting to stick, isn't it Becks?'

'Hmm. I think she'd be teased at school with that one, son. What about Margaret?' Patrick suggests.

Barry's smile slips for a second.

'Well, I mean, that's lovely. Yes, I mean, eh…Maggie or…'

'Don't worry, I'm just joking. Or Patsy? After her granddad Patrick?' Baby Patsy has a nice ring…'

'Patsy, yes... baby Patsy…it's…' I look to Barry for help.

'He's joking again, Becks. Don't mind him.'

'Very funny. Anyway, if it were a boy I'd call him Patrick for sure.'

'Ah, after a favourite father in law!' says Patrick with a nod.

'No! After Patrick Swayze. God rest his handsome soul!'

Everyone laughs. They think I'm joking.

'I mean, 'Swayze' could be nice for a girl? It's unisex.'

I look around the room for approval.

'Swayze Costello? Eh, I don't think so, Becks!'

Barry is such a kill joy.

'Right then, smarty pants. What do you suggest, then?'

I squeeze Barry's knee playfully. He's still holding the scan pictures in his hands. He plans on showing them to everyone he has ever met.

'Well, like I said before, I like Pearl.'

'Pearl?' I practically shout.

'Yes, Pearl. It's very grown up.'

'Yes, Barry. It's very grown up!'

'Really? You like it now?' hope registers on Barry's innocent face.

'Oh yes. Perfect…if you're eighty!'

Margaret laughs. 'Tricky to find a name, isn't it?'

'Ruby? Amber? Jade?' Barry interjects.

'Stop naming precious stones!' I tease.

'Well, she is a jewel, after all!'

Margaret and Patrick exchange a smile. There it is again, that lump in the throat. The pregnancy hormones are to blame.

'Will the baby be double barrelled like you, Rebecca? Baby Browne Costello?' Patrick asks.

'No, way. That would be too much of a mouth full.'

Patrick pretends to wipe his brow. 'Oh, thank goodness for that!'

Twenty five

There are one million and one places I'd rather be than in the office, but here I am. Although my in-tray is threatening to topple over at any moment, I ignore it and log on to a pregnancy website. It's a lot more interesting than overdue invoices and stationery orders.

Harry wants a word with me. I've been summoned to his office, so this must mean I've done something to tick him off. The only question is: what? There are so many things it could be. I flick through the vast catalogue of possible offences. The most likely is me leaving at lunchtime last week and not coming back to the office afterwards. I do that a lot. Oops. Next in line is that he wants to discuss me not completing any of the tasks appointed to me, bar answering the telephone if it rings. Even then, my telephone manner leaves a lot to be desired. Then againm it could be me inventing and attending fictitious antenatal appointments and not producing appointment cards. Then again, he might opt for the old reliable: getting caught on Facebook and Twitter at regular intervals.

I stick my bump out as I enter Harry's office, in the hopes that he goes easy on me.

'So, Rebecca. Please take a seat.'

Harry won't meet my eyes, which is not a good sign. I lower myself into the chair dramatically, as if I'm in sincere discomfort and am about to give birth at any moment. It might embarrass him into forgetting my alleged offense.

'OK,' Harry clears his throat, and shuffles some papers as if he is a newsreader with first night nerves. 'Now, Brendan has advised me that the Human Resources policy states that I must have a chat with any pregnant employees, in order to ... assess any risks in the workplace. It's a health and safety thing. There's a form here, I thought we could fill it in together.'

I smirk. He looks even more uncomfortable than normal. Maybe I will have some fun with this. You know, tell him my placenta hurts. Or that my nipples are leaking. I could try and get his face to go puce again. It's all that passes for entertainment in this God forsaken place.

'Oh, fine.'

'Right. Well, question one...'

We go through the form. It's pretty standard stuff, you know? Am I subject to any risks in the workplace, that kind of thing? It's clearly been copied and pasted from some other company. There are sections on bio hazards, heavy machinery and toxoplasmosis. Not exactly things you'd worry about in an office. We skim through. The last question is what I've been waiting for. It asks if the pregnant employee has any suggestions for a safer working environment. I grin.

'Well, now that you mention it...'

Harry rubs his temples. He knows what's coming next.

'I mean, you really should refurbish the office to accommodate me. You know that horrible chair that I sit in? It's definitely giving me back ache. Oh, and would a footrest be too much to ask for? This is not a torture chamber!'

The rubbing of Harry's temple is getting more intense. It looks like instead of alleviating a headache, he is going to start a fire.

'And another thing,' I'm enjoying this. 'I really need a rest room. You know? In case I come across all faint one of these days. Low blood pressure, and all. I mean, it wouldn't look good for health and safety if I passed out at my desk and banged my head. I could get concussion...'

'A rest room...' Harry looks exhausted. 'Well, I don't think the budget would stretch to...'

'Well, I might need to lie down with an ice tea and a copy of 'Heat' magazine. Black out blinds would need to be installed if I get one of my hormone headaches.'

'OK, Rebecca. Well, thank you for your input. I'm not sure we can accommodate the ...what did you call it... 'Heat' magazine and iced tea... but I'll send the form to HR. Off you go, then.'

I turn back to add that if 'Heat' magazine was unavailable, 'Hello' would suffice. I'm flexible like that. But Harry does not hear me. He is reaching for some painkillers in his desk drawer. He knocks back two with a glass of water.

Emer has convinced me to come with her to preggers' yoga after work. I nip home to feed my darling Mister Jessikins, and change his water. It's weird, he hasn't touched his breakfast, maybe I'll switch brands again.

Anyway, I'm not sure about the yoga, but Emer swears by it. She says it gives you confidence in your body and helps you to stretch and breathe and all that. Sounds like a lot of mumbo jumbo to me.

'Hey, chick!' Emer meets me outside so that we can go in together.

'Hi! You look great. Does my bump look big in this?' I pop out my stomach and laugh.

'It looks fab! Now, like I said, Rebecca, don't let them intimidate you.'

'Emer! It's a room full of pregnant women.'

'I know! It's just that some of them are a bit...competitive.' she whispers into my ear.

I notice through her t-shirt that her bellybutton has been pushed out on her perfectly rounded belly. It's like a bowling ball stuck onto the body of a gold medal winning Olympic gymnast. She's eight months gone, and is sailing through the whole damn thing.

'Some of them are not first timers like us. They're kind of... know-it-alls. Anyway, you'll love it.'

I know what she means about the know-it-alls. Over the past couple of months since I announced my pregnancy, family, friends and the general public seem to love to give me advice. They can't stop themselves. They think they have all of the answers. Just last week in Tesco, a woman came up to me and said that I shouldn't be eating ice-cream. Risk of food poisoning for the baby, apparently. Not that I was asking for her opinion. I'm just glad that the wine was buried under a mountain of waffles and pizza.

Carmel greets us as we arrive. She instantly fits into the neat stereotype I have created for a yoga teacher. Once everyone has waddled in and arranged themselves in a circle, the class kicks off with a check in. Everyone states their name, how many weeks pregnant they are and has a good whinge about any problems they are having, so that Carmel can prescribe a particular yoga move to alleviate this during the class.

OK, so I've taken the liberty of summarising the group for you. Take a peek.

TOP SECRET SPECIAL REPORT: PREGGERS YOGA CLASS OF 2017

Name of Student 1: Martha

Code name behind back: Teachers Pet

Background info: expecting her 3rd baby

Traits: smug

Fun facts: Planning home birth. Ridiculous. Home deliveries for pizzas only. I advised her to call her kid pepperoni. Not impressed.

Name of Student 2: Mary

Code name behind back: Scary Mary

Background info: expecting 2nd baby

Traits: won't shut up

Fun facts: tells everyone the horrifying details of first birth. Last delivery involved a caesarean section; wants a drug free birth this time.

Name of student 3: Nel

Code name behind back: Nervous Nelly

Background info: expecting 1st baby

Traits: sweats a lot

Fun fact: terrified. Believes in hypno-birth techniques. Totally fucked.

Name of student 4: Jenny

Code name behind back: Fort Knox

Background info: expecting 1st baby

Traits: Smug cow

Fun fact: knows sex of baby. Not telling. Has selected name for baby. Not telling. Has a birth plan. Not telling.

Name of student 5: Emer

Code name behind back: Skinny Cow

Background info: expecting 1st baby.

Traits: stinking rich

Fun facts: successful project manager. If baby arrives past deadline, will be issued with written warning.

Gulp. It's my turn to share.

'Hi everyone, I'm Rebecca.'

'Hi Rebecca,' the ladies chirp.

'This is Rebecca's first class, everyone.' Carmel nods to encourage me.

'Well, em, I'm twenty three weeks pregnant. It's a girl.'

I pause in order for them to 'ooh' and 'ahh'.

'I can't stop eating. Literally. I've got a peanut butter sandwich and half of a Twix bar in my handbag. I'm going to ask my doctor to sign me out of work for stress, because my boss is being a pig. Oh, and I've got fierce wind.'

An uneasy silence follows. I think I've shared too much.

Carmel clasps her hands together. 'Right, then! OK, everyone. Grab a mat. We're going to start with the cat position.'

I throw Emer a terrified look. I've no clue what a cat position is. The only position my cat strikes is the horizontal, drooling, unconscious type. The yoga move is much, much harder. Also, I wasn't joking about the fierce wind.

'You're doing great,' Emer catches my eye.

'Thanks. I'm better at the beached whale position. Can you believe the woman next to me keeps farting? Some people!'

After almost an hour of stretches and breathing exercises, we are invited to take a seat on our mats and welcome the guest speaker. Last week, she covered home birth. I'm so glad I missed that one. Frankly, my house has too much cream furniture and a distinct lack of pharmaceuticals on tap for any of that messing.

Next week, the guest speaker will be covering post natal exercises. You know, to keep your downstairs muscles in good order so you don't wee yourself every time you laugh, sneeze or flatten a five year old on a bouncy castle. Let's be honest, we've all been there. There's no shame in it, I don't care what the mother of that wee soaked five year old said. Oh, and apparently, this can happen a lot more once you've pushed a small person through something that, frankly, I am starting to realise shouldn't have anything pushed through.

'Ladies,' Carmel announces, 'this week, we welcome Deirdre. She's a nurse from a local breastfeeding support group who wishes to share with us the joys of breastfeeding.'

Oh, dear. Emer and I glance at each other in horror. We have had the breastfeeding conversation on the side. Although risking being frowned upon by society, Emer and I are not entirely sure that we will be giving the old breastfeeding a try. I think Emer's exact words were 'over my dead body.' She has to be back at work pretty soon after the baby arrives, and has a pretty hectic social calendar, so she'll be delegating the feeds to the nanny. Also, she is worried that it will hurt like hell. Maybe she has a point. I'll have been though enough torture. Emer argues that modern formula is just as nutritional, and is so much more advanced than it was years ago. Scientists have the whole thing figured out, she said. Finally, she sold me with the fact that choosing to breastfeed would mean excluding Barry from his night-time duties. I couldn't do that to the poor man. I'd prefer to roll over and pass out with a clear conscience!

'Now,' Deirdre scans the room, following a ten minute lecture.

'Let's see who intends on breastfeeding their baby.'

Naturally, eco mum Angie is first to shoot her eager hand into the air. Martha is next. The others follow closely after. Emer and I keep our arms firmly crossed.

'Ladies?' Deirdre looks to us for an explanation.

'Yes?' Emer keeps her cool as I sweat profusely.

'I'm just wondering why you didn't put your hand up?'

Emer stares straight into Deirdre's eyes. My gaze is fixed on my shoes, which have a sudden fascination. I pray that she won't ask me any questions.

'My hand,' Emer continues, 'was not in the air, since I do not intend on breastfeeding.'

'I see,' the nurse portrays her disappointment in just two syllables. 'And can you explain why?'

Emer is a tough cookie. She goes to board meetings with old fart directors and slashes budgets. She has fired more assistants than I've written resignation letters. Let's just say I love her to pieces, but I wouldn't want to get on her bad side.

'Well, I think that's my business. But thank you for the information and good luck to the rest of you.'

Emer reaches for her handbag and places it on her lap. This is her code for the end of a conversation.

'Of course,' Deirdre backs down. There is zero chance of converting Emer. It would be like trying to convince Buddha to join an alien worshiping cult. Or trying to convince Boy George to date women. 'It's an individual choice.'

Deidre turns to me.

'Now, Rebecca, we all know the benefits of breastfeeding for the baby. But do you know the benefits of breastfeeding for the mother?'

The whole class is looking at me now for an answer and I'm staring blankly. It's like geography class all over again.

'Who, me?'

I search for the answer. It's probably some hippy dippy thing like 'bonding' or 'attachment' or some rubbish.

'Eh...'

Deirdre folds her arms, eyebrows raised.

'Weight loss, Rebecca. That's why Selma Hayek looks so good.'

She lists off abut three well known celebrities and connects their dramatic back to bikini bodies in their music videos with their enthusiasm for breastfeeding. Now she is speaking my language.

'Well, if it's good enough for celebrities...' I sway.

'And did you know,' Deidre continues, 'that breastfeeding burns over five hundred calories a day? That's five hundred calories more you could be eating...or drinking.'

The class titter.

'No, I didn't know that...'

Deidre smiles. She knows she has peaked my interest.

'And of course you don't have to worry about that odd glass of wine. Just feed your baby first or you can do what we call a pump and dump.'

'Oh...that's handy...'

Deidre hammers on, but I'm not listening anymore. I'm thinking about Selma Hayek's smoking hot body next to my smoking hot body. We are lovers now, Selma and I. We are dressed in bikinis on a yacht, laughing and drinking large glasses of champagne, babies on our firm boobs. It's like a Duran Duran video that went a little off course.

'And you know,' Deidre continues. 'The mummies can enjoy some quiet time on the couch watching a movie while the daddies tidy up and get the dinner on– some babies take up to an hour to feed.'

Emer is shaking her head at me. Her eyes are begging me to stay on her side of the fence. It's no good – I'm straight over the fence and chomping on some greener grass.

'So, Rebecca. What do you think?'

Deirdre must collect loyalty points for every woman she converts.

'Well, I mean… if it's good for the baby…'

Twenty six

I fill Dr. Grainger in on the, ahem, awful heartburn I've been suffering.

'Oh, it's just dreadful, doctor! Dreadful.'

I clutch my chest in mock agony as she nods her head in sympathy. I remember how she had confided in me that she had suffered from this affliction during her own four pregnancies, and then Googled it. I knew it would pull on the old heart strings. It seems to be working.

Of course, I may have exaggerated the nature of my condition. Just a smidge, mind you. I might have thrown in a few Johnny Cash lyrics. You know, 'burning ring of fire', and all that. I might have said that I've tried everything and still no luck, when in fact sucking on a Rennie does the trick. Perhaps I mentioned in passing that it keeps me awake at night, when the truth is that I snore like a freight train, according to Barry who has recently bought himself a pair of ear plugs and is threatening to move into the spare bed. And the piece de resistance, the crowning glory in my sea of lies, is that I told her that I suspect that the heartburn is exacerbated by the fact that I am being bullied by my pig of a boss. There were tears flowing down cheeks and everything. The woman even put her arm around me, and rubbed my back in small circular motions.

Now, I know you think I am a bit sneaky. You're probably right. Perhaps I will burn in hell for lying to a kindly lady doctor who is only trying to help me. Promise not to tell anyone? It was a sick cert I was after. Surprise, surprise.

At first, Dr Grainger gives me a school head mistress lecture on spicy food and caffeine. She instructs me to stop eating late into the night and to quit curries. She means well. I try to explain calmly that eating is my only pleasure these days (now that the powers that be have declared that I can only enjoy one measly glass of wine on occasion. Also, separating me from a hot curry on a Friday night is like trying to separate Kerry Katona from unsuitable men: impossible!

Dr Grainger whips out her medical pad and scribbles a cert for the rest of the month. I think it reads 'acute pregnancy related gastroesophageal reflux.' That sounds so painful. There is no way Harry will challenge that one. He probably thinks I'm hooked up to an IV in some hospital ward. I post the cert along with a little yellow post-it note (I have plenty in my handbag, courtesy of the stationery supplies cupboard) to advise him that it is touch and go, but that the baby is a little fighter. Maybe he will send me flowers.

Dr Grainger says that if things are still unresolved at work and causing me distress, we can talk about it at the next appointment. There is a momentary pang of guilt, but then I remember that if I can keep the dramatics up, I might even be able to squeeze her for more time off. And who can blame me? Working while pregnant is hard! Thankfully I'm still able to help out at the animal shelter, despite Barry being Mr. worry-knickers telling me not to lift anything.

Anyway, the time off is not for me. It's for the baby. I have the time now to get ready for her. Quite frankly, work was getting in the way. I need to tick a few essential jobs off my 'to do' list: like shopping for pink mini baby swimsuits and ballet costumes, for example.

Emer meets me in Dundrum Town centre on her lunch break. I'm finishing a Butlers hot chocolate when she arrives. I try and tempt her with a bite of my double chocolate chip muffin, but she won't budge. She says that her appetite is even smaller now that the baby is running out of space. Although she only has three weeks to go, she is still not on maternity leave. In fact, her plan is to work until the day the baby is born. Last week, I told her to be careful not to give birth at her desk, but she shoos the idea away. She plans to return once the nanny has a firm grasp of everything, probably within a few weeks. She is a complete Loony Toons, and probably has it all laid out on a Ghant chart, but I do love her.

'So, chick. Ready to do some serious shopping?'

Emer and I have matching bumps, even though she is three months ahead of me. Well, I suppose she was a size eight at the off set. What chance did I have up against that?

'Defo. I've got the credit card and am ready to do some serious damage! But, listen Emer, I feel bad that you won't let me throw you a baby shower.'

'Don't be silly! Honestly, pet I'm too busy at work. I don't need one. Sure, I'll enjoy yours in a couple of months anyway.'

We make a bee line for the cosmetics department in House of Fraser. Before we shop for the baby, Emer wants some new foundation and a few make up bits. She's had her roots done and the nails are booked in. She wants to look her best when the baby arrives. David has hired a 'post natal photography consultant' to come to the hospital. Apparently, it's all very natural and flattering. It's done in an artistic, organic way, whatever that means. The photos are all black and white and framed professionally. I didn't even know that these services exist. Now I want one, too.

I officially deem baby shopping to be the very best kind of shopping there is. (Just to be crystal clear, I mean shopping for things for the baby, not actual baby shopping. That would be entertaining but morally wrong.) And that's really saying something, as there are a lot of types of shopping. Trust me, I know these things. This ranges from the dull (tiles, bathroom equipment and ovens) to the necessary (groceries and wine) and stretches to the fun (wedding dress and any kind of cake shopping). The reason I nominate baby shopping as Numero Uno, however, is that it has one simple thing that the others do not. It is guilt free. I am not spending money on myself, it's all for the baby. There is nothing to feel bad about. Also, when Barry sees the visa bill, he'll still be so enchanted by the baby scan that he won't care. Anything for our princess.

Emer has all she needs for her baby and has the hospital bags packed already. She is meticulous as always. Nothing is left to the last minute. However, to fulfil her desire to shop for baby girl things, she is going to help me get started on my baby shopping. Within minutes, she has spied a darling little number for my baby in House of Fraser. It's pink, silky and frilly. And the best bit? It has a matching headband. I balk when I see the price tag, but Emer swats my hand away.

'Forget the price! Just buy it!'

As always, she is right.

We walk past 'Weirs and Sons' jewellers. Pointing out engagement rings to my darling Barry seems like a lifetime ago. Now, it's something else sparkly that catches my eye. I used to think that baby tiaras were tacky – the type of thing a trailer trash mom might pawn her wedding ring for in an effort to get Luanne first place in the Texas beauty pageant. Loaded with diamonds, it's completely over the top. The diamond in the middle is pink. The price tag makes my eyes water. But isn't my little girl worth it? Isn't she a beauty queen?

'Buy it,' Emer insists.

'Yeah, do you think so? Will I?'

'No. Move over, I'm buying it for her. For my future daughter in law.'

Emer and I wrestle over the tiara, brandishing our credit cards.

'Put your money away, Rebecca. I'm getting this.'

'Don't be ridiculous, Emer. Stop that, I'm buying it.'

'Get that wallet back in your purse, now, do you hear me?'

'I won't. I'm not letting you buy it.'

'Rebecca, I insist, now move it.'

Judging by his smirk, the sales assistant finds us highly amusing.

In Next, we scoop up enough pink cotton sleep suits, hats and vests to deck the baby out until she is two.

'It's best to be organized', Emer maintains.

'We might as well get it all now. Ooh, look at these!'

Emer has discovered a baby outfit with an outfit for the mother to match. I just love matchy-matchy! It comes with little pearls. It's simply darling and goes straight into the basket. In Mamas and Papas, the staff swarm around Emer. It's like a scene out of 'Pretty Woman' when the snooty shop ladies realise that Richard Gere has a stash of cash and that Julia Roberts is a high class hooker who can have her pick of the frocks and order a pizza if she feels like it. I've never seen such excellent customer service before, although there's not even a whiff of a Hawaiian pizza.

'Excuse me? Yes, does this come in pink? No, not lavender. Pink. We need more pink.'

'Don't you think we have enough now, Emer?'

'Enough? No! Rebecca, babies puke on everything. Bless them. Excuse me? Do the little ducks come in pink?'

Thank God Emer insists on paying. Baby clothes ain't cheap.

'Thanks, hun.'

The staff are laying the tiny clothes in layers of pink tissue paper and placing them gently into stylish cardboard bags. Emer is rubbing her sides again.

'My pleasure, Rebecca.'

'So, Emer. Did those little niggles disappear? Was it something you ate?'

'No, they keep coming back. It's probably Braxton Hicks, you know those practice pains? My doctor says I've got to cut back at work. Can you believe the nerve of him? He hasn't a clue. I mean, I've already cut back to a nine to five day and have started taking lunch breaks. But this merger is not going to happen without me.'

She is talking a mile a minute as we go back into House of Fraser to take a peep at the top floor.

'I mean, the other day, one of the girls from the office came in and said…she said… oooh!'

'She said oooh?'

Emer doesn't reply. She's bent over. Right here by the Nespresso machines. I'm mortified.

'Emer! Get up!'

'Sorry,' she breathes. 'Just a sec.'

People are starting to stare.

'What are you like? Do you need the loo, pet?'

'Sorry, I'm grand now.' She straightens up and we continue towards the exit.

Since Emer didn't get to buy anything pink for her baby, she's getting her pink fix on mine. It's good to get it out of her system. Our next stop is to check out some little mini outfits in 'Au Pareil Du Meime.' We might even have a root through H&M for cotton bibs and bedding if it's not full of rough types.

'Sorry, the flipping Braxton Hicks are no joke, Rebecca. Honestly, now. That's the third one I've had today.'

'Do you want to sit down? We could grab a coffee and a pastry?'

I'm selflessly thinking of Emer yet again. Although, truth be told, I haven't eaten in sixty minutes and could murder a Danish in Frangos right about now. And maybe a slither of Banoffe. Or both, I can't decide.

'No, I'm grand!' laughs Emer.

We head towards the escalators, and I take her bags.

'Sure, let's keep going. We've only one more stop on the whistle-stop tour. Then I'm back at the office and then I'll be at pregnancy yoga later, are you coming? I just have to do a grocery shop beforehand at...Marks...'

She's bent over again as we get off the escalator.

'Ah, Emer. People are starting to stare, love. Here,' I pull her towards a bench. 'Sit for a bit.'

'Sorry, it'll pass in a minute. Flip sake!'

Emer can't stand anything that interrupts schedules. She makes a scene, for example, if service is slow in restaurants or if she has to queue for anything.

'You're grand. Take a minute.'

'Oh, Rebecca!' Emer shoots me a serious look.

'What?'

'Promise you won't tell anyone?'

I raise my eyebrows and give her that look. She knows. 'I promise.'

'I think I've wet myself. My pants are soaking.'

'Well,' I laugh. 'You should have used the loo.'

'Rebecca, you don't think I'm...'

There's no need for Emer to finish that sentence. We both know that an invisible red flag is waving. Her waters have trickled out, right here in Dundrum Town Centre.

'Yup,' I smile.

'Oh, God.'

'This was not in your birth plan, Emer. I'd have a word with Mother Nature if I were you. Unacceptable, I'd say. Give her a written warning.'

Our sides hurt with laughter. This is probably the first time Emer has lost control.

'Stop!' begs Emer. 'I can't believe this is happening. I really will wet myself if you don't stop laughing.'

Emer never curses, even in emergencies. And believe me, going into labour in a crowded shopping centre is what you'd call an emergency.

'Yeah, well, I think you have officially shopped 'til you dropped. Your baby is keen to catch the summer sales, is he?'

'Oh, Rebecca. I'm so glad you're here.'

She holds my hand. For a split second, Emer is vulnerable. Tears roll down her face. And then, with a laugh, she manages to pull herself together. She wipes away the stray mascara from under her eyes.

'Oh, silly me!'

'You're fine, Emer. It's going to be fine.'

Before she can protest, I'm on the phone sorting everything out.

'Right. The taxi is on its way. We will meet him out front in five minutes. Work have been informed that you're not coming back later today. David will meet us at the hospital, he's going to fetch your bags from home first. OK? Let's go.'

'Thanks pet.'

I know Emer well enough not to call an ambulance. It would be her worst nightmare. I link her right arm and balance the shopping bags on my left arm, and give her my cardigan to wrap around her waste. Please take note of this fashion rule for future reference: cream trousers are not an ideal choice when heavily pregnant and your waters break in a heavily populated area. That is all.

Twenty seven

Dublin city centre is teaming with those overly eager types who start their Christmas shopping in November. They tick off neat lists with a smug grin. Why these folks can't just make a half-assed, semi-sozzled, last-minute, cash-strapped, heart-attack-inducing attempt to shop for their loved ones at five to six on a Christmas Eve, like the baby Jesus intended, is beyond me. They think they're better than the rest of us, and they're making it tricky for the taxi to pull in outside Holles Street Hospital.

David has been waiting on the steps of the hospital entrance. He thrusts a fifty euro note at the taxi driver, and takes a calm and collected Emer by the arm. I hobble behind, like a South American mule lugging the shopping bags, up to the admissions department. Even with soggy trousers and the odd contraction, Emer is the picture of dignity. Not a highlighted hair on her head is out of place. Her makeup is still fresh – she reapplied her powder and lip-gloss in the taxi en route, while I flapped my arms hysterically and made a crazed phone call to her office. Trust her to look good, even in established labour.

David is filling in Emer's details on the clipboard, so I wish her luck and I slink off in a lather, hair plastered to head, wet patches under arms. I have an inkling that I smell worse than I look. I can't help it, I sweat when I'm nervous.

'Here, baby' I pass the bags at Barry, who has pulled up at the pavement outside Holles Street. 'Well, that was a first!'

Barry mumbles something about the traffic, leans over to open the passenger door and blasts the cold air in my direction. Bless Barry for understanding - everyone else in the world is rubbing gloved hands together and complaining about the cold, while I complain about the heat. I need a full Mars bar to calm me. Luckily, I have an impressive selection of confectionary in my handbag.

'So, is Emer OK?'

'Ah, sure you know Emer! Sailing through as usual.'

'Keep calm and carry on, eh?'

'Yeah, that's our Emer.'

This might sound unbelievably harsh, but hear me out, OK? There is a teeny tiny part of me, buried somewhere deep at the back of my subconscious, that is jealous of Emer for making everything look so easy. It's a green eyed creature so small and hidden, you'd need a microscope to find it. It's lurking next to memories of uncomfortable dates and embarrassing school episodes that I've tried to forget. The source of jealousy is seeing her sail through this entire pregnancy with enough glow and glamour to put Kate Middleton to shame!

I know it doesn't make sense. Emer is my best friend in the world, and I love her. Truly, I do. I'm pretty sure that if she needed a kidney (not that any of her organs would function below par, mind you) and I were a match, and I was guaranteed a lot of prescription medication, a truck load of 'Hello' magazines, wine for medicinal purposes and a month off work I'd definitely donate one to her. Well, I'd definitely consider it, anyway, such is the strength of my love and friendship for her.

Anyway, don't listen to me. I'm hot, hormonal and on the brink of tears every five minutes. Barry, as well as everyone else that comes into contact with me, deserves a humanitarian award.

Barry and I have got to retrieve my car in Dundrum and get Emer's back to her house. Barry insists on driving Emer's. I'm not surprised. Emer drives a black convertible Mercedes S Class with cool grey leather upholstery. Of course, her brand spanking new mummy wagon with alloys and gadgets galore has been ordered and is arriving from Japan soon.

I'm barely in the door when the phone in my handbag is beeping.

'Don't tell me there's news already?' Barry calls from the hall.

'Yeah! Unbelievable!'

I open the text message.

We are delighted to announce the prompt arrival of baby Charles Laurence, weighing nine pounds. Mother and baby are doing well. David and Emer.

'Oh my God!' Barry laughs. 'Can you believe it?!'

'I know! Who calls their kid Charles Laurence these days?'

'No, I mean... that was fast! Fair play to Emer, eh?'

'Yeah, punctual and efficient as always, eh?'

'What's wrong, Becky?'

'Nothing.'

Barry knows girl code by now. Nothing means *everything*.

'Of course it was fast. I bet it was painless, too. A veritable walk in the park, no doubt.'

'Hopefully, Becky, yeah.'

I'm hysterical, now. Jess has jumped off my lap and waddled off to the kitchen, abandoning me in my time of need. Barry's got the box of Kleenex at the ready.

'The 'Guinness Book of World Records' will probably feature her,' I sob, 'there might be a category for 'Easiest Labour', or 'Best Hair Whilst Pushing a Baby Out.'

'Okaaay…'Barry laughs. 'This is the hormones talking.'

'Not fair. Emer's brilliant at everything, and I'm just a big fat lump.'

'Don't be silly, Becky, you're doing great.'

Barry passes the chocolate to me on the couch. Jess tries to curl up on my lap but can't get comfortable, so he settles for the cushion beside me.

'No chance of this baby coming early like Emer's, eh Jess?'

I text back

Congratulations! Love, Becky & Barry xx

I've decided that Emer and David aren't going to be the only ones who can flit through life, like.... like... things that flit. Now is a good time to talk Barry into a scheme I've been scheming for some time. I've got my heart set on a baby-moon, and there's no talking me out of it. The argument for Barry whisking me away on an urgent holiday break has been edited and re-written in my head, and I'm ready to do the hard sell. For those of you who have been living under a rock for the last few years, and said rock did not have Wi-Fi or a subscription to celebrity magazines, let me explain. A baby-moon is a romantic vacation taken by parents-to-be before the birth of their baby. You know, like Kim Kardashian and Kanye West going in Paris before baby North was born. I'm giving Barry a crash course on the topic.

'Rebecca? Rebecca! Becks!'

Barry has been trying desperately to interrupt me for the last few minutes, but I'm enjoying my rant too much to quit, now.

'All of the celebrities go on one, Barry. You'll thank me for it. It's going to be our last chance to see a proper far flung exotic destination before we're grounded with nappies and bottles. Luxury, that's what we need. Five star luxury and an all-you-can-eat buffet. Emer and David went to Mauritius...'

I let that one land. Emer and David have money to burn, but I want the underlying tone to read 'don't you love me as much as David loves Emer?' Let's see him argue his way out of that one, eh?

'Rebecca, we...'

'Shush, Barry. Now, I'm thinking about booking The Maldives or India…'

'But Becks!' Barry interrupts me.

'Mum can mind Jess. Grand. I know what you're thinking. Vaccinations. But… you don't have to –'

'Becky! We're only back from our honeymoon in Mexico! That was pretty far flung and exotic.'

'That was *months* ago, Barry!'

I tut and cross my arms like a belligerent teenager.

'Yeah, so anyway, Barry. Pay attention. I was looking online, right? And because it's low season, there are some amazing special offers. I don't even care if it's the rainy season in Thailand right now. How bad can a monsoon be? I'll bring a brolly. Sure, we're used to rain here. I think we should just go for it!'

My argument is bullet proof. It's simple economics.

'Just go for it?' Barry laughs. 'Rebecca, we're still paying off the last holiday, remember? Cancun? I really think we should just…'

'Barry, you're impossible. Stop being such a stick in the mud and just enjoy yourself for once, will you? God, you're no fun, *grandad*. Anyway, it's not about you, it's about me. I'm pregnant in case you've forgotten. I'm going to need a rest before this baby comes, and…'

'Yes, and you're off on a sick cert. Rest at home!'

I mutter, but make sure he can make out the word cheapskate. He knows that I will nag at him for weeks until his head explodes. It's best for everyone if he just gives in now. Far easier all round.

'Barry, you are so ridiculous. Let me put it to you this way, OK? You're going to be exhausted getting up all night to feed this baby. So, before she arrives…'

'We can't afford it, Becky,' Barry blurts. 'We are still in debt from the honeymoon!'

I'm not listening. The IPad is logged on to the Dream Escapes website, showing The Maldives and Thailand. Even Barry has to admit, they look like heaven. A couple of weeks lying on the hot sand would be bliss.

'Rebecca, listen. I've got to tell you some news. It's about my job…'

'Right. Here it is. Look at this one. Five star. Room Service. White sand beach…Oh, Barry, look at the cute little huts with the wooden legs sticking into the water. And look at the colour of the sea. Oh my God, it's turquoise! A tan would disguise these ugly stretch marks. They're getting worse, you know…'

'Rebecca, I don't want to worry you, but…'

'Now, hear me out, OK? I won't be able to fly from February onwards. Eight months preggers is the cut-off point. Silly, I know. Airline policy. Set in stone, apparently. They're afraid that if you pop one out at twenty thousand feet, it might get a little messy for the other passengers, ha-ha. Anyway, that just leaves from now until…'

When I count out the dates on my fingers, the pause for breath is Barry's chance to jump in.

'Redundancy!'

It's like a red flag flounced in the face of a bull. He has caught my attention.

'What?!'

Barry holds his head in his hands and sighs.

'OK… so a couple of months ago, Nigel called me into his office.'

'Oh, God,' I breathe.

'Look, it's going to be OK, but… well, the company is going to go into liquidation. All of the staff are going to be made redundant.'

'Even you?'

''Fraid so, Becks. Nigel is going out on his own as a sole trader. So that means that one month from now, the job will finish.'

'Hang on. Wait a sec. A couple of months ago, you said?'

'Yeah, well…'

'Why didn't you tell me straight away? Barry! I can't believe you didn't tell me before.'

'It's just… I didn't want to worry you until I found another job, you know? Soften the blow and all that.'

'And have you? Found another job?'

'No, not yet. I went for an interview a couple of weeks ago. It went great. Really thought I'd nailed it, you know? It was for a big company in the IFSC. Nice package, too. Permanent role. Remember Stephen from college? He works there, tipped me off.'

I'm silent as Barry ploughs on. I wonder whether Barry has rehearsed this news over and over in his head, afraid to tell me. Saying things out loud means that they are real.

'But, anyway. I didn't get it, baby. Apparently it was a close call between me and some other guy internally. Really disappointing. I'm keeping my eyes peeled. I know I'll click something before the time runs out.'

Barry is smiling, but his forehead is creased and his foot is tapping uncontrollably.

'OK.' I nod my head slowly, place my fork on the coffee table and push my plate away.

I open my mouth, but nothing comes out. Questions bubble to the surface like pockets of air from a gaping fish. My eyes are fixed and glassy.

'But, look... We'll be OK for a few months, Becky. We don't have much in the way of savings, but the redundancy package is not bad. It'll buy us some time. I can talk to mum and dad if things get a bit tight.'

'OK.'

My voice is small when I eventually find it. The sound is as if I am underwater. I concentrate on the heat from Jess' small body against mine, and stroke his fur.

'Listen, it's only a matter of time before I find another job, OK? I don't want to set up on my own. Too risky. We'll hold tight until something comes along.'

A thought creeps into my head. 'But ...I'll only be paid for the first six months of the maternity leave. The rest is unpaid leave. It's how it works.'

'I know, baby. It'll be fine.'

Jessie is back on my lap, purring softly. On TV, Sally Webster is having a stand up row with Gail Platt in the Rovers Return. I stare at the flickering colours, but cannot interpret them. I barely blink.

'Eat your dinner, Becks. Come on, love.'

Barry passes the loaded dinner plate back to me.

'Thanks,' I accept the plate and place it on my lap.

The smell of the basmati rice and chicken tikka masala make my stomach loop. Barry watches as I poke about aimlessly with the fork.

Twenty eight

On my way up to the Merion Wing, I stop off to buy a teddy bear wearing a blue sweater tied to a balloon. The door to Emer's private room is open and I see her before she spots me. She is cradling a small bundle in a blue blanket.

'Honey,' I knock as I enter. 'Congratulations.'

I place the present on her locker, and perch on the side of her bed.

'Oh, Rebecca! Thanks for everything yesterday. Can't believe how fast it all happened. You were great.'

'Sure, it was nothing,' I wave my hand. 'I mean, if Noel Edmunds is looking for nominations for 'Modern Day Angels', you could drop him a line. You know, no pressure, or anything.'

Emer laughs. 'Here's the little man himself. Say hello to Charlie.'

He is simply beautiful. There is no other way to describe him. I know it sounds like a cliché from a Hallmark card, but it's true. I mean, have you ever heard me describe a baby as beautiful before? Not counting my own on the monitor during the scan, of course. But, sure that doesn't count. Everyone likes their own babies. It's part of the deal, apparently. When I first saw the pink line on the pregnancy test, and went on to have a full on knicker fit, Barry told me that kids are like farts – nobody minds their own. How eloquent of him.

'Oh, Emer,' I put my hand over my mouth. 'I can't believe it. He's absolutely perfect.'

Charlie is dressed in a white cotton sleep suit and is curled up on her chest, his face nestled into her neck. His eyes are closed and his hands are little fists. Her fine blonde hair moves gently with his breath. Emer rubs his back in small patting motions. She is humming without realising it. I can't say another word. My throat is restricted, as if there is an invisible hand around it, and my eyes sting.

'At least we got to finish the shopping, eh Rebecca! Sorry I gave you a bit of a fright.'

'It's fine. So…'

I brace myself as I pose the inevitable question.

'…How was it?'

Emer and I have a pact. We decided way back that we will be really honest with each other. We have come across two distinct categories of women during our pregnancies, and we swear not to morph into either. According to the Rebecca Costello nee Brown comprehensive dictionary, these categories of women can be defined thus:

1.*The Delusionals.* (pronounced dih-loo-zh*uh*-nls), adjective.
Definition: those who have false or unrealistic beliefs or opinions; ladies who dramatically play down the trauma of birth in order to preserve the fragile feelings of the pregnant person to whom they are speaking.
Example: my mother, since she insists that I, in fact, 'swam out' into her arms and went on to become a saint of a child. Both claims are highly questionable. She also maintains that contractions are purely muscular pains, and that there is nothing to worry about. Common exclamations: 'Ah sure, it was grand!'

2. *The Horror Story Tellers* (pronounced h⬚r-ər stawr-
ee tel-er), noun.
Definition: a person who entertains or fascinates by
shocking or frightening, especially by an emphasis on
bloodshed or supernatural forces.

Example: Most of the women in my office. Prone to
exaggeration, their birth stories have enough blood and
guts to shock the director of a Stephen King movie, and
leave your stomach churning.

Common exclamations: 'I had stiches. Down there.'
Usually uttered, despite protestations that you are
trying to enjoy your lunch.

'OK, then...' Emer eyeballs me.

'Go on. I'm ready.'

I take a deep breath, in through the nose and out
through the mouth. This is it, my only chance to hear
the truth. I've got to face it sooner or later, and Emer is
the only friend I can trust to tell me honestly.

'It hurts...'

'Right.' The blood drains from my crumpled face. That's
it, then. Game over. Maybe I'm better off not knowing
the rest. Emer is holding her hand up so that I don't
interrupt her.

'But listen, Rebecca, it's OK. You can totally do it.'

'Oh, Emer, I don't know. You've a higher pain threshold
than I do.'

It's true. Once, Emer went to work despite having a
raging kidney infection and accompanying fever. She
was on antibiotics and prescription painkillers, and she

said that her back felt like she'd been kicked by a donkey. I'd have taken a month off to recover from that one.

'Ok, Rebecca. When it's your turn, you need to do two things, right? Now, remember all the yoga stuff Carmel showed us. Honestly, it works. And ask for the epidural as soon as you're admitted. It's good stuff. The rest was fine. I was lucky, he took just over an hour from the time we arrived.'

'Jammy wagon.'

'I know. Thanks.'

'And how did David find it? Didn't pass out or anything?'

'Ah, no, sure he was grand. He was very good, really. The staff were brilliant. You'll be well looked after. Will you look at the state of me, though?'

I give her the once over. Her hair looks freshly blow dried. Her nails are a dark red.

'Eh hardly, Emer! And listen, he's lovely and calm now, but did he cry all night? Is it not totally scary now that he's really here? I haven't got a clue what to do with babies.'

Emer smiles. 'Me neither. I'm learning fast, though! He loves the bottle thank goodness. And no, the nurses topped up my meds and then took him to the nursery all night. Dropped him back to me when the breakfast came. I got a great sleep, actually. Really needed it.'

'Ah nice...' my voice trails off.

A staff member knocks on the door and discreetly collects the lunch menu.

'What's up, Rebecca?'

'What? Nothing!' I force a smile. It is crooked, and Emer holds my gaze until it cracks and I give in.

'It's nothing, really. Just a bit of worrying news with Barry. It'll be grand.'

I feel bad. Emer has a new baby in her arms and I'm spilling my problems on top of her, but there's no one I trust more, and she's always my go to girl.

'What happened?'

'His law firm are going into liquidation in just four weeks. He's being made redundant.'

'Oh no. That's terrible. And they only gave him four weeks notice, that's horrible!'

'Well... turns out they told him two months ago. He didn't want to worry me. Idiot.'

'Ah no.'

'Yeah, he's been carrying that worry around all this time, afraid of upsetting me. Maybe he thought that I'd flip out with all these hormones, eh? Anyway, he's looking for a new job. No luck so far.'

'You'll be fine. Solicitors are always in demand. He's highly qualified.'

'Suppose. So, where's David?'

'Oh, he's at home assembling Charlie's cot. The interior designer is just putting the finishing touches on the nursery. It's all go.'

Emer's cream and cappuccino nursery will be like something out of 'House and Home' magazine. So far, our nursery is a spare bedroom which currently contains an ironing board, a broken TV and a random collection of shoes. Barry will have to get his skates on.

'And Emer, your text said that Charlie weighs nine pounds! Bit of a bruiser, eh?'

'I know! My God! The consultant didn't see that one coming. Imagine if I wasn't three weeks early?'

'Yikes.' My mind flashes back to baby Barry and his melon head.

'Anyway, I got in touch with the new nanny, told her that Charlie here decided to come a bit earlier than expected. She has just finished with a family in Zurich and will fly over next week to get started. I'll have to hang in there 'til she arrives!'

'Wow, Zurich...'

Even Emer's nannies are the best. Her IPhone buzzes.

'Sorry, pet. It's the office.'

'Emer! Tell me you're not going to answer that!' I point to the sleeping baby on her chest.

'Yeah, you're right,' Emer puts the phone on silent.

Lunch is being served, complete with little posh doilies under the coffee pot.

'Listen, Emer, I'll go.'

'No! Stick around. Here,' Emer passes the bundle in the blue blanket in my direction.

'No, don't, it's fine… don't wake him! Emer!'

It's too late. Emer has expertly manoeuvred Baby Charlie from her chest with a scoop, and he is in my arms. I'm stiff like Dolly Parton's hairdo. He squirms momentarily, and I think for a frozen second of horror that he might wake and then cry and that I might be forced to do something. What that something might be, I have absolutely no idea. There is a myth that I would like to dispel right now. It can't wait a second longer. Most people think that all women are born with a baby-expert-microchip in their brains. Well, I am here to inform you that either that myth is wrong, or I am faulty. Charlie is small and vulnerable, and I'm prone to dropping things. His head is floppy and I'm awkward.

Soon, then he nestles down, and I resume breathing.

'See? You're fine! He's fine.'

Emer gives me a grin.

Tears roll down my face. In just three months time, I'll have a little bundle in a blanket. I won't be able to hand her back if she cries. And chances are, she will cry. That's what babies do, apparently. Barry will be at work eight hours a day, and I'll have to figure it out for myself. The thought is terrifying.

'Rebecca, what's wrong?'

'Sorry, it's just…'

'What, chick?'

Charlie's fine blonde hair tickles like feathers against my skin.

'It's just that… oh, God, Emer…'

'What, love?'

'Oh,' I wipe a tear away. 'I'm just rubbish with babies.'

I'm laughing and crying at the same time, and Emer joins in. We're like hormonal, hysterical hyenas. The nurses in the nurses' station down the corridor can hear us cackling.

Twenty nine

Barry says I was mumbling in my sleep last night. Something about shopping, he maintains. Although I deny it vehemently, he insists that I was shouting about my credit card, and was standing at the foot of the bed demanding my purse. It's all highly questionable. I mean, I'm not the shouty, demanding kind. Barry thinks it's hilarious. He will probably use it as an amusing anecdote at the next dinner party we're invited to.

'I've no idea what you're talking about,' I declare as I roll over. 'Maybe you dreamed the whole thing.'

The truth is that I remember the dream with a shocking clarity, but I'm not about to admit that to Barry. Well, it was more of a nightmare. You see, the dream involved our baby coming early. I know, I know. I'm only six months gone and that it's all quite unlikely. But anyway, tell that to my subconscious, it clearly didn't get the memo!

The odd thing about the dream was that I wasn't all that bothered about having a premature baby. Immature lungs and incubators were not the main focus, *per se*. There were no nose tubes or frantic prayers for her to pull through. The cause for my utter meltdown was the thought that we have bought nothing for the baby besides sleep suits and a beautiful, if not slightly impractical, diamond tiara. I was inconsolable that she had no-where to sleep. I was traumatised that she had no buggy in which to be paraded through town, with me wearing something swanky. I was devastated that I have no baby changing unit, and would have to slum it by peeling stinkers off the tots bum on the couch.

And then, like any self respecting dream, I was running. Out I ran, hospital gown flapping at the back, granny pants on display for all and sundry to see. Past the teeny baby and past the staff and my gaping husband I ran. I believe I hailed a taxi to some remote supermarket. Then I was caught up in one of those trolley dash jobs, and Dale Winton was there. His skin was a deep orange, and his teeth a dazzling white. He told me to shove as many baby things as I can into the trolley and race to the checkout before the timer ran out. An audience was clapping and cheering. Against the clock, I was tipping highchairs and cots and potties into a large trolley, and pushing it towards the neon lit checkout.

Anika Rice was there too, in a shiny yellow tracksuit and all out of breath. I'm not sure if she was trying to help me or whether we were competing, but I told her that I was a fan. We may have also snogged during the dream. There was definitely some lesbo running of fingers through silky blonde hair and washing-machine-tongue action. I am going to have to Google 'hot steamy lesbian tendencies whilst pregnant' later when I have a minute. The hormones have me all confused.

Anyway, I digress! The entire point of the dream, if you will allow me a little self analysis, is that it represents a fear of being unprepared for baby's arrival. It's a no brainer. I know what I'm talking about. I used to own a dream interpretation book that I bought at a car boot sale. Also, you know how I hate to brag, but I did take a whole semester in psychology at college back in the late nineties. I mean, I'm a naturally enlightened spirit.

My night time antics, namely the screeching and credit card thrusting, can be explained by a primal urge to shop, coming from my deep subconscious. I'm sure this urge dates back to pregnancies in the stone-age, and everything.

When I wake again, the house is empty, so I call Emer and then Barry.

'Hello?'

Barry hates being interrupted at work, but this is important. Personally, I couldn't be stuffed going in to the office myself, I have far too much to do. I'll squeeze out a few tears to Dr Grainger later in the week and say that Harry the Horrible is being his usual bullying, obnoxious self. I'll say I'm emotional and vulnerable. I'll use the word overwhelmed. I'll have a tremor in my shaken little voice when I declare my woes. That should do it.

'Barry? Yeah, hi. We have to talk. I've been thinking.'

'Oh dear, here we go.'

'Ha-ha, very funny. Anyway, listen, Barry, the baby has flip all. I'm not organized!'

'What are you talking about? We've loads of time. And sure, didn't yourself and Emer not go flipping crazy with the credit card a month ago? Remember? You shopped the poor woman into early labour?'

'Yes, we did pick up the most adorable little pink outfits, but don't joke about poor Emer, Barry. Anyway, this is serious. Our little girl...'

I pause for dramatic purposes. I learned that trick at stage school as a kid. Gets 'em every time. I also try to sound as if I might be sobbing softly in the background, it usually works a treat. Now, the use of the words 'our little girl' are about as subtle as a 'TOWIE' tan.

'…has nowhere to sleep. No buggy to be pushed about in. No nappy changing unit for her little bottom to lie on. What if our baby arrives early and needs to be incubated with a drip in her little arm, and then comes home to no cot?'

Barry is silent, but I just know, deep down in my core, that he is rolling his eyes. I can practically hear it. I move in for the kill.

'Won't someone please think of the children?' I sniff.

'Ah, here,' Barry is having none of it. 'Don't exaggerate, Becks. We have ages left. And listen, I'm sorry to have to remind you about our …' he lowers his voice. '…current financial difficulties?'

I knew he'd try and talk me out of it, but I won't be dissuaded. I've made my mind up. I'm only calling to give him a heads up on the credit card bill out of pure courtesy. It's time to pull out the big guns. I sob at a high pitched level. It's annoying, even at this end of the phone.

'Becky! Look, fine. I mean, yeah, you're right. We do need *a few* baby things. Of course we do. She needs a cot. I just don't see what all the panic is about. Let's go in together at the weekend and take a look, yeah?'

'No way! You know nothing about baby stuff, Barry. You'd choose a buggy just because it comes with the best coffee cup holder, you know what you're like when it comes to gadgets. I'm not falling for that. Besides, Emer is all set to go. She knows about these things. You can see it later. You'd be bored.'

'Fine, fine.'

I know that he's only agreeing in order to get me off the phone, but who cares?

'Just…Becks? One more thing. Don't go crazy, OK? Just get what we really need. I'm sure we'll get loads of presents from our family, so we don't need to buy absolutely everything in one day…'

'Yeah. Yeah. Love you. Toodle pip!'

He hasn't a clue.

I'm dressed in a flash and ready to go. I've decided to press pause on the whole redundancy worry. Simple as that. I mean, I know we're broke, but I'm shopping for our baby. Whether Barry finds work or not, the fact remains that we need all of this stuff. I won't go overboard. It was ludicrous of Barry to suggest such a thing.

Emer has parked in the mother and baby space outside Mothercare in Carrickmines Retail Park. Even though Charlie is not yet a month old, she's all set to go. She says she is not one for hanging about the house and is feeling the cabin fever creeping in already. We have plans to make absolute pigs of ourselves at Vanilla Pod afterwards. They do the best fries ever. Having said that, I think Emer's idea of making a pig of herself is having dressing on her salad. Some people just don't know how to live a little.

We air kiss outside Mothercare. The cold air makes my nose glow red. It's the first week of December, and the promise of Christmas lingers in the air. Twinkly fairy lights glow faintly, waiting patiently for darkness to creep in so that they can dazzle.

'Oh my God, Emer. You look …amazing!'

Emer is back in her skinny jeans and high heeled boots already.

'Are you sure you didn't have a nip and tuck while you were in there?'

'Don't be silly! I was so glad to get your call, I was going stir crazy being in the house all day, and no work to go to!'

I peep into the buggy. The angelic child is unconscious and tucked up all cosy. He is like a miniature version of Brian O'Driscoll in a teensy preppy Irish rugby jersey and cream slacks. I think he's got Timberland boots on, too. You know, in case he decides to go hiking. What a handsome son in law he will make. I think I'll let him call me Becks when he starts dating my daughter. Mrs. Costello is so formal!

'Ah, look! Hello, baby Charlie. Emer, are you not up to your eyes with him all day?'

'Not at all. Honestly, Rebecca, it's so easy. He literally sleeps, like, all the time.'

'Is that normal?'

'Hmm? Oh, I've no idea. And listen, the nanny is great. Emily. No, Amelia. Or Amelie. Something like that. I just needed to get out of the house, you know? I mean, I'm back doing my marathon training every evening, so that's good.'

'Oh, I know what you mean. I might take up running once this big lug evacuates. Might even join you in the marathon.'

'Really?'

'Absolutely!'

What is so ridiculous about the idea of me running a marathon? How hard can it be? I'll just get a pink spandex stretchy suit thing, a water bottle and a nice pair of spongy runners, and off I go. Just you try and stop me. Twenty six miles probably just sounds worse that it actually is, you know? Anyway, a bus runs through the Phoenix Park, if the going gets tough.

We start off by choosing a gorgeous pine cot and matching baby changing station. Barry would be proud of my thrifty ways, they are fifty percent off in the pre-Christmas sale.

'Ah, would you look!' Emer has spotted an adorable cream and beige rocking chair.

'You have to have that, too. It's part of the matching set. And Barry will look so cute rocking back and forward in it when he does the night feeds!'

She's right. Who am I to break up a furniture set? They might *pine* for each other, get it? Pine? Oh, never mind, I'll explain it to you later. Besides, I want Barry to be comfortable when he does the night shifts. I don't want him grumbling about a sore back, waking me up. That would be awful!

At the till, I present my credit card. I feel better already. There is no chance of being caught out with an early baby and nothing bought, now. Take that, deep subconscious fears! In your face, disorganisation! Creepy dream: nil, Rebecca Costello: one.

'Oh, I just thought of something,' Emer's forehead creases subtly. The Botox won't allow for much of a crumple, just enough to portray a vague concern.

'What?'

A teenage employee from Mothercare is struggling to jam all of the gear into Barry's Jag. I don't know if it's all going to fit. This is hilarious when it happens to other people, you know, those distressed souls who try to cram an Ikea wardrobe into a Nissan Micra, but not so much when it's you.

'Hey! Watch the paintwork. Goodness!'

'Well,' Emer's mouth turns down. 'I think all of this is self assembly. You know, like flat pack? Will Barry go mad?'

'Don't worry about Barry!' I click my tongue. 'He will just have to get his screwdriver out...or Alan key, or whatever it is people use to build furniture these days. Sure, it'll be a nice project at the weekend for him, like jigsaws for grownups.'

'True, Rebecca. He's a man. He'll figure it out!'

'There are pink jobs and there are blue jobs. This is a blue job. Anyway, today is the last day of his work. Nothing else lined up, I'm afraid. He might have loads of time on his hands, you know?' I'm cracking a joke, but the fear is not far beneath. My lip wobbles a bit.

'Oh my goodness, Rebecca. That came around so fast. I can't believe today is the last day already. You must be so worried.'

'No, I mean... yes, I suppose a little. Just a matter of time, I guess, before he finds something else. Terrible time to be job hunting with Christmas so close, but I'm sure he'll click something soon.'

I turn to the teenager so that Emer doesn't see the tears building up in my eye. The teenager finally manages to squeeze the furniture into the boot of the car by lying the back seats down flat. It took him long enough to figure it out. If he wants a tip, he can have one. Here it is: stay in school. There, don't say I'm not generous.

'Course, he will, pet. Course he will. I'll ask David to keep his eyes peeled in case something comes up. Anyway! We still have no buggy. Let's go on a little excursion to 'Le Petit Bebe', they have buggies there to die for.'

Charlie is still unconscious when we finish our grub at Vanilla Pod and hit Le Petit Bebe. I wish babies would just sleep like that until they go to college. It's all far more civilised when mummies can finish their moccachinos in peace.

'Here,' Emer points. 'That's the same buggy that I have. It's amazing. They have all the latest models here.'

I never thought I could be excited by a buggy before. Surely they are dull but necessary things, like wallpaper? But Emer has whipped up an excitement inside me. They are trendy, and they come in a choice of hot colours. They have these little muff things for babies to snuggle into in the winter months, and come with a matching baby changer bag. Emer says I desperately need one of those, too. She says they are essential.

'Oh my goodness, would you just look!'

I've just spotted one in hot pink! It's a shade up from my lipstick and a shade lower than my shoes. It's just the right kind of pink, really.

'See? Isn't it pretty?'

'Wow, I'm tempted, Emer,' I confess. 'They are so nice. And they're made from titanium, you say? That's why they're so light?'

'So glad you like them. And imagine! When we go for walks in Marley park,' Emer is clapping her hands, attracting attention from shoppers. 'We will have matching buggies, but in different colours. Yours in 'hot pink promise' and mine in 'electric blue babe'. And our babies will fall in love with each other and go on dates and then on to have babies of their own. And then those babies will be pushed in pretty buggies, too!'

Her excitement is contagious, and we are whooping and clapping right there in the middle of the store. Fellow shoppers have stopped to look at us. The shop assistant resists the urge to block her ears to shield her from the shrieking.

'Oh, we shall be so fabulous,' I declare. 'Matching buggies!'

We high-five on the words 'matching buggies.'

I'm routing in my handbag for my credit card. I don't think I can retrieve it fast enough.

'Oh, Emer,' I laugh as I pull out keys and lipsticks in search of my purse. 'Barry will go mad when he sees the price of it. I mean… oh, he's on the phone now. Look at my screen. How hilarious! He must have a device that beeps when I spend too much money!'

'Hey, Barry.'

I'm laughing so hard, it's hard to talk. When I hang up, I'm deflated.

'What's wrong, babes? Rebecca?'

'Barry is such a meanie. He's thrilled with the sound of the cot and changing table. Naturally, I didn't mention the rocking chair.'

'Naturally.'

'But, Emer, I was telling him about the buggy, you know? I even mentioned the cute cappuccino cup holder and the speedometer on the handlebar, right? He said it sounds amazing.'

'So what's wrong, Rebecca?'

'When I told him the price...' my voice trails off.

'Don't worry about it,' Emer declares, grinning.

The shop assistant is pretending to straighten high chairs, but is listening to our little melodrama unfold.

'Well, I mean, I can't just go and buy it now. Barry wants me to wait until the weekend, maybe see if there's one on sale somewhere, or ...second hand...'

'I said don't worry about it.'

'What?' I dab at my nose with a tissue.

'OK, look. I've been trying to figure out what to get you, right? You're my best friend!'

'Emer, you don't need to get me anything. You've done so much for me already.'

'Shush! Now, David said I have you to thank for getting me to the hospital safely. He's really grateful to you. He said I should just bring you here and see what your reaction was, and that if you genuinely liked it, I should just get it. From Charlie.'

'Emer, no way. It's amazing, but no. It's too much. Way too much.'

Emer passes her platinum credit card to the sales assistant who has reappeared at our side, the smell of commission in the air.

'Please put the 'hot pink promise' deluxe model through on my card,' she instructs.

'Thanks, Emer.'

I sob into her shoulder. There is mascara and snot on her one hundred percent wool coat. It's such a rollercoaster!

Thirty

Barry sits with his head in his hands at his empty desk. The walls and bookshelves of the office are now bare. There is a sad little cardboard box in the corner with all of his personal stuff in it – his framed law degree which once took pride of place in the centre of the wall, a photograph of Rebecca, some law reference books, and all the stationery he could get his hands on.

Today is the last day before the solicitors firm ceases to exist. Nigel's office desk, filing cabinet and a handful of other items have been delivered to his new office in Gallery Quay, where he'll be operating solo from now on.

'Don't forget, everyone is meeting for drinks at five,' Janice from reception pops her head around the door. Barry throws her a half-hearted smile. He is really not in the mood.

Having to tell Rebecca not to buy the buggy was a pride crushing moment. Thank God he caught her before she put the amount through on the credit card. I mean, sure, the baby will need a new buggy (on top of a staggering amount of other stuff), and she will get everything she needs. Of course she will. But what was Rebecca thinking spending a grand on a buggy right now in their financial position? It's a total joke!

Allowing Emer to pay for the buggy, or deluxe *travel system* as she called it, was a low point. She might as well have taken a three inch high heel and stamped all over his manhood. He's grateful to her, though. This way, Rebecca gets the buggy she really wants, the one she deserves. Whatever keeps her happy is of upmost importance these days. It's best not to rock the boat where Rebecca and her hormones are concerned. Emer gets to feel good about getting a present for her best friend that she can easily afford, and Barry doesn't have to worry about another grand piling on to Debt Mountain.

'Coming for a farewell drink at five, Barry?' Nigel interrupts Barry's stare into space.

The least that Nigel can do is buy him a stiff drink after all that he has put him through these last few months. But Barry is too irritated to face anyone. He can't even afford to buy his own kid a buggy. One or two of his colleagues have secured new jobs over the last three months, but most are in the same boat as Barry. He wishes he could go along and rub a new job in Nigel's face.

'No, thanks. Not really in the mood. Catch you another time.'

Barry knows there won't be another time. This is it – the last hurrah.

On Monday morning, he will have no job to go to, and there are no more interviews lined up that he can pin his hopes to. The P45 will be in the post. The dole queue will become a reality. Going it alone as a solicitor is one option, of course. But there's office rent to think of and building up a client base, and Barry never was one for taking chances. It would be better to hold off for a job with a steady income, holiday pay and a pension.

He and Rebecca have pretty minimal savings after the honeymoon excess – he will just have to put elastic on what little they have. If things continue like this, he'll have to hit the Bank of Mum and Dad for a loan to carry them through. No wonder he's finding it hard to drop off to sleep at night.

Barry's mobile rings, and 'Stephen' appears on the display screen. For a fleeting moment, he considers not answering it. Trying to fake polite conversation is going to draw on his reserves at this point, and his supply of patience is dwindling.

'Alright, mate, how's it going?'

'Grand, Barry. How's the wife?'

'Blooming! Shopping for Ireland, but that's nothing new.'

'Yeah?'

There is a shred of hope still clinging on, like a barnacle to a sinking ship. Men don't call other men for chats or to discuss the weather. Maybe Stephen has seen the sinking ship's distress flare and is coming to the rescue.

'Well, look, another job has come up here. Now, it might not be your cup of tea, you know? Probably not of interest at all, in fact...'

'Try me,' Barry surprises himself with a laugh.

'Yeah, you never know. It's just that, well, like I said... it's a big company, lots of movement here, you know?'

'Yeah?'

'Yeah, the guy who got the solicitor job you applied for... well, he was a legal counsellor before that. Had been in the company a long time. Anyway, looks like his old job is up for grabs now that he's in the new job.'

'Oh?'

'Yeah, I mean, look – I don't think it pays as well as the job you originally went for. About five grand less, I heard. Something like that. They're looking for an immediate start. I mean, it might not be suitable for you. But, look, if you think you'd be interested... you'd be a total shoo in. I mean, you're overqualified, really. They'd be lucky to have you. I just thought that you could use it as a foot in the door, you know? Your one Sue in HR asked me to suss you out, see if you're interested at all. Being the runner up for the last job and that...'

'Yeah, I mean...'

'You could keep your eyes peeled for other openings once you're in, you know?'

Barry pictures the one hundred and ninety euro per week job seekers allowance. Rebecca would spend that just on shoes. A salary of five grand less than his own job, which is currently circling the drains, doesn't seem too shabby. It beats the dole queue, hands down.

'Listen, Barry. I'm putting you on the spot, here. Have a chat to Rebecca and sleep on it. Sure, give us a buzz tomorrow, yeah?'

Barry pictures the buggy with the price tag. He remembers the worry on Rebecca's face when he revealed the news about the redundancy.

'You know what, Stephen? Yeah. Tell them I'm interested.'

'Really? Nice one. OK, then. Listen, I'll get Sue in HR to give you a call later to thrash out the details. She can send you a job description, get the contract sorted and all that jazz. We can grab some lunch next week then, yeah?'

'Nice one, mate. Owe you one.'

Only ten minutes have passed when Sue from the Human Resources department calls. Naturally, Barry plays it cool. By the end of their brief conversation, Barry has negotiated a marginal increase in the salary. It's a token amount, but he is feeling good about it. A lifeline has been thrown just in time, and he has grabbed it with both hands.

He dials Rebecca's number immediately. He can practically hear her smiling. He can feel the relief pouring down the phone.

'I knew you would do it,' she cheers. 'Thank God.'

'Thanks, baby. I'll pick up some takeaway on my way home tonight. Might be a little late.'

At five minutes to five o'clock, Nigel shuffles past Barry's office door with his coat on.

'Nigel? Nigel!,' Barry calls to him.

'Yes?'

'Yeah, I think I'll let you buy me that drink, after all. Better make it a double.'

Thirty One

The animal shelter was such a joy on Sunday. Even though Tammie insists on doing all of the lifting, she was glad to have my help. Last week, a gorgeous cat called Marmalade had been found on the side of the road, and then gave birth to five kittens. We have named them Cosmo, Marguerita, Mojito, Mimosa and Harvey Wallbanger. In between walking Bailey, our poodle in residence, and organising feeds, I watched the kittens snuggle into Marmalade as she purred and licked their little heads.

Monday morning came quickly, and I made the journey into the office. The great thing about being eight months pregnant in February is that you can wear layer after layer of knitwear to try and cover up your now monster sized bump. It's bloody freezing out, and the man on the radio said that there is a chance of snow. I've got a chunky cardigan and a scarf over a polo neck jumper in the naïve hopes that people might think that the thickness of the cable knit explains my bulk. The only trouble is that this bump refuses to be disguised. I catch sight of myself in the car door as I stand sideways. The little girl from next door gawps in her driveway. I'm the size of a small country at this stage and feeling absolutely pants about myself. Speaking of pants, they just don't make them big enough lately.

The weight gain is probably nothing to worry about. I'm sure it's totally normal. After all, Dr Grainger would tell me to lay off the pies if there was a problem. Everybody piles on the pounds when they're expecting their first baby, don't they? Look at poor Jessica Simpson. She's foxy now, though. And, I mean, I'll totally work it off after the baby comes. No, really I will. I'll talk to Barry again about the personal trainer to help whip me back into shape. Posh Spice makes it look easy, and she's popped a few out by now, hasn't she? It's not too late for me. I could be skinny again one day, like the day I skipped down the aisle, tightly packed into a glorious size ten.

Emer says that post pregnancy weight loss is a multi million Euro business. It must be. Look at all of the 'Mommy and me' gym classes advertised around the place. I think some of them use their babies as weights to work off those mommy bingo wings. It looks hilarious; I sometimes watch them through the window of the gym café and lick the chocolate off an éclair.

It's simple, really. Once baby arrives, I'll just switch to a no-carb /low-fat diet and take up running. Or cycling. Or pole dancing. Done! I saw Amanda Holden on 'Britain's Got Talent' days after popping another kid out. I'm sure I could do the same. Not the judging in front of a live audience bit, the looking stunning part. And I'm sure that the stretch marks will simply melt away when the fat does. Easy peasy!

The sweat is pumping out as I waddle into the office and remove the scarf and cardigan. It's not my intention to do any actual work, you understand. Fat chance of that when there is a little acrobat doing somersaults inside my body and using my bladder as a safety net every five flipping minutes! I mean, I'm far too poorly to jump through Harry's hoops like Fifi the over zealous circus poodle. Even sitting at a desk all day would be totally out of the question. Why, you ask? Plenty of women work all the way through their pregnancy without missing a day, you say? Get over yourself and get some work done, you think? Well, you asked! As I may have mentioned, I've got the bladder of a small child in potty training, and need the loo approximately every three minutes. I'm not joking. It's hardly conducive to a productive days work, now is it? My temper is shorter than a Kerry Katona marriage. Also, my knickers are riding up my bum and I am unable to retrieve them, which has put me in foul form. Honestly, don't annoy me today – it won't end well for you. I'm constipated and trumping like a fog horn all at once. It's ironic, really. It would be in violation of people's right to health and safety in the workplace if I were to clog up their air with my putrid emissions. I couldn't do it to them. My back aches like a ninety year old woman who has been pushing a granny trolley about town. Lugging this brute of a child about the place is exhausting. I've been on a sick cert on and off for ages, thanks to the generosity and understanding ways of Dr Grainger. Also, I couldn't be bothered. Sorry, but it's true. I have more important things on my mind. Like, for example, how in God's name I'm going to birth this whale of a child and survive to tell the sorry tale.

So, why am I trudging my lard ass all the way into work, you ask? Well, I got a fat tip off from Judy that there might be a little office send-off for a certain pregnant elephant of a dedicated employee (that's yours truly.) She said it will be like a mini office baby shower kinda thing. Belinda has had four send-offs. They even had gifts and balloons at hers. I attended all four, purely for the goodies.

Anyway, Judy overheard Harry say that my sick cert runs out today, and that I might be gracing them with a rare appearance. He said that today might be the only chance to catch me before I go out sick again. Cheeky wretch! Little does he know that Dr Grainger has furnished me with another cert which I shall be flitting under his nose this afternoon. It's only fair to establish expectations as soon as I arrive. I don't want him disappointed when he realizes that I'm only here for the party and then limping back to my sick bed.

Dr Grainger has been great – she is money well spent if you ask me. She simply popped another sick cert in the post, seeing as how my back is still in agony. Also, I called her secretary on the hour every hour until she sent it. Like Jesus always said, 'God helps those who help themselves to whatever they want.' Oh, and I think the bible also says something like 'blessed are the pregnant, for they will rule the world.' It's so true.

Anyway, here I am back in the office, all be it reluctantly. I mean, it would be rude not to show up to my own party. All going well, I can go home for a nap afterwards, and then catch a movie on Netflicks. Besides, there is always cake at these affairs, and I could really use some cake right about now.

'Ah, Rebecca. You're in today!'

Harry doesn't say welcome back. He doesn't ask how I'm feeling. I stoop over a bit, like a decrepit woman.

'Yes. I've surfaced from my sick bed. I can't tell you the agony I've been in. Still am, truth be told.'

I wince a little and rub my lower back. I forget which side is meant to hurt, so I alternate. Best to hedge my bets.

'Right. OK, then. Let me introduce you to your replacement.'

Replacement? I wasn't expecting this.

We walk towards Harry's office. Or rather, he walks briskly and I waddle behind him like a morbidly obese duck. I put the palm of my hand on my spine to show him how much pain I'm in, but he doesn't notice. There's no chance of a bit of sympathy from the old git!

Harry has dark circles under puffy eyes. For a fleeting moment, I feel sorry for him. I mean, yes the man has been utterly intolerable and if I had the skill to make a voodoo doll I'd insert pins into his beady eyes. He has been a big fat meanie and is always so demanding. But just think about it for a second. The poor man will probably be landed with some useless temp for the duration of my absence. I bet she will be practically ancient – someone who is just punching in time, typing a few crappy letters before she retires and then dies. I mean, how can he possibly manage without me? Poor, sad, horrid, silly Harry.

Harry's hand reaches for the glass door to his office. I see a slender silhouette perched on a chair, legs crossed. Long hair cascades down slim shoulders.

'Rebecca, this is Mandy. She started last week. She has kindly agreed to start work before your maternity leave officially begins in order to cover your…eh…*sick leave*.'

'Rebecca, how lovely to meet you. I've heard all about you.'

The young woman can be no more than nineteen. She stretches her hand out to me. Instead of shaking her hand, I look to Harry for an explanation.

Is this some kind of sick joke? She's a flipping foetus! There are laws against child labour! This isn't a garment workshop in Malaysia, last time I checked! Is there a candid camera trained on me? Is the lighting man hiding amongst the potted plants?

'Harry?'

This is insane. For starters, this young one couldn't know the first thing about my complex, highly skilled job. It took me years to perfect my profession. I'm an artist! She is too immature to have any real qualifications. I bet she doesn't even know where the power button on my PC tower is.

Her hand is still outstretched, so I reluctantly shake it. Otherwise, I'd be rude, and that's so not like me.

'Hi.'

Right. I was caught off guard there for a second, but I've got it figured out, now. The reason for her recruitment is as obvious as a slap in the face – she is a total knock out. There is no other explanation. Harry is a dirty old man and wants a sexy assistant. What a cliché. He should be royally ashamed of himself.

'Mandy has a degree in Business Studies and experience as an office manager with PWC.'

'Oh,' is all I can manage. I have an Arts degree, but I've never once heard Harry tell anyone about it. Work experience in Price Waterhouse Cooper is pretty impressive. Maybe she graduated when she was twelve. It could happen.

'Everyone has been so friendly,' Mandy continues. I notice that her teeth are perfectly straight and Hollywood white.

'I bet they have...'

I decide that every male employee with a pulse has been swarming around her like bees on honey.

'So, I suppose Harry expects me to spend all day showing you the ropes, eh?'

I rub my back to show how painful a process that will be. It will be utterly inconvenient. I mean, 'Murder She Wrote' is starting in an hour.

'Well, I mean, I think I'm up to date.'

'Up to date? Sorry? Up? ...To date?'

'Well, yes. I ... Harry showed me the invoice tracking system. It's a little out of date, so I upgraded the software, you know? Made it a bit more efficient? It can run reports now. Much more user friendly.'

I'm staring at her boobs. I'm sorry, I don't mean to. Is that odd of me? It's just that they are so perky. It can't be normal. They are gravity defying. My head is tilted to the side, I'm trying to predict what would happen if I accidentally bumped into her. Would they deploy like airbags? Or are they rock hard like footballs?

'Well, I mean, yes...' I try to pull my gaze up to her face. That's perfect, too. Symmetrical, and friendly and fresh. There is a pout to her lips.

'I didn't get around to that... software thingy... What with the crippling pain in my back and all...Oh, that reminds me. This is for you, Harry.'

Harry doesn't need to open the folded white sheet to know that it's a cert. He knows the drill by now.

It turns out that Mandy has already replaced me. Can you imagine? She has accessed my computer files. One of the traitors in IT got her logged in without my password, or my permission for that matter. I feel completely and utterly violated. No doubt by now, she will have stumbled upon my draft resignation letters in the 'personal' folder. The ones which insult Harry's bald patches. She will, of course, have seen my job applications to 'Vogue' magazine. She will have stumbled on to my internet browser history and discovered my penchant for celebrity news and candy crush. It will be just my luck if she has discovered my obsessive posting on www.mypregnancy.com and uncovered emails in my sent box marked with high importance to the Dr Grainger's secretary demanding that my ante natal appointments do not clash with my heavy soap opera commitments.

I swallow some panic bile. She might even have rummaged through the personal photos that I uploaded from my digital camera. There are some pretty racy ones from my hen night on there. Let's just say they involve a male stripper dressed as a Tom Cruise style pilot, a can of whipped cream and a large banana. We're talking baby oil a go-go, here. I'm sure you can work the rest out. I haven't had time to sweep the computer clean before my departure. She will have seen everything by now!

'So,' Mandy smiles at me. 'When are you due?'

I'm so on to her. I can see right through her act. Pretending to take an interest in my pregnancy is the lowest of the low.

'Four weeks,' I sulk. It's so unfair that I've got to be nice to this awful, perky teenager.

She plays the role of perfect princess well, I'll give her that. I imagine that she is one of those goody-two-shoes types who shows up to work before ten o'clock - an ungodly hour, if you ask me. Maybe she stays until five in the evening, or worse still, five past five. That's what a lick would do. I bet she doesn't even know that there's flexi time. Well, sorry, but I'm not going to enlighten her.

'Very exciting for you,' she twitters on.

I make a bet with myself that she is also the type to hand reports in *before* the deadline. I wager that she also types like the wind, and take minutes at board meetings without drifting off to daydreams about George Clooney. Perhaps, like her neat and tidy clothing, her sick leave record is equally unblemished. It would make you sick.

'Oh, by the way. I couldn't find any templates, so I made some. Hope that's OK?' she grins.

This girl is far too upbeat for my liking. Something must be done.

'Templates? Oh, yes…didn't find any, you say? Gosh! That's odd.'

I emphasise the word 'odd.'. I have absolutely zero idea what a template is, but I am looking at her like she is a complete simpleton for asking me. She has a flipping nerve.

'Anyway,' Harry interrupts. 'Let's all make our way into the conference room for some, eh… tea.'

The silly old fart still thinks that I will be surprised by his lame attempt at a party. I'll have to drop my jaw and say 'oh my goodness, what a surprise!' when I see everyone gathered around a cake. It has better be chocolate cake!

'I'll just say a quick hello to Judy. See you there in five,' I back away, remembering to limp and drag my left foot.

Judy is typing frantically at her desk.

'Judy, what the actual *hell* is going on in this God forsaken place? What do you make of perky tits over there replacing me? I mean, wow! Is she *awful*? Tell me she's awful. I need to hear how awful she is. On a scale of one to ten, describe the awfulness of the situation... one being 'you want to tear your hair out when she talks' and ten being 'she is the worst human being you have ever had the misfortune to meet'. Which one? Pick!'

Judy stops typing.

'Hi! Actually, Becks, she's really...nice.'

It's official. Judy has had a lobotomy in my absence.

'Nice? Oh, right. I see.'

Fine! Message received. Judy and Mandy are probably new office BFF's now. They probably have girly chats over salads at lunchtime and bond over cosmopolitans on a Friday night. They might have some private jokes by now. It's like secondary school all over again. Tara dropped me for the new girl who joined our class. She was skinny, smart, blonde and little miss perfect. I can see on Facebook that Tara got really fat. Ha!

'C'mon, Rebecca. Let's go to your party.'

I storm off towards the canteen, forgetting to limp. A small collection of colleagues have gathered in the conference room for my sad little excuse of a party. There is a cake on the table with 'good luck, Rebecca' written in swirly icing. Mandy and her perky boobs are here too, she is grinning at me like we are lifelong friends. Harry is clearing his throat. Oh, no. I think he's about to give a speech.

'Well, eh, welcome everyone. Rebecca, thanks for being here.'

There is a snigger from Brendan in Human Resources. I glare at him. He'd have a pretty shocking sick leave record too if he had a bowling ball with arms and legs, pressing against his spleen. I'd like to see how funny he'd find that.

I have forced my hand to my face in mock surprise, as Harry continues his insincere speech. 'We're all assembled here to wish Rebecca the very best of luck with her maternity leave and her journey into motherhood. I'm sure we'll all …eh, miss you and… eh, stay in touch.'

Stay in touch? What is the senile bat talking about, now? I'm hardly trekking unaccompanied to Outer Mongolia with only a pair of snow boots and a compass for company. I'm not about to fall off the face of the earth just because I'm having a baby. It's not like I'll be chained to the kitchen flipping sink! Once I secure a childminder (by which I mean of course mum, as she is free) I'll be off socializing and drinking low fat extra foam mocha frappaccinos with a shot of vanilla, with the best of them.

'Oh, and I almost forgot…' Harry is rummaging under the desk and retrieves a fancy gift bag with pale yellow tissue paper protruding from the inside. He thrusts it into my outstretched hand.

Finally, a gift! It's about time. Let's see what this tightwad has splashed out on. I've given the man the best years of my career. Scratch that, I've given him the best years of my life! I hope it's a solid gold watch. I could have it melted down at some 'Cash Your Gold' joint and go shopping. Or maybe it's some expensive Molten Brown bath products. Ooh! Or perhaps it's a fluffy robe for relaxing in, complete with matching slippers like the ones you get in a five star spa. It's a pretty big bag, so I'm guessing it's a bumper crop.

'It's from all of us.'

The entire room is looking expectantly at me as I fumble with the packaging.

'Thanks, guys.'

I tear at the bag while someone slices up the cake.

'What the…?'

'Do you like it?' Suzie the receptionist is waiting for my response.

'It's a…'

I have no idea what it is. How awkward is that? I can only describe it to you as a kind of an alien pod shape and it's plastic. There's a picture of a gurgling baby on the box. All I know is that it's not something for me. It's something for the flipping baby. The baby who, let me remind you, gets everything while I, having done all the hard work, get nothing.

I've never been great at the old fake-reaction-to-crap-gifts charade. I'm working on it. You see, my face is too obvious. One Christmas, Barry's mum gave me this hideous jumper. Honestly, my first reaction was to laugh. It was completely awful. It had a reindeer on it with a fluffy red nose and everything. I recall saying

'Ha-ha, Margaret, very funny.' Thankfully Barry interrupted me before I asked where my real present was. It was mortifying. I mean, I know that funky Christmas jumpers are all the rage now, but this one was desperate. Poor Margaret is the best mother in law you could ask for, so I wear it every Christmas just to show her what a wonderful daughter-in-law I am.

My colleagues are still staring at me. I'd better say something quickly.

'It's... lovely.'

'You don't have one already, do you?' Mandy is fluttering her ridiculously long eyelashes. They must be false. No-one is this good looking for real.

'No, I...'

Clearly I don't have an alien pod thing already. It would be ridiculous to have two. Unless, I guess, aliens need a spare in case they can't get home? But wait! It's got a picture of a milk bottle on the side. That's a clue.

'Oh thank goodness!' Suzie cheers. 'Cake, Rebecca?'

'Yeah. Large slice, please.'

'Judy! Judy!' I hiss. 'What the flip is it?' I point to the gift, which I have shoved back in the bag, upside down. 'And why is there nothing for me?'

'What? Oh, I've no idea. Must be some ...baby equipment or other? Sure, I wouldn't know.'

'It's a baby bottle sterilizer,' Mandy startles me.

'Of course it is!' I laugh. 'Ha-ha, got you! Yes, I was just seeing if Judy knew. She's crap with babies, ha-ha, crap. Not a clue! Isn't that right, Judy?'

Judy is now in deep conversation with the ridiculously attractive but ridiculously young intern.

'Well, my sister had one for my nephew Ben,' Mandy gushes. 'He's three now. Such a cutie. Oh, I just love babies.'

I hope to God she doesn't show me a photo of him. He might have sticky out ears and I might laugh and then that would be cringey.

'Oh, Rebecca, I'm so envious of you.'

'Yes, well. Thank you, Mandy. I'm sure when you are all grown up, you'll meet someone nice and... Anyway. Being pregnant is great. I mean, I just love it so much! Such fun! The magic of ... eh, life. Apart from the crippling back ache. And the heartburn. And the piles. God, the piles are a nightmare.'

'Oh...I see.'

'Yeah. So, anyway,' I take Mandy by the elbow for a private word.

'About Harry. Total plonker. Don't let him fool you, right? He'll be all nicey-nicey to you at first, and then wham! It'll be all, 'oooh, Mandy, fax this' and 'oooh Mandy copy that'. Seriously. Don't be a door mat, you hear? If I were you, I'd tell him where to go. Works for me. The man's a real slave driver He'll respect you for it in the long term. Go on, tell him now.'

'Harry? Ah, no. He's being great.'

'So, Rebecca. Not long to go now, eh?' Suzie interrupts us.

'No, just four weeks.'

'Wow. And listen, are you sure you're not carrying a litter in there, ha-ha.'

'I'm sure.'

That joke is beyond wearing thin, but I remind myself to be on my best behaviour for the next twenty minutes until the cake runs out and I can get out of here.

'Oh, this one will be a bruiser for sure, ha-ha! But seriously though, Rebecca...' Suzie leans in closer and whispers. 'Is your doctor concerned about the size at all?'

'What? No...'

'The baby's not... a bit on the big side, then?

'No!'

'Right. Good. Of course not. Great. I'm sure there's nothing to worry about. Oh, did you hear about my niece Holly? Had a very rough time of it with her labour. Now, the baby's fine. Thank goodness. It's just that Holly had severe pelvic bone damage...'

'Oh. Ugh. Will you excuse me a moment, I just have to...' I try to dream up an escape plan on the spot.

'She's in severe pain, Rebecca. She can't walk or anything. Might need surgery.'

'Thanks Suzie. Thanks a flaming bunch.'

It might be a bit like jumping from the frying pan and into the fire, but I've managed to escape Suzie and her horror story fiasco in favour of Amanda from accounts. Now, yes, I know what you're thinking. Isn't Amanda a total and utter bore? Yes, she is. Thanks for remembering. But! She hasn't got any kids, and therefore doesn't have much of an opinion on pregnancy and labour. Hurrah! I might get to finish my third slice of cake in peace if I'm lucky.

'So, how are you feeling these days?' Amanda enquires. She's not having any cake. Says she has a gluten intolerance, but judging by her protruding collar bone, and tiny figure, I doubt it.

'Dreadful, Amanda. Dreadful. Been off with back ache. Can't lift a finger at home, either.'

I think I detect a smirk, but it's gone before I'm sure.

'Oh, and don't get me started on the heartburn and flatulence, either. Awful.'

'Oh…'

I'm like a whoopee cushion these days, I'm trying hard to not to let any air escape, but it's no good.

'Oh, sorry. Full of wind.'

'Oh… so, have you thought of any baby names you like yet?'

'Ehh…'

Amanda has touched a nerve. Barry and I have yet to agree on a baby name. There's still time, but it's making me a little edgy. Naturally, I've Googled celebrity baby names for inspiration, but Barry simply poo-poo's every one of them with a snort. All we can agree on so far is that we don't want anything common like Brad (even though Brad Pitt is a hottie) or Brittney (even though Brittney Spears is one of the best performers of our time). We also don't want anything kooky or sickening like Apple or Princess. The name must be classy like me, with an air of importance. I don't want anything boring that every second child has, either. Who wants their kid to raise their pudgy little hand in school along with five others, when their name is called out at role call?

'Well, Amanda, I like the name...'

I'm cautious. I don't want her scrunching up her nose when I announce a name that I adore. That would be like a pin to my balloon. A couple of years ago, Belinda in the office announced that she was expecting another boy and planned on calling him Ethan. We all smiled politely and nodded our heads in encouragement. Some said 'lovely.' Some said 'great.' I said 'Oh yes, like Ethan Hawk – I fancy him!' However, one of our accountancy colleagues with zero people skills decided to make an unforgivable faux pas. She announced that she found the name pretentious, and said that since Danni Minogue had named her first born Ethan a few years back, it was no longer unusual. Cue burning cheeks on Belinda, and uncomfortable shuffling amongst the rest of us. She could have at least had the decency to wait until her back was turned so that we could say it behind her back like normal people do.

'Oh, I just don't know!'

Thirty two

Barry's new job is so jammy. Not only does his contract state that he is entitled to loads of sick leave and holidays, he's even allowed time off to attend an ante natal visit with me. You'd never catch that Nasty Nigel giving him any time off. When the time comes, Barry will get three weeks paternity leave on full pay. Just as well, he'll be exhausted from all of the nappy and bottle duties while I recover. It will take all of my strength just to ring my little bell.

We've put it off for ages, but here we are at the public health centre, all signed up for a day long ante natal course. I've got a pretty good idea now about what to expect from the labour, but poor Barry hasn't got a clue. As the old saying goes, ignorance is bliss. The other thing about the course is that Barry will get a few tips on how to bath the baby and change nappies and what not. He can fill me in once he gets the hang of it.

'Pull in there,' I instruct Barry.

'Where, Queen of Sheba?'

Oh, that's just my nick name. Don't worry, Barry is saying it ironically. He wouldn't be brave enough to say it otherwise. It all started a couple of weeks ago when I flat out refused to drive anymore. Unless of course there's an emergency, such as if I was alone and ran out of crisps, or there's a flash sale on in Next. Barry is like my chauffer on the weekends, now. He refuses to wear a hat and call me madam when he opens the door.

My reluctance to drive is due to two issues: Firstly, I'm tired. Concentrating for long periods makes me sleepy and my attention span is rubbish. Secondly, I'm fat. I mean it! I'm not even saying it so that you can say 'ah, no, you're not!' and then I can feel better about myself and enjoy a slice of cake without feeling guilty. I'd know you were lying to my plump face. Anyway, when you have the belly of a sumo wrestler, getting in and out of the driver's seat in Barry's Jag is pretty tricky. Like my fat ass these days, the car is low to the ground.

On the rare occasions that I drive, I have to recline the seat all the way back to home-boy-in–an–R&B-music-video proportions in order for my bump to avoid the wheel. I'm just not sure that I'm cool enough to pull it off! Also, last week, on a desperate nachos run to Tesco, I got wedged in the car. I might need some counselling to ever truly get over the horror of it. Don't laugh, it was traumatizing. Imagine a whale in a bathtub and you're on the right track. In a nutshell, I'd parked too close to the next car, and had convinced myself that I was svelte enough to slip out. Turns out I was not. Lesson learned. In future, I have to find two empty parking spaces together so that I've plenty of room to waddle out.

'Pull in, Barry!'

'I can't, baby' he circles the car park again. 'The only space left is a parent and child space.'

'Exactly, you nutter.'

In other news, I am now getting away with calling Barry a nutter. I don't mean it, really. It's the hormones talking. I don't know why, but he's not arguing back about anything these days. Says he's worried about my blood pressure. It's hilarious. I'm like a toddler without boundaries. I might even have a full-on tantrum in the sweetie aisle in Dunnes Stores, and see what happens.

'We can't park there, Queen of Sheba. We don't have a child with us.'

'Eh, hello? What do you call this, Barry? A football?'

I laugh and gesture to my belly to make my point. He reverses the car and parks. Like I say, I'm getting away with holy murder. I might try my hand at some serious demands later, and see if he objects.

A woman with twins in a double buggy throws Barry a dirty look as she walks through the car park and sees that we have parked in the parent space but have no accompanying brat in our back seat. By the sound of the crying tots and the redness of their thighs, I'd guess they've just had their vaccinations. Remind me to delegate this task to a nanny when I hire one. I'm not great with needles.

'Come on, Barry. We don't want to be late.'

It's fun playing the Queen of Sheba and getting away with it. I feel like your one out of Dynasty. You know her, she married that oil tycoon and wears big sunglasses. Alexis Carrington, that's her. I just need a nice big hat and a fur coat to swan about in and I'm all set.

'Here, hold my bag, will you baby?'

'Why?' Barry attempts to challenge me. In fairness, a pink leather handbag is not a good look on him.

'It's heavy, Barry. I'm not supposed to lift things. Remember?'

'Good lord, what have you got in there?'

'Don't be ridiculous, Barry. You exhaust me.'

'I'm serious, Becky. It weighs a ton.'

'Nothing! Goodness! Just a can of deodorant, right? I get sweaty. And spare shoes. And some lunch. And a two litre bottle of Coke.'

He's looking at me like my marbles are skittering across the car park.

'I'm hypoglycaemic! I get the shakes if I don't eat!' I can't say it with a straight face.

Barry shakes his head as he holds the main door open for me.

Judith is the public health nurse delivering the course. She says she has been delivering babies for forty years. I'd say she's seen some ugly ones on her time. I'll ask her later. Judith is making her way through the group to make introductions. As per most of these cringe-inducing courses, we are arranged in a circle and must introduce ourselves aloud.

'Hiiiiiiiiiii,' the first couple simpers in unison. They are holding hands and their heads are tilted towards each other.

'She's Babs,' says the man.

'And he's Gavs,' says the woman.

'Babs and Gavs,' they laugh.

They think they are so cute just because their names rhyme. Also, I suspect that they rehearsed that little introduction. It's unforgivable, I tell you. They think that they are cuter than us. I roll my eyes. They are one of those annoying couples who finish each other's sentences. It should be banned for reasons of being too smug.

'Welcome,' Judith smiles.

I've decided that I'm going to address them only as Barbara and Gavin to show them who's boss.

'We are thirty eight weeks pregnant,' Barbara grins.

'Pfft. *We!*' I nudge Barry with a snort. 'She said we*!* Although, they do have matching bellies!' I crack myself up.

'Anyway,' Barbara continues. 'The pregnancy is going great. It has brought us closer together.'

'Huh! What is this? Couples counselling? Flipping 'Share Your Emotions week'? Who asked them, anyway?' I snigger to Barry. He shushes me and says I need to keep my voice down.

'Of course,' Gavin jumps in. 'Since Babs can't enjoy a drink, I'm off the gargle as well.'

'Pfftl!' I nudge Barry. He doesn't respond.

'Might help with his beer gut, though.' I whisper and poke Barry in the ribs. 'You could do the same.'

Barry has his index finger over his lips like a five year old in a junior infant's class obeying the command 'ciunas.'

'In fact,' Gavin drones on. He is starting to bore me now. I don't recall Judith requesting a detailed life story.

'Anything on the naughty list right now is off limits for me, too. No soft cheese, pate, shellfish ...'

'Thank God I don't eat anything fishy or foreign. Hey, what have you given up for me, eh?' I hiss at Barry.

He doesn't reply. He doesn't want to get in trouble for talking in class.

'Great! Well, let's hear from the next couple,' Judith is looking at Barry and I. It's our time to shine. I send Barry a telepathic message to stay quiet and let me do the talking. If we're the soul mates that I think we are, he'll receive it. It's a test.

'Hiiiiiiiiii everyone', I smile at the group. I tilt my head towards Barry and try to hold his hand, but his arms are folded, and I can't reach his fingers. He knows nothing about body language. Barry and I need to be the best couple here. *We can nail this!*

'I'm Rebecca, this is Barry. Becky and Baz!'

Barry shoots me a look. He detests his name being shortened in any fashion. I plough on, undeterred.

'I'm due in three weeks. It's a girl.'

Cue dramatic pause so that everyone can revel in how cute we are.

'We're going to call her Swayze. You know? After Patrick Swayze.'

Barry's eyes widen. 'Eh, well, the jury is still out on that one, ha-ha.'

Barry obviously didn't receive the telepathic message. We need to work on our non-verbal communication if we're to be the best couple. He needs to take this more seriously.

'We'll see what you have to say about that when they show the video, darling. Ha-ha.'

'What video?'

'Shush, love. Anyway, I know what you mean about sacrifices, Gavin. I myself am only having one drink. Instead of wine, I enjoy a Baileys these days. Sure, that's made out of milk. Great for the calcium. Baby's bones, and all that jazz. Also, I only drink Sangria if it's made from real fruit. Vitamin C is very important for, like, skin... and stuff. Barry's off the booze, too, aren't you, baby?'

Barry nods mutely. There is a sharp intake of breath. The group are staring. They will probably get straight on to the 'Joe Duffy' radio talk show after this and report what a heroic brave person they met today. 'Only one drink' they will say. 'Baileys for the calcium!' The might nominate me for 'best pregnant person 2016' in some humanitarian award. It could happen.

'Ok, then,' Judith has made her way through the six couples in attendance.

There is a pretty cute French couple. He gives her foot rubs and back massages. I'll be having words with Barry later to get him to step up his game. I won't bore you with the details: let's just say that we're the best couple by far.

Sure enough, the TV is being rolled out on a trolley and is hooked up to a VCR machine.

'Now for a little video,' Judith blows a layer of dust off the old video cassette and inserts it into the ancient machine.

'Told you, Barry.'

Judith presses play and I take a deep breath. Emer warned me about this. Apparently, they play the same 1970s birth video on this course every year. It features some hippy, mellow couple with matching perms. My eyes are squeezed shut for most of the film. Let's just say that this movie was made prior to the invention of waxing. Nightmares tonight are a distinct possibility.

The French chap, Philippe, leaves the room, pretending to have a coughing fit. He's closely followed by a heavily pregnant Adele. This definitely bumps Barry and I up to the position of number one couple. Philippe's cough mysteriously disappears as soon as he is through the double doors in into the safety of the corridor. I recognise a faker when I see one. I use this technique myself when Harry the Horrible quizzes me over petty cash.

'There,' Judith presses the power button as we exhale. 'That wasn't so bad, now, was it?'

I glance over at Barry. He's pale.

'Bit icky, wasn't it? Barry? You OK?'

Dear angels,

Please don't let my darling Barry faint. Besides inspiring zero confidence in him as a birth partner for the Impending blood bath, it's not the type of thing that a winning couple does. I don't want Philippe and Adele to beat us.

Ta.

PS if he does faint, don't let him bang his head. He can't drive me home if he's concussed.

'Hmm? No, it was fine,' Barry clears his throat. 'Fine.'

'Good.'

Barry is a terrible liar. Bless him.

Judith proceeds to pull a plastic pelvis and a naked black plastic baby doll from a canvas bag. There are some nervous sniggers from around the room. Judith simply wants to show how the baby's head passes easily through the pelvis and into the birth canal.

'Sorry about this, folks,' Judith is pushing and shoving the upside down doll through the pelvis, but it won't budge.

'Must have packed the wrong doll. Just a sec.'

Finally, the doll's head pops through the plastic pelvis, but the shoulders are wedged. The head is dented with the force of the shove. Phillippe stands, and is suddenly in need of a glass of water.

Barry smiles, but his knuckles are white on the handles of the chair. I don't think he can take much more.

Judith has gone through all of the pain relief options. I still don't believe that sucking on gas and air actually qualifies as pain relief. A brown paper bag would probably be more effective. As for the deep breathing and yoga positions, after six sessions of pregnancy yoga, I'm not so sure. Judith demonstrates the tens machine, but it looks like the 'Ab Pro Belly Fat Burner' that Barry bought me one Christmas (the Christmas where we had a huge fight and I accused him of calling me fat.). There's also something called pethidine, which is injected into the thigh.

We break for some coffee. Barbara and Gavin are both off caffeine. They say it's bad for the baby. They are really starting to get on my nerves.

'Now,' Judith starts the final portion of the class. 'Let's have a practical demonstration.'

The naked black baby dolly is back in action, and the distinct indentation on the tot's head is still obvious. Hopefully it's not permanent, or she will be bullied at dolly Montessori. Judith dips the dolly in and out of the bath, holding the doll in the crook of her arm. We all have a turn at the tiny nappy.

Adele used to work in a crèche. Frankly, she is quite the know-it-all. Barbara is expecting her third. I don't know why she's even on the course, she could run the damn thing herself. I think she's just here to show off. Barry and I put the nappy on backwards. He has never held a real baby in his life, and my experience is limited to say the least. I drop the dolly on her head when lifting her from the bath. She must have brain damage by now. In my defence, wet babies are slippery.

Back in the car, I turn my phone back on. I can see that there are three missed calls from mum. Barry has one also. We exchange a look.

'Mum? Everything OK?'

'Hi, darling. Sorry to interrupt the class.'

'It's over. What's up?'

'Are you on the way home, darling?'

'Yes. Why?'

'OK, darling. It's the cat.'

'Jess?'

'Yes, my lovely. I popped in to drop off some groceries…'

'And…'

'He's gone, darling. Just slipped away in his sleep.'

'What?!'

Barry is quizzing me, but I shush him.

'So sorry, darling. He looks very peaceful. I tried to move him to check, but he's gone.'

I can't speak. I'm afraid that if I do, I'll start crying and I won't be able to stop.

'He was very old, love. He had a great life. The best. If there's a cat heaven, he's in it. I'm just here in your house. Just come home and we'll talk OK?'

'OK,' I hang up and look at Barry.

'What happened?' Barry's eyebrows knit together.

'Jess died,' I manage.

A hot tear spills down my flushed face. Barry puts his hand on my chubby knee and keeps driving.

'I'm sorry, Becks.'

I don't know why Barry is apologising. This is entirely my fault. How did I not know Jess was going to die? How did I let this happen? Was he in pain? Did he suffer? Did I ignore him? Am I so wrapped up in the baby that I missed something? Our kid will probably have an indented plastic head, and severe nappy rash, since her parents don't know what on earth they are doing. We can't manage a black plastic dolly, and we can't even keep an elderly cat alive!

Thirty three

I have crossed over from sick leave into proper maternity leave today. That means that, presuming the baby is punctual, there are only two weeks to go until she comes.

A typical day consists of:

1.Lolling about in fetching fleece pyjamas (in a size 'large' which makes me feel yuk) and pink fluffy slippers. I refuse to get dressed, apart from at the weekends when Barry takes me out to a posh lunch. During the week, there is no point in dressing. Wearing the same maternity clothes on a loop is depressing. Besides, the maternity outfit choices are becoming even more limited as my girth increases. I don't want to morph into one of those Vikki Polard types, with their shirts riding up on a bare pregnant belly, stretchmarks on display for all and sundry. I have some pride, I'll have you know.
2. Calling Tammie for cat, dog and the occasional donkey update.
3. Reading trash magazines. I'm up to date on the celeb gossip, and can tell you who is getting a divorce and who hasn't lost the pregnancy pounds. However, I have crossed into new territory: I don't care.
4. Eating. And not just for two. We have gone way, way past that. Be quiet.
5. TV. It's not the same without 'Jess-the-amazing-water-bottle-cat' curled up on my lap.

I know what you're thinking: it sounds like bliss. I mean, it is. It's just that it's wearing a bit thin now, you know? I'm starting to feel a bit silly sitting around all week with nothing to do. I know I should enjoy the peace and quiet while it lasts. My little girl will be here in all of her pink glory in no time. I guess I should make the most of it.

I wonder what they're doing in the office right now. It's two o'clock on a Friday, which means I'd be in the middle of a Candy Crush tournament with Judy. The memories of the baby party are well and truly dead, like the flowers they bought me. I was too busy to put them in water. Judy's new BFF Mandy has probably made my role so uber-efficient that it will be barely be recognisable when I reluctantly shuffle back next year. If it wasn't for this pesky mortgage, I'd tell her to bloody well keep it. She will have de-cluttered my clutter, un-picked the chewing gum from beneath my desk, discovered my secret hoard of crisp wrappers, and charmed the entire board of directors into liking her more than me. She will have reorganised my entire filing system, robot style, which is entirely unnecessary. I already have a clear method when it comes to filing: items are either shoved under B for 'Bin it' or K for 'Keep it'. No need to complicate things. She and Harry are most likely scheming behind my back.

Still, I'm relieved to have finally broken free of that office slash hell hole. The inevitable is inching closer day by day. The sands in the hour glass are slipping downwards, and there are only a few grains left. The impending labour is starting to feel very real. At night, I dream of the bashed doll's head and the plastic pelvis. Who knows which day will be The Day? Will it be today? Will it be tomorrow? Will it be two weeks after my due date, with me in a frantic, crazed wall-climbing state? In a way, it's a bit like a band aid — it's better to rip the flipping thing off as soon as possible and get it over with than to slowly, painfully drag it out. Do you know what I mean? Of course you don't. No-one understands.

I dial Barry's number and tell the receptionist it's urgent.

'Becks? Is the baby coming?'

'What? No! Stop being so dramatic, Barry. Honest to God, what are you like?'

'But the receptionist. She said it was urgent. I was pulled from an important meeting with a client.'

'What? Oh right. Anyway, it is urgent, silly.'

'What is it Rebecca?'

Uh-oh. He's pronouncing Rebecca through his teeth, again. I suppose I deserve it. Yesterday, I left a message at reception for him that I was all out of Hagen Daz and to hurry home. The day before, I text him ten times until he stood up from the meeting and called me back to discuss my thighs. You see, I'd discovered a stretch mark on a thigh, which is preposterous, and absolutely not my fault. His patience is running thin.

'I've changed my mind.'

'What?' I can hear Barry clicking on his keyboard in the background, which means he's not giving me his full attention.

'Don't take that tone with me, Barry. I've decided. I can't go through with it. It's too awful. The baby will just have to stay put.'

'Right... Can we talk about this when I get home?'

Barry sounds tired. He says he hasn't been sleeping for the last few weeks. Something about a mysterious fog horn sound emanating from my side of the bed. Well, I can't help it if I can't sleep on my side anymore and have to roll onto my back, OK? Once he doesn't wake me, that's the main thing.

'Fine,' I hang up with a heavy hand.

According to the final chapters of 'What to Expect When You're Expecting', I'm meant to be nesting by now. I don't think tidying the contents of the digital recorder box counts. The definition of nesting is as follows: the overwhelming desire during the latter stages of pregnancy to move furniture about, re-slate the roof and clean curtains until you exhaust yourself. Well, no thanks. I don't feel the urge. Maybe I could delegate the nesting to Barry. He'd love that.

I call Emer. No answer. Since she went back to work, she's back to the full slave driver pace. I picture her whipping the subordinates who have been slacking off in her short absence. With any luck, my baby might come early, like Charlie did. My patience, like my view of my feet, is slipping away. I plea bargain with Jesus. He owes me one.

Hi JC,

I'm still preggers. Not long to go, hopefully. Listen, I know you're like, super busy and stuff. All that drama in poor countries, or whatever. It's all very sad. But listen, whatever you do, don't let me go so far over my due date that I go from drama queen to completely irrational. I'm not the type to be neurotic as you know, but that would seriously be pushing me too far! A few days early would be super fab.

PS, did you not get my message about the stretchmarks? Honestly! They're getting worse!

I pick up my baby book, but quickly put it down again. The chapter on Caesarean sections (and the bit about slicing through muscle) is putting me off my six pack of Monster Munch. You see, there's something else niggling about in my brain. My cousin once knew a girl in her office, whose neighbour's best friend's auntie did not bond with her child. What if that happens to me? I'm not exactly the type to win 'most likely to be a kick-ass mom' in a high school year book. What if I look at her little face and don't think she is the most beautiful thing that I have ever seen? What if I don't find her adorable or funny or charming?

Let's face it, most babies are born pink, squealing and wrinkled. My friend Tracey's baby was like a little old man in a white cotton sleep suit, and had the temperament to match. I might turn to my baby after delivery, and instead of gushing some mushy sentiment such as 'I knew I loved you before I met you', might say something wildly inappropriate such as 'that's nice, but does she come in blonde?' It's possible! The midwife would then raise the alarm, call social services, and brand me an unsuitable mother.

What if this whole parenthood thing just doesn't work out? What if, like the owner of the bedraggled dog in the 'A puppy is for life, not just for Christmas' adverts, I'm bored of the whole thing and decide that walking, pooper scooping and feeding are a drag? A baby is even more work than a puppy. Babies cry more, produce more poop and are not as cute. It's far too late to suggest adopting a dog to Barry, he seems really sold on this whole baby thing.

And the pesky thing about kids these days is that they are non returnable. I mean, they are a permanent fixture, like a tattoo. I don't know why this is only occurring to me now. Even in the mid-season sales at Dundrum, I can change my mind within fourteen days. It does not affect my statutory rights, apparently. I can march back up to the counter at Brown Thomas and say to the super skinny sales clerk that I have decided that peach is in fact *not* the new pink, and furthermore the jeans made my bum look big when I took them home, tried them on in front of a less flattering mirror and caught my husband stifling a snigger. No such luck with a baby. You just walk right out of the hospital whether you're equipped or not. Even a dog requires a licence!

I don't bake. I don't sew. I don't kiss sore knees better and apply plasters. Will I be like Tiffany, one of the teen mums I saw on MTV's '16 and Pregnant' show, who screams at her toddlers whilst riding public transport, wearing a tracksuit? Eighteen years of responsibility is suddenly like an invisible chain that hangs around my plump neck, pulling me to the ground.

Emer says it's just nerves, and that it's time to cop the flip on. This baby will be loved, there is no doubt about it. I soothe myself with thoughts of a year off work, and the sparkling diamond eternity ring which Barry no doubt has already selected. It had better make it a blinder!

Mum lets herself in with her spare key and pops her head around the sitting room door.

'Hi, darling. Just a quick hello.

Mum clatters around the kitchen, putting enough treats in the fridge to feed Michelle, Jim-bob and their nineteen-and-counting kids.

'I'm on my way to Bridge Club, darling. Any sign of my grandbaby yet? She will surely be running out of room any day now, ha-ha. I'm popping in later to see Nuala after her hip operation, then having my hair done, then to the post office. I'll swing past after that.'

'Fine.' Trust mum to prioritise retirement club soirees, postage stamps and senile old biddies with dodgy hips.

Thirty four

Emer is such a pet. She has organized a whole day of pampering. She knows this salon in Dundrum that has a pregnancy package, and I'm booked in for the works. Apparently that yummy mummy from TV3 goes there all the time.

'Won't it be tricky to get out for a whole Saturday without baby Charlie?'

'Not at all,' Emer scoffs. 'We're training in a new nanny. It'll give them a chance to get to know each other better. Did I tell you the last one turned out to be a total disaster, by the way? Only lasted a month. Kept asking for weekends off! And me taking on the company restructuring, can you imagine? Had to let her go. The new girl is great. Marla. Or Marlena. Martha. Something like that. Works every hour God sends and sends the money home. Honestly, Rebecca, you'll have to be so selective, now, when you're recruiting one. I can recommend a good agency if you need it.'

'Great.'

Barry would choke if I suggested one of Emer's expensive agencies.

'And are you not exhausted being back at work? I mean, Charlie is just three months now. Didn't they allow you more time off? I think it's EU law or something...'

'Nah, sure what's the point in me staying home? The nanny has everything under control. Anyway, the office was falling apart without me. There's a bit of a mess needs sorting out.'

Charlie is a model baby. He has been smiling since he was six weeks old, which is two weeks ahead of the developmental milestone, whatever that means. And Emer says it definitely wasn't wind, it was a proper, gummy smile. This indicates a high IQ, she says. He's been on a strict 'Gina Ford' baby schedule and thriving on it, apparently. Every minute of his day is monitored with German precision. He attends something called 'baby sensory classes', and Emer says he's top of the class. I'm not exactly clear what the criteria for excellence is, but I think that infants staying conscious for long enough for the enthusiastic teacher to jingle a bell in their fat faces would suffice? Apparently, there's a lot more to it than that. Go figure.

Oh, and have I mentioned that he is sleeping through the night? Of course he is. Was there ever any flicker of doubt that he wouldn't? Of course not. Emer says he has been sleeping through the night since the hospital. He just glugs ten ounces and passes out. It sounds like a night in the pub for Barry. Already the kid is an over achiever like his mummy. Oh, and he has a tooth already, too. Didn't even cry. Perhaps that's how future presidents teethe. I wouldn't know.

'Anyway, lovey. I'll get some shopping in while you're having your treatments done. I want to update my wardrobe. Then we'll go for our blow dry after, yeah?'

By the time Emer and I meet three hours later, I'm floating on air. The pregnancy massage was incredible, and the manicure pedicure has me feeling like a million dollars. Even though my feet are so swollen that they look like they belong to the elephant man, the beautician wasn't afraid to give them a good rub and soak. The French polish dresses them up a bit and although they are still hideous, they are at least semi-presentable now. Sadly, the only shoes that still fit now are a pair of purple crocs that are ghastly and don't match any outfit.

Emer's new seven seater mummy wagon is so slick. She's only got one kid and doesn't plan on having any more, but there's plenty of room to ferry Charlie and his pals about when he's playing rugby for Ireland, or travelling to his advanced chess tournaments. It's got Bluetooth and touch screen sat nav, in case you get lost on the school run. Each child seat in the back has its own cup holder and DVD screen: excellent for keeping the little darlings quiet. We're cruising down the M50 towards 'Hair by Franc' in Sandyford.

Half an hour later, my hair has never looked better. All the guy did was blow dry it, spray it and charge Emer a staggering amount, but it's fab. I can't stop touching it and checking myself out in her passenger seat mirror.

'Thanks for a fab morning, babe' I kiss Emer on the cheek as she clicks her seatbelt in. 'Honestly, it was just what I needed.'

'Let's pop into your mum on the way home, yeah?' Emer suggests as we veer onto the M50 exit. 'You can show off the fab hairdo.'

'Sounds good. Not sure if she's in, but sure we can swing by.'

When mum answers the door, she's all dressed up.

Ah, sorry mum',' my face falls. 'You're obviously on your way out, are you? We just thought we'd stop by after our pampering morning.'

'Not at all, love. Pop in for a cuppa. I'm expecting some ladies for a little afternoon tea later on. Come in, Emer.'

Mums kitchen is full of pink balloons and there are a dozen ladies clapping as I enter. A banner with 'baby shower' dangles from the kitchen press. The dining table is full of pink cupcakes on a fancy cake stand.

'Oh my God!' is all I can manage.

I scan the room and see my aunties and friends.

'Emer, I can't believe it!'

She is beaming. 'Surprise!'

'Well,' mum grins. 'We couldn't let you go without a baby shower, now, could we?'

'Sure any excuse for a bit of an 'auld party, eh?' Margaret kisses me hello.

In keeping with the theme, the champagne is pink. I think Emer picked it up on one of her wine runs to France recently. I don't want to gossip, right, but I think that's another reason for the seven seater mammy wagon. You can fit so much booze in around the baby seat and the boot is big enough to house your own defibrillator resuscitation kit, should you overdo it. You can bring a shed load of booze across on the Ferry, no hassle. It's definitely something I'll bear in mind when I trade my car in. You have to be practical about these things.

'God, that's good champers, Emer,' we clink glasses. 'Cheers, my dears.'

'Glad you like it. There's a case for you to take home and pop when baby arrives.'

'Ah. You think of everything!'

I shove another pink cupcake into my gob. The pink butter cream would make you cry, it's like it came straight from heaven. There are cute little baby things decorating the tops. Mine has a little pram made out of icing. The chatter in the room is deafening. I suppose that's what happens when you put a dozen ladies together. Karen is in full flight, knocking back a gin and tonic and chatting to my aunties about her little ones at home. Joyce is nursing a lemonade and has dropped the bombshell that she's expecting again. Some people are gluttons for punishment.

'Emer,' mum announces. 'Have you met Ian's partner Cindi?'

'Yes, of course. Hi, Cindi. How are you? And you've only two weeks to go as well!'

Cindi is looking good. I hate to admit it. Emer nods politely as Cindi explains her thoughts on raising her kid a vegan. I'm busy weighing up the cost of being caught topping up my champers glass with the benefit of the glorious thirst quenching bubbles.

'Best of luck, anyway,' Emer excuses herself. 'I'll just pop to the loo.'

Emer flashes a wide grin as she passes. Now I'm trapped with Cindi.

'So, the cousins will get to meet each other soon, eh?' Cindi smiles.

'Yes! Although, I have a feeling I might deliver early, you know?'

I'll be damned if I let Cindi win the race. I'm not going to be Paddy last while she parades her baby about.

'Yes, who knows.'

'So, you didn't have a baby shower yourself, then,' I dig.

'No,' admits Cindi. 'I mean, your mum offered to throw me one...'

I bet she's trying to steal my mum.

'You know, seeing as how my own mum passed away and all...'

'Oh. Oh, I didn't know that.'

Oh, great! Now I feel like a cow. And at my very own baby shower, too. Thanks a bunch!

'It's OK. It was a long time ago. We were very close, though. Really miss her these days.'

There is a stake being driven into my shrunken, jealous heart. I've been so unkind to this girl, and she doesn't even have a mammy to call her own. I should be ashamed of myself. I vow to make it up to her.

'And your mum has been like a mum to me. She's the best.'

It's true, my mum is the best. And who am I to hog her? There's room in mum's heart for one more daughter, and I've never had a sister. The ice in my frozen heart melts. Maybe there is hope for Cindi and I. Maybe we could learn to love each other. Maybe we could be kindred spirits, soul mate BFFs. Maybe...

.

'Besides, baby showers are so commercial! It's all just a money making racket developed by the greedy multinational corporations, you know? It's a conspiracy.'

Then again…

'Right…a conspiracy…Mum?!'

Mum click clacks over in her high heels to top up my champers glass.

'Ah, cheers mum. Bottoms up, Cindi. I'll just knock this one back and then I'd best dash to the loo. Bladder is the size a postage stamp these days, ha-ha.'

'Rebecca! I can't believe you're drinking alcohol!' Cindi is wide eyed.

'Well,' I bluster. 'I can't believe you're not! Honestly, it's lush. Want a sip? Emer only buys the best. So cute that it's pink, isn't it? Here, try it. Looks yummier than that sugar free Fair Trade lemonade you have, you don't know what you're missing.'

Emer covers the lip of her glass as I try to fill it.

'Sure, make it a spritzer, Cindi!'

'Don't you know the damage you're doing? Research on foetal alcohol syndrome shows-'

Cindi is so dull, so I wave my hand dramatically. The champagne is making me kind of giddy, and I don't want a lecture during my 'pink champagne elegant baby shower' thank you very much. She can sling her Greenpeace- supporting, hippy-dippy, holier-than-thou hook.

'Not at all, Cindi. It's grand. My consultant is a real doll. She believes it's absolutely fine to have a tiddly bit. You know, on *special occasions*?'

I gesture around the room to emphasize the special occasion bit, and to show how only fun people like me get parties thrown in their honour.

'Time for presents!' mum diffuses the building tension.

Thank God! Cindi was starting to ruin my buzz. We move excitedly into the sitting room, where Emer and I perch next to each other on the couch.

'OMG!' she mouths as I giggle. She had been ear-wigging the whole time, and can't believe what a drag Cindi is being.

'OK, bags going first with the pressies. Here, chicks!' Emer presents a small package in pink tissue paper with a pink bow on top.

'But, Emer! You already gave me a present! The super fab buggy, remember? And the pamper morning?'

'Yes, yes, but this is a little something *just* for you!'

Mum and her sisters crane their necks. I strip off the tissue paper and laugh. It's the case of pink champagne she promised me. Classic!

'Well, you seem to like it so much!' Emer nudges me.

Everyone cheers except Cindi.

Mum passes me an envelope. Inside the ornate card she has written 'to my darling daughter on her baby shower. We are so proud of you.' Everyone smiles as I open up the white paper folded neatly inside. There's a voucher for a family session with a photographer.

'Oh wow, mum. So thoughtful. Thank you.'

Margaret has lovingly made a new mummy survival kit. It's both hilarious and touching. There are eye shades, body lotions and little luxuries. I squeeze her hand in appreciation. Joy presents me with a little pink outfit for the baby.

'And here's mine,' Cindi passes me a parcel wrapped in brown paper. I'm guessing it's eco-friendly recycled paper.

'Thanks so much, Cindi,' I smile sweetly. 'Wow, thanks, it's a...'

'It's a baby sling,' Cindi proudly announces. 'I hope you don't already have one? It's great for carrying the baby about with you everywhere you go. Great for bonding.'

'It's... lovely,' mum attempts. 'So... clever.'

It's made out of hemp, whatever the hell that is.

'Smashing, thank you.'

Mum clears away the wrapping paper and tops up the glasses. Emer is passing about some cocktail sausages and miniature quiches. I polish off a plate, it's great for soakage. Cindi refuses anything. She has brought her own, unappetizing food. Being a vegan must be so annoying. Also, tofu tastes like cardboard. I'm just saying.

Karen's on her third G&T, and is getting quite animated when describing her kids vomiting bug last month.

'Tell us again about the curtains getting splashed,' Auntie Marie laughs.

'Girls, honestly, it was like the house had the plague. I started answering the phone, like, 'hello? Mrs. Murphy's launderette, can I help you?'' she wipes away tears of laughter. 'There was that much washing to get through. And sure, my husband was the worst patient of the lot. He didn't think he was going to make it!'

The room erupts with raucous laughter.

'Everything OK, Cindi?' mum's kneels next to Cindi, who is squirming on the couch.

'Fine, thanks Joan. Fine.'

'You don't look fine, love.'

'Just a bit of a cramp. Nothing, really.'

Cindi rubs her belly and smiles.

'Might be the 'I-can't-believe-it's-not-chicken' nuggets? Or the fakin-bacon butty? Maybe the Quorn sausage rolls aren't rolling right?' I suggest. I like to be helpful, it's just in my nature.

Cindi doesn't come back with a smart quip. That's odd.

'You don't think maybe you should go home for a rest, do you?' mum offers.

'I can call Ian to come and pick you up?'

'Yes,' I add. 'Best head home.'

Cindi is just being an attention seeking party pooper. If she dares go into labour at my 'pink champagne elegant baby shower' party, I'll never speak to her again.

Ian arrives ten minutes later, and carts Cindi home for a rest. My shoulders drop in relief. This has been the best day ever. Maybe Barry and I can have another baby next year. It might be the pink champagne talking, but being pregnant is fab!

Thirty five

Being pregnant sucks! There are only two days until my due date and I've had enough. There's nothing much on telly this morning and Netflix is on the fritz. Our broadband is down due to the bad weather outside. First world problems are such a pain!

Here's a newsflash for you. Remember how Cindi went home during the baby shower? I thought she had indigestion from the vegetarian food? Well, it turns out she was in early labour. Thankfully, she didn't steal my thunder by popping a baby out during my champagne elegant baby shower' party. Luckily, she didn't ruin mums upholstery with leaking waters. I'd say that's a nightmare to get out. No, it turns out that she was in one of those slow labours that goes on for days.

I was trying to sprawl in peace on the couch nursing a pink champagne hangover, and Ian was on the phone to mum every shagging five minutes with an update. Of course, I told Ian to hang up and just call mum back when the baby arrives. The updates kept interrupting Corrie! Mum secretly loves the drama of it all. She has been back and forward from their flat to her house like a tennis ball at a Wimbledon match. There was much pep talking, mopping of brow and drinking of organic nettle tea.

Three days later, Cindi went into 'proper' labour, and went to Holles Street. This lasted around forty eight hours, and she was in excruciating pain throughout. Mum, despite my protests, has told me all of the gory details. I tried sticking my fingers in my ears and saying 'la la la la' but she kept talking, and some of the horror got through to my ears. Cindi refused an epidural, intervention or drugs of any kind. The mind boggles.

Anyway, finally baby Oisin was born. Mum says that he has a glorious head of black hair on him just like when Ian was born, and that he's the most handsome little chap she has ever seen. Ian sent me a picture text of him. In fairness, he's pretty cute, even if he is a mixture of Ian and Cindi's genes. Mother Nature is a wonder.

Cindi has been breastfeeding around the clock and she checked herself and the baby out of the hospital as soon as she was medically fit to do so. She wanted to get away from the 'artificial' setting and get home. I'll probably get around to seeing them when I'm not so busy.

Last I heard, the baby cries all night. It has cheered me up somewhat to hear, but I'm still fed up. You see, it's official: Cindi has won the race. She popped one out before me. And the grand prize? Oisin is now mum and dad's first grandchild. Yes, I know they will love our little girl just as much, I get it. But the first one is special. You know it's true, so don't try and tell me otherwise. Mum has been crying at the drop of a hat and is so caught up in the emotion of it all. I worry if she'll be as excited about the arrival of our little one.

A text comes in from Emer.

Hey chicks. Hang in there. Not long now! Hope u have UR feet up XX

I look down at my swollen feet on the leather poof. Yes, they are up, but they are amid crisp packets and half cups of cold tea. I'm not sure how I didn't notice it before, but the place is a flipping mess. I've been too busy wallowing about to see that the house is far too filthy to bring home a baby. I mean, would you place a new-born in a Petri dish? Probably not.

The bedroom is like a war zone, and the bedroom is like a bomb went off. These two rooms have been my main living quarters since I finished work, so it's no surprise that the rooms are in complete disarray. The kitchen would shock even Kim and Aggie, and they've seen it all. Everything looks dirty. Things looks out of place. All of a sudden, I can see a thick layer of dust everywhere. Pictures are not hanging straight on the walls. There is a creepy looking spider web trailing from the chandelier in the sitting room to the flat screen telly. It's as if my rose coloured glasses have been swapped for smudged, streaked ones.

I call Barry in a panic.

'Barry, you need to come home this *minute.*'

'Jesus, has it started? I can be there in, like, ten minutes...'

'Don't be stupid, Barry. I'm not in labour.'

'Oh? Something wrong, Becks?'

'Yes, Barry. Something's wrong. Have you failed to notice that our house resembles a homeless man's armpit? Has it escaped your attention that we are about to bring a helpless infant into this den of germs?'

'Well, I mean, it needs a damn good tidy, but... listen, Becks. I'm at work now, so can we chat about this later?'

'No we cannot. *Later* might be too late. *Later*, I might be pushing our baby into the world. *Later*, I might be in excruciating pain. *Later*...'

'OK, I get it.'

'Did you see how filthy the curtains are? And I don't think the stains on the landing carpet are going to come out. And, Barry, I think that we need to replace the tiles in the kitchen. They're too dirty to clean.'

'Sounds like a serious case of nesting. That's a good sign, I hear.'

'Don't be ridiculous, Barry. This has nothing to do with nesting. I'm not a flipping *bird* for Christ's sake! I'm telling you Barry, I looked around and it's like our house was suddenly invaded by aliens overnight. Very messy, filthy, litter bug aliens!'

I can hear Barry talking to someone in the background. His hand is over the mouthpiece, trying to muffle the conversation, but he is fooling no-one.

'Everything's fine. I'll be back into the meeting in two secs. OK.'

His hand is off the mouthpiece now.

'Becks. Listen, relax. I'll ask mum to pop round. Give you a hand.'

'Eh, no you will not. No way. I'm not having my mother in law discovering my secret shame, Barry. There's a new programme on Channel Four just like that. Will you organize a cleaner? I'll supervise. I'm good at supervising.'

'Becks, we can't go splashing out on cleaners right now.'

'Oh, fine! FINE! I'll just pop up on the roof and fix the loose slate, shall I? Absolutely. Oh, and I'll defrost the freezer on my hands and knees while I'm at it, eh? I can scrub the carpets by hand. No problem!'

'Rebecca. I'm at work. Chat later. I'll call mum.'

Click!

'No!'

It's too late. The eejit has hung up on me! And me *with child*, and everything! That's strike one! I will Google DIY-divorce later, he is really asking for it. Any judge in the land will see my side of the story. He might even have to face a prison sentence for cruelty to a pregnant person. That would be just smashing.

A bed of sweat is forming on my forehead. Bear in mind that it's March and about two degrees outside. That's panic sweat, if ever I saw it. His mother only lives ten minutes away. She could arrive here and discover my horror home before you can say 'lime scale'. I mean, this is the reason I don't invite in-laws around! I don't like cleaning! I dial Barry back, but he doesn't answer. His mobile is engaged. That means he's talking to her right now! That's strike two!

Within five minutes, I'm dressed. I'm not taking any chances that my mother in law will not only discover my dust bowl house, but will find me in my pyjamas at lunchtime. I race around like an escaped lunatic.

Half an hour has passed and I'm red in the face from the sudden burst of activity. The downstairs has been hovered and the floors mopped. If the doorbell rings now, at least the floors are clean, so she'll think I'm only a semi slob. I even got that nasty spider web (and hopefully its creator) sucked up into the vacuum hose.

Ten more minutes pass as I slap on a full face of makeup. If Margaret was going to come, she'd be here by now. I'm probably worrying over nothing. I think I'll click the kettle on and try and catch an episode of 'Keeping Up Appearances.' That Hyacinth is such a hoot. The rest can wait until later.

The doorbell rings just as Daisy and Rose are getting out of Onslow's backfiring car. I haven't even finished my tea yet. Through the grubby curtains, I can see two figures at the doorstep. Surely not!

I fire off a quick panic prayer.

Hey, God, me again. Waynetta Slob, here. Any-who, quick one for ya. Please, please, please don't let that be my mother in law at the door. She can't see the house looking like this. I'd be scarlet if she saw my Landry pile! Worse than a crown of thorns. Worse than being nailed to a cross. Let it be some bible basher, and I swear I'll invite them in for tea and not laugh at them. Let it be a charity fundraiser, and I swear I'll sign up for a monthly donation to help build wells in Africa. Anything!

Over and out, Becks.

The doorbell rings again, through the frosted glass, I can make out two short figures shuffling restlessly. Maybe God has his out-of-office sign on, because he has declined my request. This is just not my day. There's no point in hiding under the duvet. There is no point in pretending I'm not in. One of the shapes is peering through the letterbox while the other shape is fumbling in her purse for a key.

'Ah feck!'

With reluctance, I open the door.

'Mum. Margaret. What a surprise.'

Margaret is wearing jeans. I've only ever seen her in pearls, nude heels and Chanel inspired jackets. I didn't even know she owned a pair of jeans! They look brand new and she has teamed the jeans with an immaculate sweater and pumps. Mum is in some sort of tracksuit bottom and sneaker combo. Her hair is held back with a hair band. It's like they've had some kind of a make-under.

'Hi, darling. We're here to help. The cavalry has arrived!' Mum is decidedly giddy.

'Come in. What's going on?' I'm on my best behaviour because Margaret is standing next to mum.

'Barry called, Rebecca,' Margaret smiles. 'Said you could use a wee hand with getting the place ship-shape before the big arrival. Let's get stuck in.'

Before I can protest, Margaret is doubling back to the Volvo to get some supplies. She returns with a steam cleaner and bag of various attachments for tackling tricky corners, a feather duster and a plastic bucket of cloths, furniture polish and detergents.

'So. Was anyone hurt, Becks?'

'No, mum,' I deadpan.

'When the bomb went off, I mean ha-ha.'

'Ha-ha mum, very funny.'

'Now, how are you feeling, dear?' simpers Margaret, but does not wait for an answer.

'I was telling Joan how wretched I felt when I was expecting my Barry. Two weeks over, he was.'

She turns to mum and stage whispers. 'Eleven pounds, Joan. Quite the drama.'

'Goodness, Margaret.'

My fake smile is slipping. This is a new kind of hell. I love mum and Margaret, but cleaning with them all day will be like being prodded in the posterior by devils.

Margaret says that like a professional cleaning crew, we will start from the top of the house and work our way downwards. She is quite naïve to use the word we, since I'm too huge to give it much wellie. I kind of hover over them as they work, offering cups of tea and listening to their waffle.

'This is fun!' Margaret cheers as sheets of dust flit off the bedroom lightshade, much to my total mortification. It's quite sad that this is her idea of fun.

I don't mean to be disloyal to Jesus, right, but my silent begging is going out into the universe and I don't care who answers. God, Buddha, Allah. The tooth Fairy... I don't mind. Just don't, whatever you do, let anyone open the wardrobes and uncover where I have shoved all of the bedroom clutter this morning. Also, I am screwed if anyone opens the hot press. Mum reads my mind and goes straight to that very location.

'Good lord,' she declares. 'Just as well I enjoy folding, eh?'

Who actually *enjoys* folding?

Next, mum tackles Laundry Mountain. She will need an oxygen mask and a mountain climber stick to reach the top. I place the items on hangers and fold the clothes away in wardrobes as she whittles down the load. Soon, the mountain is shrinking.

'Ah,' mum takes a damp cloth to the window sills, which resemble a dead insect cemetery, and fills a little rubbish bag with dirt and dead flies. 'Our little grandbaby will have such a sparkling house now.'

Despite my deep, crippling shame, I'm starting to enjoy watching the house take shape. Mum and Margaret have become close pals since the engagement, and now they have a grandchild in common. It gives them something to bond over. It gives them something to fill their dull lives. I feel my eyes sting with tears. It's either from the emotion of it all, or else due to the fact that mum is Fabreezing everything in sight. It's probably a little from column A and a little from column B.

Now, for legal reasons, I feel I must mention the following. I don't want anyone in the family to sue me, should a life threatening cleaning related accident occur on my watch.

1.Margaret is in her early seventies. Don't be fooled, she's pretty sprightly. If she says she is well able to lift my mattress without being crushed to death, in order to Hoover under it, then who am I to argue? I don't want to insult her. That would be ageist, and I'm against anything that ends with 'ist'. Think about it. Nothing good ends with -ist. There's terrorist, sexist, masochist. I rest my case.
2. Margaret's house is pristine, like a stately home. She did everything for Barry when he was living at home, including cooking gourmet meals. She spoon fed him and wiped his bottom until he was six. I suspect that Barry is smuggling out some of his shirts to her at the weekend for starching and pressing, as I've noticed that

they have disappeared from the laundry basket, and I sure as hell am not doing them. Also, he eats for Ireland when he visits. Margaret shops at Donneybrook Fair and always has top nosh. Barry makes me look bad by playing the starving kitten routine at her house. This is strike three, by the way.

3. Just because mum has a dodgy hip and I'm all grown up doesn't mean she's off the hook. I'm her child and always will be, no matter what age I am. She's tied to me until one of us dies. That's just nature, I'm afraid. I didn't write the rules.

4. Margaret is keen to demonstrate her new steam mop. She bought it off one of these infomercials on the TV, which is very trendy of her, and is very proud of her new addition. She calls it Steamy Sam. I don't think I've ever named a kitchen appliance before, but who am I to judge? It costs a bomb, but she thinks it was a steal. She says that my mop is useless and should go in the bin. She is going to buy me one of these little beauties, and that I can chose the colour. I don't know whether to be grateful or highly insulted on behalf of my limp, smelly grey mop which has now been cast into the wheelie bin.

'No, sorry. No, I don't think I have the hang of it yet. Show me again, Margaret?'

She's on a roll with Steamy Sam, so I'd hate to interrupt her. I'm standing there looking dumb as she demonstrates in every room of the house – the thing has an attachment for every crevice and surface you can imagine. The kitchen tiles have never sparkled to such a high sheen. They're like something out of a show house.

'Let's have a little peep at the nursery, Rebecca,' mum tip-toes towards what used to be the spare room. Barry has transformed it. What was once a dumping ground for un-hung pictures, the battered ironing board and the overflowing laundry hamper, is now a haven of peace and tranquillity. The only thing missing is a sleeping baby. It's overflowing with cuteness. Barry is a not great man for the DIY, but I must admit, he has poured his heart and soul into the nursery, bless his eager little heart. There is an intake of breath as the door is opened.

'Oh my Goodness.'

Margaret places her hand over her mouth and her eyes fill up. 'Isn't Barry marvellous?'

'Would you just look at that,' mum puts her arm around me, and I well up too.

Major brownie points have been awarded to Barry. His title of 'Golden Boy' with Margaret remains unchallenged. You see, I'd delegated this particular task to him. Men are better at building and assembling things. Besides, I'm busy building and assembling a baby from scratch, and with no instruction manual. In fairness, Barry has done a great job. His three strikes evaporate.

Despite my constant teasing, Barry has managed to assemble the flat pack wooden cot, changing table and rocking chair. The cream teddy bear wallpaper border matches the curtains and lightshade. An old fashioned teddy bear sits at the head of the cot, next to a folded blanket. I never knew that Barry had an eye for interiors. Perhaps I should stop shushing him so much the next time we're in Ikea.

We stop for a tea break, and I rustle up some hobnobs and slice up the chocolate fudge cake that mum brought from Marks & Spencers. It's lush, and just what the doctor ordered.

'Ah, this brings me back,' Margaret smiles. 'Before Barry was born, I remember the nesting period. Honestly, I was like a mad woman. I even painted the ceiling! Can you imagine me?'

'I went mad with the nesting, too. When I was expecting Ian, Rebecca was only two and a half. And quite the little minx, too, let me tell you. Anyway, I got it into my head that all of the walls needed cleaning. I was convinced that they were slightly yellow looking. By God, they were shining when I was done!'

Barry arrives home at a six o'clock.

'Hi, baby,' he kisses my forehead. 'And hello baby,' he rubs my belly.

'Well, now!' he turns to Margaret and mum. 'Would you take a look at you lot! Sitting around drinking tea, is it? Here, pass us a choccie bikkie. I thought you'd be dusting the ceiling by now.'

'A well-earned pit stop for the workers,' mum chips in. 'We've been busy.'

'Great job on the nursery, love' Margaret beams. 'You put a lot of work in there.'

'Well worth it. Nothing's too much trouble for our jellybean,' Barry smiles.

Barry exchanges his suit and tie for jeans and a t-shirt. We are like the crew from 'Sixty Minute Makeover', tackling the kitchen presses with a bottle of Flash and a packet of J cloths. After another hour, the house has lost its sticky, dusty feel and I feel my anxiety slip away.

Thirty six

Honest to God, if that flipping mobile phone beeps with another 'good luck' text or an 'any news?' phone call, I will throw the shagging thing down the toilet and give it a hard flush. My mobile battery, as well as my patience, is running low.

Please, whatever you do, don't tell me to hang in there. If you were overdue by nine days and feeling like a watermelon on legs, you'd be cranky too. I never thought that I'd say this out loud before, but I'm sick of TV. Reading a book demands too much concentration, since I have now developed baby brain and cannot focus on anything but the pregnancy and how crazy it is making me.

Mum is the biggest culprit, bless her, but I know she means well. She takes the gold medal. Not only does she call me on the half hour every hour (even Sky News cannot boast the same dedication to the pursuit of news), she calls to the house, too. OK, she brings goodies, otherwise, I wouldn't let her in the door.

Barry is in second place, taking the silver. Yes, yes, he's terribly worried about me, and is just anxious that everything will go well. I know! He's all stressed about his first baby, I get it. But seriously! He's acting like he has nothing to do all day in the office but ring me for updates.

Margaret is in third place, taking the bronze. I know I should cut her some slack. Barry is her only child and this is her first (and probably *last* judging by my foul mood) grandchild whose arrival is fairly imminent. Everyone needs to calm down, OK?

Instead of asking 'any news?' Emer asks 'how are you feeling?' It's marginally better. Also, she sent me flowers yesterday, with a note that read 'thinking of you, babes', so she remains in my good books.

'Hey, baby.' Barry is home from work, and undoing his tie.

'Any news?'

'Don't.'

'What, baby?'

'Just don't.'

'I'm only asking.'

'Well, don't. If there's news you'll be the first to know. Followed secondly by mum and then Margaret, and then Emer... and then the whole flipping world, since they are texting me every five minutes!'

'Ah, Rebecca. They mean well.'

'I know, Barry. I've had enough. I'm like Moby bloody Dick over here. Her head is, like, weighing down on my pancreas. I can't even walk properly. Look at my swollen feet! This is ridiculous.'

'Yeah, well, not long now, eh?'

'That's what you said last week.'

'Yeah, but Dr Grainger said it'd be any day now, didn't she? Said the head was fully engaged or diluted or whatever.'

'Dilated, Barry, not diluted. She's not a bottle of orange squash. Anyway, what would she know? She won't admit me or give the baby her marching orders. Says I have to wait.'

'Okaaay… so wait, then.'

Barry retreats to the kitchen to make the dinner. He knows there's absolutely no point in arguing with a forty weeks pregnant woman. Even as a highly skilled solicitor with mediation skills under his belt, this is one battle he will never win. In fact, there are no winners in this situation. It's just a big fat pile of misery.

I try to console myself with an episode of 'Murder She Wrote.' It's a repeat, which takes all the joy out of it. There is no point in watching, because I already know that it was the butter-wouldn't-melt niece that bopped her elderly auntie over the head with a bronze bust from the ball room, and then pushed her down the stairs and tried to make it look like an accident in order to inherit the country mansion with extensive stables. It's so obvious, now. I don't know why Jessica Fletcher didn't cop on to her wicked ways sooner. Senile old bat.

Barry peeps his head out of the kitchen to ask me if I'd like some tea.

'Yeah, Barry. Thanks. And sorry. But listen, Dr Grainger said that if I don't have the baby by Wednesday, she'll induce me.'

I push back the tears. I have come to fear the word induction as it becomes a distinct possibility lurking in my future. Emer says that this involves breaking your waters with a knitting needle kinda thing.'

'That's good,' Barry calls from the kitchen.

'Good? Eh, no, Barry, that's bad! I do not want to have some gel stuff inserted you know where, and then have to writhe in pain for days on end in ward three, thank you very much. I've done my research. I'm not going to let that happen.'

'OK.'

That's all Barry says these days – OK. I could tell him I have decided to shave my head and join a cult on a spaceship and he'd say OK. I think he's afraid of me.

'What is this?' I stare in disgust at the tea that Barry has just handed me. I'm not being paranoid, it smells funny.

'Raspberry leaf tea, baby.'

'Eh, pardon?'

'One of the ladies in the office said that it was good for getting labour started, you know? So I stopped off at the health food shop on the way home.'

'Oh, I see!' I laugh. 'Telling all the girls in the office, eh?' I wink. 'What did you say? That I'm a total grump and you can't take it anymore? Poor Barry, having to listen to me, ha-ha. Well, the baby has been served an eviction notice but has no immediate plans to vacate the premises.'

'Ha-ha, very funny. Anyway, I thought it would help.'

Thanks.' I sip the tea. It's heinous, so I spit it out and make a toddler face. Barry guffaws.

'Ah, Barry, what the hell are you trying to do to me?' It's so bad I'm in stitches, and it hurts to laugh so hard. I think I may have sprayed Barry with the tea.

Sorry! So, what's for dinner? Smells nice. I'm famished, haven't eaten in a whole hour.'

'Curry.'

'Ooh, nice one, Barry.'

'Chicken vindaloo. Nice and spicy. The girls in the office also said this might do the trick. You know, get things moving.'

'Worth a try.'

The curry is delicious, but it would burn the backside off Satan. If I didn't know better, I'd check myself in the mirror to see if steam is escaping from my ears. Thankfully, I've a stomach lining made of lead, having built up my resistance to Indian food over the years. Barry is gulping back the water and mopping his brow.

'Oh my God! Listen, Becks, if this doesn't work, there's another method that we can try. You know, seeing as how uncomfortable you are and all.'

'Oh?' Barry is such a pet. I take back all the moody things I've said to him. Well, most of them.

'Yeah, we could, you know... have sex. It's meant to get the old labour starter... I mean, if you...'

'No,' I cut him off. I've a face like Anne Robinson swallowing glass. Barry is the 'Weakest Link' here, no question. 'No chance. Barry, I can't even make it up the stairs without gasping for air. Cop on, will you?'

Barry just laughs. 'Ah, worth a try!'

'Right. That's it. I literally can't be pregnant a day longer.'

'Ah, hang in there baby,'

'No. I've had enough. Let's get this baby out.'

'Becky, you know as well as I do that we have to just wait it out, OK?

'No.'

'Baby, I'm afraid you don't have much choice in the matter.'

'Get the car started, Barry.'

'What? Eh, no need to kick me out, ha-ha. You need me here in case the labour starts.'

'And fetch my luggage. We're going to Holles Street.'

'But… are you in labour? Does it hurt anywhere? Have your waters gone?'

'No, Barry. Don't be silly. I just need to go in and, oh I don't know…ask them to get the baby moving, or check me in. Come on.'

'Ah Becks. Listen, Dr. Granger told us only to go in if the contractions start. I know you feel like you're off-side, but the referee is about to blow the whistle. You're into injury time now, you know?'

Whenever Barry talks in football metaphors, I'm lost. I mean, fashion and shopping metaphors are fine, but sports are sweaty and unnecessarily complicated.

Barry can tell by my eye rolling that his little coach pep talk has not landed.

'OK. Fine, Becky. Let them check you over. They'll probably just send us home.'

Barry manages to get me off the couch like a crane lifting a tonne of cement, and I waddle to the car. It reminds me of those awful American TV shows where there is an intervention for some poor morbidly obese chap who has gained so much weight that he is trapped in his house and keeps ringing for pizzas. Have you seen that show? It takes five of them to get him in the ambulance and all the toothless neighbours are gawping on their front porch. When they lift his arm they find the remote control and some sweet wrappers between his bracelets of fat. No joke, Barry says I'm being silly, but I'm telling you that I'll be heading in that direction if this pregnancy goes on any longer!

Barry hits every pothole on the way to the hospital. He says he's not doing it on purpose and that's just the state that Irish roads are in, bloody politicians and county councils have a lot to answer for. I should have used the loo before we left.

When we arrive at Holles Street, we're directed to the first floor and to the admissions desk. There's a pointy faced woman in her early fifties sitting behind a desk, and a mountain of paperwork in orange files surrounding her. She looks as though her day is going worse than mine.

'Hi, Barry smiles. 'This is Rebecca Costello. We'd like to see a doctor, please.'

He hands her the orange maternity folder with all of my details.

'See a doctor?' she peers over the spectacles at the end of her nose. 'Are you in labour, Mrs. Costello?'

'Well, eh, she's…very uncomfortable,' Barry attempts.

'Yes,' I snap. 'Today's the day. Yippee.'

The pesky paperwork has to be completed before this drill sergeant here will allow me through the double doors into where they keep the drugs. The power of the clipboard has gone straight to her head. Minutes later, I'm escorted to an examination room and a doctor pokes and prods me.

'So, you say your waters haven't gone and you're not in any pain as such...'

'Yes, I am in pain, *actually*.'

'OK, Rebecca. Where does it hurt?'

I know it's wrong of me, but I've decided that I've got to exaggerate. If I give some vague wishy-washy answer, they'll send me home, and I'll be back to square one. Even if they induce me now, something I've dreaded all along, at least I won't have to go back to the endless waiting game. Right. It's time to dig deep and remember my time at Mrs. Higgins stage school for gifted girls.

'Well, I mean, it's total *agony,* doctor... eh, when I walk. Baby is pressing on my, eh, appendix, or something. And my back is totally wrecked.'

The doctor, who by the way looks all of eighteen, is unimpressed. He rubs his eyes, probably on the last stretch of an eighteen hour shift, by the looks of him.

'Right. It's just that according to your medical history here, you had your appendix out in 1997.' He points to the offending orange folder.

'Did I say appendix? I meant my spleen. My spleen hurts. The baby is squashing it and needs to come out now.'

Barry's looking desperately worried about my spleen, but the doctor's expression hasn't changed. I'm about to demand that they page my real doctor, who Barry is paying for dearly, when inspiration strikes.

'Oh, yes... and I'm worried about the baby. Really, eh, worried...'

'Oh?' I've got his attention now. 'How so?'

'Well, come to think of it, she hasn't kicked in ages. She is so squashed in there, being nine days over. Probably crushing her own organs as well as mine.'

God, I'm good. Even I'm scared now. Maybe the baby really is in trouble!

'So, no kicks for the last hour, then?'

Dear Holy Mary,

I know that lying to a priest is a sin. I'm clear on that. I also know that telling porky pies to a policeman is against the law. But telling fibs to a junior over worked doctor on an eighteen hour shift in a maternity hospital? Hardly! Anyway, surely you know that lies in this case are absolutely acceptable. I've had enough. I want the doctors to give the baby a bit of a nudge. Not, like in a violent way. Just in a gentle 'get a move on' kind of way. I'm sure you understand, although I bet the baby Jesus wasn't this much trouble.

Ta,

Rebecca.

'Eh...' I pretend to think really hard about the question. My acting skills know no limit. The truth is that this kid is like an octopus on amphetamines, and my inner organs are probably black and blue right about now.

'No, I don't think so... no, nothing. Best to check me in. Maybe get the labour going and all that, yeah? Probably the best thing for the baby.'

'OK, let's get you to just lie here and we'll attach this monitor to your stomach. Just take a few sips of water every few minutes. I'll be back in half an hour to look at the results.'

Barry's eyes are wide. 'Rebecca, is the baby not kicking? Why didn't you mention that?'

'Relax the cacks, Barry. I just want them to admit me and get the baby moving.'

Barry is shaking his head. I don't care, he doesn't understand me.

'Rebecca, you can't just... *decide*... that the baby is coming. She will come when she's ready.'

'What evs.'

The doctor is back and is looking puzzled. Apparently, the baby is very active indeed, and not showing signs of any stress. None, whatsoever. In fact, she's having a gay old time in there.

'How strange! Thank goodness, doctor. Still, best to admit me, though. Get the baby moving?'

'Try going for a long walk,' the Dougie Houser look alike suggests.

'Sorry? A *long walk*, did you say?'

'Yes, it gets things moving along nicely.'

'Does it, now?'

'Yes, you could…'

'OK, let me lay this out for you, *Dougie*. Let me make this crystal clear. I am overdue by nine days. *Nine days*. That's two hundred and sixteen hours pregnant on top of the usual nine months pregnancy, and frankly -.'

'Yes, but I think if you can just…'

'Get… this… baby… out… now.'

I'm calm, but in a creepy kind of way. My teeth are on show, but I'm not shouting. You know when a boiling hot lava of rage is bubbling underneath the cracked surface, getting ready to spew the scalding magma all over anyone within a one mile radius, horrifically burning their skin and scarring them for life? Yeah, like that.

'Rebecca,' Barry takes my hand. 'Baby, let's go.'

Barry is not on my radar right now. I have a score to settle with this little teenage mutant hero turtle here, and I'm not going anywhere until he is firmly back in his box.

'I mean, what more do you people want from me, huh? You need to admit me and get this labour started off, quick smart. Get my private doctor on the line. Tell her it's urgent.'

'I'm not going to admit you. You can go home now and get some rest.'

I'm vaguely aware of Barry tugging at my wrist. The dense black warning smoke that precedes a volcanic eruption is thick in the air. Stand back! Run for your lives! The villagers are scattering, leaving their precious belongings behind. This is going to be a nine point nine on the Richter scale, baby!

'Listen to me, you little pip squeak. I've got t-shirts older than you. Not that they fit me anymore, but that's not the point. I demand to see a real doctor. Preferably someone who is old enough to remember the twin towers collapsing. Ideally, someone whose stethoscope wasn't manufactured by Fisher Price. Someone whose medical degree is not written in crayons. Perhaps one who is mature enough to grow facial hair and vote and…'

I've been asked to leave. The utter shame. I've been ejected from a maternity hospital. Barry is keeping quiet as he clicks his seatbelt in case I turn on him. We drive past the front entrance in silence. Even the ruffians on the front steps with their massive bumps sticking out as they drag on their cigarettes are welcome to stay when I am not.

'Sorry, Barry. So sorry.' I am suddenly very tired and emotional. I burst into tears.

'It's OK, baby. Let's just go home.'

We continue in silence for a few miles.

'I'm a big bag of raging hormones.'

'It's OK, baby.'

'And Barry?'

'Yes, sweetheart.'

'Please don't tell anyone what happened.'

'Don't worry. They wouldn't believe us anyway!'

Thirty seven

Its midnight and I can't sleep. It's impossible! I keep replaying my Jerry Springer-guest-type melt down. There's literally no position that is conducive to sleep then you are nine months plus ten days pregnant. Barry is oblivious, mouth agape. The poor sod has put up so well with my hormone fuelled rants. He's probably dreaming about fancy Belgian blonde beers and Cabernet Sauvignon and other things on my banned list, while I lie here, maternity pillow between legs, trying to get comfy.

I rub my enormous stomach. 'Ready to meet you, baby. Any time you're ready...'

Barry stirs momentarily and snorts. The baby outstaying her welcome is not all that's bothering me. Those niggling twinges are back. I noticed them when we got home from the hospital, and they are still there. It's nothing, really. I'm afraid to get my hopes up in case it's a false alarm. I squirm and pull at the duvet, which Barry has been hogging.

'Everything OK, baby?' Barry mumbles in his sleep. He's snoring before I have an opportunity to reply.

Best let him sleep. If this is the real thing, he'll need to stay vigilant when they're dishing out the drugs to make sure I don't miss out. The house is silent apart from Barry's deep breathing and the occasional 'divine' and 'sugar crush' from Candy Crush on the IPad. I'm on level three squillion now. When I close my eyes, I can see the candy balls lining up. I think I might have a mini addition.

By four o'clock, the niggles have become cramps and are coming every few minutes. I'm trying to breathe just like Carmel showed me in yoga class, but all I can do is ball my fists and scrunch up my eyes. I don't think I'm a natural at this yoga thing. Never mind, I can't be amazing at everything! I try to ignore the twinges and log onto Facebook, so I can roll my eyes at people's happy news.

At five o'clock, I sit on the loo. I just don't know what else to do. I daren't wake Barry in case it's another false alarm, because then I'll feel like a fruit cake drama queen all over again. It's becoming harder to ignore the pains, and I realize that I'm clutching the side of bath. I think this is it!

'Right,' I deliver my pep talk. 'Time to put operation GLAM into action.'

Oh, did I not mention this before? I've invented a new programme and its fab. It might catch on, and then I'll release a DVD and make a wheelbarrow full of cold hard cash. It could happen. Basically, I have decided that I'm not going to be one of those bedraggled mummies that you see in baby's first photo album. You know the ones? Think bed-head and panda eyes and you're in the right ball park. They clutch their new-borns looking like they've been dragged through a bush backwards, sans makeup. But that won't be me. Oh, no!

Look, I'm not delusional. I know labour is going to be hard. And long. I finally brought myself to read the last few chapters of 'What to Expect when You're Expecting' last week, and it wasn't pretty. This baby is going to rip out of my nether regions no matter what I do. I get it. But who's to say I can't look my best whilst doing so?

Now, some people have a birth plan. Each to their own. I have a GLAM plan. You see, there are certain steps that a mum-in-waiting can take when the signs of labour begin. Like the scouts say, 'always be prepared.' OK! So, I'll give you a quick run down.

G is for Gel nails. No matter how rough labour gets, these bad boys will not chip. Now, luckily, Emer's day spa package a few weeks ago covered this, and I had a quick top up coat done yesterday. The hot pink beauties are looking glorious, if I do say so myself. It would take a blow torch to crack them. No-one wants to visit a baby and have to look at the mother's ragged cuticles. I mean, come on! Mishka at the salon even did my toes also, as I can't even reach my feet anymore. They will look great in my peep-toe black fluffy kitten heel mule slippers as I totter about the maternity ward doing whatever it is that mothers do. I bought and packed a dressing gown to match too. So pretty!

L is for Lovely Locks. I'm lucky that, unlike Emer, I've gone into labour at home and I've time to preen myself. Believe me, I'm thanking my lucky stars. My roots were expertly done last week, so all I need to do now is to sculpt my hair with enough hairspray to ensure that it doesn't move an inch from my head.

A is for Apply the slap. I don't just mean put a bit of lippie on. God forbid! I'm talking a full face of makeup here, people. Labour could last hours. Days, even. I could sweat profusely. I could cry. The makeup needs to be applied with a shovel and powdered to cement-like proportions so that it stays on. Three layers of lipstick need to be applied, followed closely by a lip coating to make sure it's going no-where in a hurry. What's more, I could really use another layer of tan. I hear those harsh fluorescent lights they have in hospitals are not in the least but flattering. I strip down to my pants and flick open the tanning cream. Don't worry, I won't go overboard. I don't want them to think I'm some Essex wag with a bun in the proverbial oven.

M is for Medication, and lots of it. My first word when we arrive at the hospital will be 'epidural', and I won't tolerate any flitting about in that regard. I want to be dignified and pain free. Barry is under strict instructions to speak on my behalf if I'm in too much agony. We have devised a clever hand signal and everything. It involves a middle finger.

I text mum.

Hi. R u awake?

A text comes back at lightning speed.

Yes. What's wrong?

Ah, bless! My darling mum has obviously been afraid to sleep heavily in case there is news. She has probably been imagining all kinds of far fetched dramatic outcomes – the kind of things she has seen on 'Corrie.'

Ten minutes later, I hear her key in the hall door downstairs. By now, I've got the tan setting nicely and am halfway through the makeup. I've got an industrial strength can of hairspray balancing on top of the loo. In between contractions, I'm getting through my to-do list. All is going to plan.

'Rebecca! What on earth are you doing? All OK?'

Mum is in her dressing gown and slippers and has driven from Foxrock like the clappers.

'Hi mum, will you pass me that...'

I'm bent over the edge of the bath for about thirty seconds.

'Goodness, is this it?'

'…hairspray. Thanks. It's grand, we've loads of time. Everyone says to tough it out at home for as long as possible. Don't want another false alarm and then be either sent home or put into ward…three…'

I'm bent over again. I can't help it.

'Where's Barry? Darling?'

I point frantically, just as Barry pops his head around the bathroom door.

'Becky? Oh, hi Joan. What's up? Is it happening? Getting yourself all worked up in Holles Street probably got things moving, Becky.'

Barry rubs his eyes. He looks like an oversized child on Christmas morning. Except instead of Spiderman pyjamas, he's wearing Calvin Klein boxers and has the start of a beard.

'Barry,' my mum instructs. 'Yes, she's in labour. We need to get Rebecca in now, she seems to have started, alright.'

'Nonsense,' I wave my hand. 'Loads of time. It only started at midnight.'

'Midnight? Becky! Why didn't you call me? Have you been awake and in pain all this time?'

'Yup. Just let me finish my mascara and then…'

I'm gone again. This time, I can't straighten up for a full minute and it hurts like you wouldn't believe. I've never been punched in the gut, but now I've a pretty good idea of what that might feel like. I try to explain, but can't. For once in my life I have no choice but to shut up.

'Barry, will you fetch her a tracksuit or something easy to put on, and get the bags in the car.'

'The …pink …tracksuit,' I manage with great difficulty. 'Juicy…couture…with…diamantes…'

Barry needs very clear instructions when it comes to fashion. If he were left to his own devices, he would find some hideous woollen poncho at the back of my wardrobe that I'd forgotten all about, and team it with a pair of clogs or something hideous. That clearly is not fitting with operation GLAM, now, is it? Honestly, you've no idea. He needs guidance! Thankfully, I had left the tracksuit out on the spare bed next to the hospital cases, so even Barry couldn't mess it up.

Mum helps me into the tracksuit while Barry runs to our bedroom to throw his jeans on. He's wide awake now, and taking his daddy role very seriously.

'Right!' says Barry. 'OK. Right!'

Barry's eyes dart from me to mum. He's frozen to the spot.

'The car? The bags?' mum reminds him. 'Go on, Barry. I'll get Rebecca downstairs.'

Barry's tasks are very simple. I'm doing all the tough stuff (of which I will remind him every day until I die.) All flipping Barry has to do is:

1.Carry my matching Louis Vuitton luggage and purse to the car and into the hospital when we arrive.

2.Drive me to the hospital and make sure we get there in one piece. As much as he'd simply adore to whiz through a couple of red lights, 'Miami Vice' style, and explain to a cop that his wife is in labour, he has been warned to behave.

3. Allow me to squeeze his hand like you see in the movies. I'll really crush it just to make my point, you know? I've been practicing in order to build up the strength in my hand.

4. Not panic.

5.Make sure I get the drugs.

I will tolerate a little messing up from point 1 through to 4, but by God, he will feel my wrath if he messes up the last one.

In the car, I grip the upholstery. It's six in the morning and the traffic is minimal.

'Are you OK, baby? Want me to speed up?'

'I'm fine, Barry. We could have waited at home a bit …longer.'

'You're in pain. No point in taking any chances, baby. Damn! Every bloody light is red! I think I'll just step on it'

'Barry! Will you relax!.'

Barry manages to get a pretty jammy parking spot right outside the main entrance of Holles Street. He drags the two small pull-along suitcases in his right hand and holds my elbow with his left. We are escorted into the lift and up to the second floor. The same sour puss woman is sitting in the admissions office. I've decided to christen her Ms. Snootington.

'We're back,' I deadpan. 'Surprise!'

Ms. Snootington doesn't acknowledge me, and addresses Barry by glancing over the spectacles at the bottom of her nose.

'If she can fill in the necessary paperwork …*again*…and sign here, here and …here.'

'Eh, pardon?' I roll up the sleeves of my tracksuit top, ready to give her a piece of my mind. 'I'll have you know I'm in no state for flipping paper work, you….little…'

Barry looks relieved that I cannot finish the sentence.

'Here,' Barry plays peacekeeper and reaches for the clipboard. 'I'll fill it all in. Can you notify Dr Grainger that we are here, please?'

Barry has rushed through the paperwork.

'Everything's going to be fine,' he rubs my back.

I suddenly realise what a great dad he's going to be, and I'm picturing him placing a Band-Aid on a scratched knee and giving cuddles to child covered in chicken pox. I must have done something in a past life to deserve him. A warm trickle rolls down my trouser leg and pools at Ms. Snootington's desk.

'Oops. Sorry!' I smirk.

'Becks! Did your waters just break?' Barry smiles.

The look on Ms. Snootington' s face is glorious, it almost makes me forget the pain. A perky nurse in her early forties appears and, presses the clipboard to her chest.

'Hi Rebecca. If you'd like to come this way, please?'

We are escorted to the Merion wing. It's just as plush as I'd been hoping for.

'Now, Rebecca, hop up on that bed and we'll take a look at you.'

When you're pregnant, there are many requests to 'hop up' on examination beds. It's not as easy as you'd think when you're:

a. Wearing soggy tracksuit bottoms.

b. In pain. Not, like, bone crushing agony or anything, but medium pain. Stepping —on-a-piece-of Lego-barefoot kind of pain. Maybe I have a high pain threshold. I'd Google it, but they don't have Wi-Fi. I already asked.

c. Trying to manoeuvre a bowling ball.

Still, I obey orders and hop - as best a soggy, cranky, nine months and ten days pregnant woman can hop.

Epidural,' I hiss at Barry. 'Tell her I want an epidural. Tell her!'

Barry shushes me. He actually shushes a woman in labour. That's against human rights. Amnesty International will want to hear about that one!

'Let them examine you first, baby.'

I try to throw him a dirty look, but a wave of pain is building up.

'Having some contractions, then?' the nurse smiles.

'Yeah, she is. Every few minutes. I'm sorry about Rebecca, she's a bit anxious. It's our first.'

'It's fine. Rebecca? Rebecca, tell me when the contraction passes, dear. I'll just need to examine you then.'

The nurse turns to Barry and whispers as she examines me. 'She might not be in established labour, you know? These first babies can take quite a while... oh!'

'Everything OK?'

'Everything's fine. It's just that you don't look like someone in the throws of labour, but...'

'Operation GLAM,' I mumble.

'Pardon?' the nurse looks at me as if I have lost the plot.

'Operation GLAM. I stayed at home doing my makeup until the pains got bad.'

'Well, good for you. The good news is that you're about two centimetres.'

'Great, baby,' Barry beams. 'You're doing great.'

'Will Dr Grainger be coming in shortly?' Barry enquires.

'She's on her way.'

'Epidural,' my voice is tinged with a hint of desperation. 'When are you going to get the epidural?'

'Oh, it's a bit early for that. Tell you what. I'll just hook you up to this monitor here. Check baby is doing well. Make sure he's tolerating the contractions.'

'She,' Barry and I correct her in unison.

'Oh, she? Very nice. I'll keep checking on you. You can have the epidural when you're a bit further along, say about four centimetres. OK? Try some deep breathing in the mean time. You can take a puff on the gas if you need it.'

'Gas?' I'd give her the death stare, but she's too busy swapping smiley faces with Barry who is thanking her profusely.

I'd have more luck hyperventilating into a paper bag. Still, I give the gas a try. We are paying top dollar for this, I want to try everything. It's not bad: kind of like having a gin and tonic.

'Pace yourself on the gas, Rebecca. Tea?' the nurse chirps.

'Oh, yes please. Milk, two sugars,' Barry beams.

'Not you, Barry. She meant me! Goodness!'

'Sorry, pet, I was actually offering Barry,' the nurse tilts her head to the side. 'I can't give you anything to eat or drink I'm afraid. In case you're sick, pet. Just water if you need it.'

Five minutes later, she presents Barry with tea in a fancy cup and saucer. There is even a chocolate digestive on the side. The biscuit taunts me, waving it's tantalizing little chocolate arms at me. The nurse presents the 'Irish Times' newspaper for Barry.

'Barry?'

'Yes, sweetie?'

'Eat that biscuit…'

'Yes, baby?'

'…and die.'

Thirty eight

It's been two hours since that excuse for a nurse first refused to provide me with the drugs. She will pay dearly for what she has done to me. I will hunt her down and skin her alive. You think that I'm joking, don't you? You think I'll forget all about it when this is all over, yeah? You don't know what I'm capable of. I've filed that away forever, like a serial killer.

Ok, yes, she flits in and out of the room in her clickety clack white clogs and smiles at Barry. But I, for the record, do not smile back. Yes, she fills in her little paperwork files and checks the baby's heart monitor. Big whoop! She has yet to provide me with the epidural. It's not like I haven't asked for it. I ask every time she pops her cheerful little head around the door. She says it's too early. I don't know what in God's name she is waiting for. Do I have to be clawing at the ceiling before she will give me the goods? Do I have to stand on my head and beg? Because I'll do it. I'll do whatever she tells me to.

She's back. Here's my chance.

'Well, now Rebecca. How are we doing?'

I roll my eyes.

'*We* feel like *we* have been punched in the face over and over. *We* are in absolute agony. *We* need an epidural. *We* are going to sue if *we* don't get one!'

Barry apologises. He's been doing a lot of that lately.

'Barry?' I'm suddenly tearful. 'If I don't make it? Give my shoe collection to Emer. She appreciates couture.'

'Right! Sounds like someone is progressing in their labour. Let's check you again, shall we?'

'Lets!' I drip with sarcasm.

Barry throws me a look. I'm being rude, apparently. Well, fine. Whatever my personal pain threshold is, I've reached it. I've been pinched like a pin cushion and squeezed like a supermarket melon. I'm sorry that I'm not some super trooper that doesn't complain and just gets through labour by deep breathing and thinking happy thoughts about sunflowers. I'm sorry I'm not a martyr. I'm sorry I'm not some rough type who can take inordinate pain levels because they are so used to getting tattoos and eyebrow piercings. I have smooth, delicate skin. I was pampered as a child. I'm a lightweight. There, I've said it.

Dr Grainger is no-where to be seen. She's carrying out a caesarean on another patient, apparently, which is so inconvenient. The nurse is having a great old poke and prod about. She announces that I'm five centimetres dilated and is picking up the phone to request an epidural.

'About time!'

I instruct Barry to call off the lawsuit, the drugs are coming. Relief sweeps across his face. He's sympathetic, but doesn't grasp the level of pain. The closest thing he's ever known in the pain category is that he once had a root canal. Now, I know that is a painful procedure, but he would have had a local anaesthetic for it.

Oh, and by the way, the hand clutching is going great, thanks for asking. I don't know my own strength! As you know, Mishka did a fab job on the nails. When she enquired as to whether I'd like them square or oval, I asked her to make them pointy. I said for her to imagine vampires. They are really doing the trick. I think I may have even drawn blood on poor Barry. The angel on my shoulder says to go easy on him, that he's doing a great job and remaining calm. The devil says that it's his fault for filling me full of champagne, and telling me I looked pretty on the wedding day.

Finally, the moment of bliss is upon me. I don't care that the anaesthetist needs to insert a needle the length of my fist into my spine to administer the epidural. Sweet numbness sweeps through me in seconds and my smile returns. Barry looks like he might cry. It's hard to tell whether it's the pain in his hand or the relief that his beloved wife will soon be pain-free and rational again. The safe money is on a number two.

'Oh, thank God,' Barry shakes the anaesthetist hand. 'I didn't know how much more I could have taken.'

'Don't be such a drama queen, Barry.'

Honestly, he is making a show of himself.

The next four hours pass easily with the help of the latest 'Hello' magazine. The nurse checks me regularly. Barry is under strict instructions to stop pacing as he is driving me bonkers. Also, he keeps nipping out of the room and I highly suspect him of sneaking Mars bars at the vending machine. That is not cool.

The nurse is back. It turns out she is, in fact, not the spawn of Satan or out to get me. I'm so glad that whole paranoid / I'm-going-to-claw-my-own-face-off phase has passed. I don't know how those 'au natural' types do it, bless their hippy hearts. Still, it just leaves more drugs for the rest of us.

'Good news, Rebecca.'

'Oh?'

'Dr Grainger has arrived and you're nearly fully dilated. You're nearly ready to push your baby out. Not long now.'

Barry looks chuffed. 'Well done. We're on the home stretch.'

Before I've finished an article about Katie Price's new baby (another one, I know! How does she do it?) the machine I'm hooked up to starts making some weird beeping noise. I'm sure it's nothing, but worry-wart Barry is squinting at the machine, trying to interpret the data. You know men and machinery, they think they know it all. He's pacing again, yet I've made it perfectly clear that I am against pacing.

'Barry! Will you stop?'

Dr Grainger peeps at the paper readout from the machine, and reaches for the red panic button by the wall.

'Nothing to worry about, Rebecca. Heartbeat is a little slow. The baby's not tolerating the labour as well as we'd like, that's all. It looks like she's getting a bit stressed.'

Barry is the one who looks a bit stressed. Next thing you know, the room is full. Now, you know I love an audience, right? Well, not like this! I'm naked from the waist down, and not exactly feeling sociable at the moment. A gaggle of medical students have also snuck in with all the commotion, having a great gawp.

'Rebecca,' Dr Grainger is suddenly all business. She doesn't want to make small talk about what baby names I like anymore. 'You're going to have to start pushing, dear. Alright? We need to get baby out as quickly as we can.'

I have a go. I've seen more babies delivered on 'One Born Every Minute' than Ulrika Johnson's had facelifts. You just scrunch your face up and, like the tennis pros, you grunt a bit. You know, just to show that you're trying.

'How was that? Is the baby out yet?'

'No Rebecca. I really need you to focus, now. Put your chin to your chest, dear, and push.'

'Yeah, Becks,' worry is splashed all over Barry's tired face. 'Please, love. Just go for it.'

I'm about to tell Barry to 'just go for it' himself and see how he likes it, but I stop. Dr Grainger keeps glancing from the monitor to a clock which is mounted high on the wall. The staff are all gathered around the bed. I overhear someone on the phone instructing a colleague to prep the theatre for an emergency caesarean, so I know that plan B is waiting in the wings. I close my eyes.

With three mega pushes, she is out. It's like reaching the top of Mount Everest. But before I can say 'smashing! Now, top up the epidural', a team of blue scrubs swallows up my tiny baby. Dr Grainger takes control.

Someone cuts the cord and we are separated. I haven't even seen my baby's face yet, she was just scooped up before I could reach for her. I can't see her lying on the table, the doctors are blocking my view. But I know that she is not moving. I know that she is not breathing. Barry's face is grey.

I hold my breath and pray.

Dear Jesus,

Forget every other favour I've ever asked of you this week. Scrap them. But please. Please don't do this. I want her. I know I said I wasn't sure. I know I said I'd be a rubbish mummy. But I know, now. Please…

There's a tiny cry and I exhale for the first time in a full minute. Barry's head is in his hands as he sits on the side of the bed.

'Everything's fine,' Dr Grainger reassures us. 'Just needed a bit of oxygen, there. Here, mummy wants to hold you.'

She places the baby on my chest as Barry scrambles for a camera, pink vest, sleep suit and hat.

'Hello sweetheart,' I kiss her tiny head.

'She's perfect,' Barry kisses us both. 'Well done, Rebecca. You did great. Wow, let's take a look at her.'

'Dr Grainger? I just have one question,' my head is tilted sideways in confusion.

'Yes, Rebecca?'

'She's absolutely gorgeous. But… why does she have a willy?'

The doctor laughs. Barry lifts the baby's leg and sure enough, we have ourselves a strapping baby boy.

'Oh my God, a boy,' Barry laughs. 'So, *Patrick* it is, then!'

'Sometimes we don't always get it right from the scan. Congratulations,' Dr Grainger grins. 'I'll leave the three of you alone for a moment.'

'Hello, Patrick,' I smile at his handsome face. His eyes flick open for just a moment. They are a deep crystal blue. Just like his daddy's.

'I'm your mummy.'

Printed in Great Britain
by Amazon